Sent from her favouit

Kind regards

Mark Tilbury

The Last One to See Her - Text copyright © Mark Tilbury 2020
Cover Art by Emmy Ellis @ studioenp.com © 2020

All Rights Reserved

THE LAST ONE TO SEE HER

Mark Tilbury

PROLOGUE

2 a.m. August. 12 years earlier.

The baseball bat is wet and sticky with blood as Paul Whittacker opens the door to the master bedroom. He's already killed the young boy and the young girl. Sleep tight, little ones. Now it's the parents' turn to die.

The landing light, probably left on for the children, casts shadows across the bedroom and turns it into an old black-and-white movie set. Even the blood on the bat appears grey and less indicative of its macabre history.

He stands for a while, catching his breath, observing, listening. His arms are shaking from the exertion of the kill. He needs a fix. To slip into the warm syrupy blanket of oblivion. But there is still much to do before he can allow his body to succumb to the needle.

He takes a few steps into the room and stops. His heartbeat pulsates in his ears. Sweat dribbles down his back. He tells himself to calm down and make ready for the kill.

The man snores and makes a strange gurgling noise in his throat. He smacks his lips and rolls over to face his wife. Hesitancy, that powerful adversary to careful planning, suggests it might be better to use a knife on him, but he doesn't want to waste time going downstairs to look for one.

He creeps towards the bed, weapon raised, threat-level raised, blood pressure raised. He makes ready to strike. The woman sighs. It's a seductive sound that arouses him. He considers raping her once he's finished with hubby, but that means getting into a whole new area of forensic jiggery-pokery.

Sweat dribbles into his eyes. He stops, bat hovering two feet above the man's face. He wipes an arm across his forehead. He's seized with an uncontrollable urge to laugh when a bright-pink moth flies across the bedroom and lands on the wall just above the headboard. It's strikingly beautiful in this black-and-white movie. He knows it's just a hallucination. Residual imagery from last night's acid trip.

He raises the bat and brings it crashing down on the side of Hubby's head. The man responds by pawing his wife's face as if trying to provoke foreplay. His legs kick out under the duvet.

Whittacker smashes the bat down again, this time eliciting a muffled scream from the victim, who raises his head six inches off the pillow. The bat wastes no time sending that head right back to where it came from. This time he is motionless. Not so much as a whimper.

Whittacker considers checking the man's pulse, but his wife is now awake and exercising her right to scream. Her arms flail in what appears to be an attempt to defy physics and fly.

Whittacker steadies himself, takes aim, and raises the bat. But he is stopped by a sudden sharp pain between his shoulder blades. At first, he thinks he's having a seizure. This thought is replaced by a more serious self-diagnosis – a heart attack brought on by stress.

The pain comes again, accompanied by a wet slapping sound. He cries out, blood bubbling on his lips. He drops the bat, legs bucking, spilling him to the floor.

Too many drugs spoil the moth.

He checks above the bed for the bright-pink insect, but the only splash of colour in this black-and-white world has gone. Something warm and sticky runs down his back. Sweat? Too thick. The golden-brown liquid from every needle he's ever jabbed into his veins? Too painful.

The woman screams again. The sound bounces around the walls and pounds on his eardrums. This can't be happening. Not now. Not when he is so close to…

The room suddenly goes quiet. Deathly quiet, you might say. Paul Whittacker doesn't hear the woman wailing like a malfunctioning police siren. He doesn't feel his body being turned over, or hear a male voice trying to soothe Mrs Wailing Siren with assurances that everything will be all right.

By the time the police arrive twenty minutes later, Paul Whittacker is lying on the bedroom floor in a pool of his own blood. The baseball bat lies next to him, pieces of skull and tufts of hair decorating the wood like ghoulish artwork.

The ceiling light has now switched the room from black and white to high-definition colour. Blood drips onto a white rug next to the bed, and Hubby's gore saturates the pillows and duvet.

Whittacker doesn't hear a policeman walk into the room and tell his colleague that there appears to be two child fatalities. One male, one female. He doesn't hear Mrs Siren sobbing on the deathbed.

The world is now as black and silent as death itself.

CHAPTER ONE

At six-foot-two, with a knee-length black Burberry coat and an umbrella tucked underneath one arm, Mathew Hillock appeared to be the only man in Feelham who was unaware of the heatwave sucking all the air out of the town.

He crossed the road to Abbasi's Convenience Store and plucked a *Daily Telegraph* from the display stand. Entering the shop, he joined a small queue at the counter. Mr Abbasi was talking to an elderly man about the stifling heat.

'This goes on much longer, I'm emigrating to Iceland.'

Mr Abbasi gave the man his change. 'You need to get air conditioning.'

'I've got a fan, but it ain't much use.'

'That's because it only swirls the heat around.'

The old man picked up his cigarettes. 'I can't afford any of that newfangled stuff on my pension. Barely enough money to eat as it is.'

Mathew didn't understand why people always talked about the weather. It wasn't as if they could do anything about it. And people who couldn't afford food shouldn't waste their money on cigarettes either, but that was a thought best left inside his head unless he wanted to start an argument. Which he didn't.

By the time he reached the front of the queue, it was almost ten past six. That meant he had enough time to sit on the bench at the corner of Croft Road for twenty minutes before heading home for his tea.

Mr Abbasi smiled, his moustache curled up at the ends. 'Hello, Mathew.'

Mathew returned the grin. 'Can I have a big bag of Skittles, please?'

The shopkeeper reached up and plucked the sweets from a display behind the empty chocolate stand. All the bars had been transferred to the fridge because of the heat. 'Isn't it a bit warm for that coat?'

Mathew shook his head. 'Might be a storm tonight.'

A man browsing the magazines turned around. 'Are you for real?'

Mathew ignored him. For a man of thirty, Jim Bentley was childish and ignorant.

Abbasi scanned the paper and the skittles. 'Anything else, Mathew?'

'No thanks.' And then, without any conscious thought, 'Someone's going to die.'

Abbasi squinted at Mathew. 'Pardon me?'

Mathew picked up the Skittles and stuffed them into his coat pocket.

'He's off his fucking trolley,' Jim Bentley said, the words slurred.

'Please don't swear.' Abbasi turned back to Mathew. 'Who's going to die?'

Mathew scooped up his paper and shrugged. 'I don't know.'

The door chimed. A young girl walked in. Maybe ten or eleven years old, brown hair scraped back in a tight ponytail.

Bentley stood behind Mathew. 'Who you gonna kill, retard?'

Mathew smelled the foul odour of tobacco and alcohol on Bentley's breath. He ignored him and walked out. He didn't want to discuss anything with the likes of Jim Bentley, especially something as serious as death.

'Maybe it's you who's gonna die,' Bentley shouted as the door clanged shut.

Mathew ran a hand through his tangled mop of hair. His mother said it had a mind of its own, which was daft, because everyone knew hair didn't have a brain. His brother, Gareth, sometimes called him "hair-brained", but Mathew knew that meant something different altogether. The English language was strange. So many words, so many different meanings.

A slight breeze whispered promises of relief from the heat. Mathew found it difficult to sleep at night, even with the ceiling fan whirring above him. His mother kept telling him to open the window, but he would never do that. There were moths, spiders, and other creepy things hanging around outside at night just waiting for an opportunity to come inside.

He was proud of himself for not responding to Bentley's stupid comments. Gareth had told Mathew that Bentley had spent time in prison once and considered himself a big man. The only thing *big* about him as far as Mathew was concerned was his mouth. Bentley had even told Mr Abbasi to go back to Pakistan once, which was not only rude, but stupid, because Mr Abbasi was from India.

Mathew sat on the bench. He stretched out his legs, sending a group of ants scuttling for cover. The blood-red sun hung above Feelham like a huge all-seeing eye. He stood the umbrella on the ground, clamped it between his legs, and pulled the newspaper out of his pocket to fish out the Skittles. He only liked the yellow, orange, and purple ones. It had nothing to do with flavours and everything to do with colours. Red always seemed to make him feel anxious, and green reminded him of peas, and he hated peas more than Brussel sprouts. But not quite as much as broad beans. God must have been having an off day when he'd created those disgusting things.

He cursed under his breath as Jim Bentley headed towards him. Shoving the Skittles back in his pocket, he opened the paper and pretended to read.

Bentley stopped near the bench and lit a cigarette. 'What you doing with a newspaper? I thought Mummy only bought you picture books.'

Mathew told himself Bentley would go away if he ignored him. He was only trying to wind him up. Push his buttons. He wasn't worth wasting his breath on.

'So, you gonna tell me who's gonna die?'

The sun beat down on the top of Mathew's head as if trying to melt his thoughts. He wanted to go home and take off the coat. Relieve himself of the stab vest he always wore beneath his tee-shirt. The newspaper text was nothing more than an indistinguishable blur. Several of the letters appeared to march across the page like ants.

'Why are you dressed for the fucking Artic?'

Go away. Go away. Go away.

Bentley sat next to him. 'You know what I think, retard?' He didn't wait for an answer. 'I think you're a fucking accident waiting to happen. If I had my way, you'd be locked up in Fairacres where they can shoot a few thousand volts up your arse. You never know, they might even find your brain while they're about it.'

Sticks and stones may break my bones, but —

'Wassamatta, you lost the ability to speak?'

Mathew shook his head.

'So, who you gonna kill?'

'No one. I just say stuff sometimes.'

'You're like a fucking doughnut with no jam.'

'I don't like jam.'

Bentley pointed at him. 'You trying to be funny?'

'No.'

9

'You wanna slap?'

'No.'

'You know what they say about retards?'

'I'm not a retard.'

'They're the result of in-breeding. Maybe your mummy got it on with one of your uncles. One fuck, and BAM!' Bentley thumped the bench. 'One fuck-up of epic proportions.'

Mathew counted from one to ten and back again. The voice in his head told him to knock Bentley to the ground and squish him. But he'd only get into trouble with the police and upset his mum, which was the last thing he wanted to do.

'Tell me how come your brother's normal and you're as mad as a shithouse rat?'

Ignore him.

'I mean, I know he's your brother and all that, but something ain't right.'

'Leave me alone.'

'Maybe your old lady dropped you on your head when you was a baby.'

'Go away.'

The young girl who'd been in the shop walked towards them, a four-pint carton of milk in one hand and a mobile phone in the other.

'You gonna make me a cup of tea, love?' Bentley asked.

The girl glanced at him and hurried past without speaking.

'Kids,' Bentley said. 'No manners these days.'

'Maybe she doesn't talk to strangers.'

Bentley stood. 'And maybe she took one look at your ugly mug and pissed her pants. Anyway, I gotta go. Things to do and people to see.'

Mathew had to restrain himself from punching the air in delight. He watched Bentley follow the girl along St John's Road until a sharp bend obscured them from view. Hopefully, Bentley would walk in front of a bus and get squished.

Towards the end of St John's Road, there was a gate leading to the Bunky line – a disused railway line running from Feelham to Chorley. About a mile along the track, there was a derelict farmhouse where a guy called Calum Sheppard had imprisoned a schoolgirl some ten years ago. He'd starved her to death because she'd refused to marry him.

Mathew shuddered, remembering the gory details of the murder. 'Bad things happen to good people in Feelham,' he whispered.

And he couldn't help wondering if something terrible was going to happen to the young girl.

CHAPTER TWO

Alison Willis glanced at the kitchen clock and her stomach flipped over. Nearly 7 p.m. Her daughter, Jodie, had gone to Abbasi's to get milk almost an hour ago. It was only a ten-minute walk. Maybe she'd met one of her friends on the way and was chatting. Jodie could talk for England on a quiet day.

Jodie was a good kid. Feisty. Or spirited, depending on which side of the Jodie-fence you sat. But she had a heart of gold. Loved animals and wanted to be a vet when she grew up. That was a long way off, and she would probably change her mind a dozen times before she reached eighteen. At least being a vet was a more realistic prospect than being a princess (aged seven), a ballerina (aged eight) and a pop star (aged ten).

Jodie's father had walked out on them two years after her birth. A painter and decorator by trade, and the world's biggest arsehole by nature, Colin Pitman had proved to be about as reliable as a knackered car in a scrapyard. He'd moved in with some tart he'd been working for on the Pinehurst Estate.

The next few years had been the hardest of her life, but at least she'd been able to find part-time work as a playground monitor when Jodie had started school. With her mother pitching in to babysit, life had been just about bearable by the time she'd met her current partner, Terry Stevens, on a rare night out. Terry was funny, good-natured, and a breath of fresh air after Colin.

7 p.m. Alison grabbed her phone off the kitchen table and called her daughter's mobile. Straight to answerphone. Her heart stalled as she hit redial and got the same automated message requesting her to speak after the tone. She tossed the phone on the table as if it was personally responsible for her daughter's absence.

Alison called Terry's mobile. Asked where he was.

'At the Cross Keys. Why?'

No surprise there. He liked to have a couple of beers and unwind after work. 'Have you seen Jodie?'

'No. Why?'

'Because she went to Abbasi's an hour ago to get some milk and she hasn't come home.'

'Maybe she got talking to a mate. Why don't you call her?'

'I have. It went straight to voicemail.'

'She's probably got it switched off.'

'She never switches it off.'

'Out of charge?'

Alison gnawed her lip. 'I need you to come home.'

'Okay. I'll see if I can get someone to give me a lift.'

Alison disconnected the call and tried Jodie's number again. Voicemail again. 'Please leave a message after the tone.' The woman's automated voice seemed to be mocking her. Talking down to her as if she was just a frantic mother worrying over nothing.

This time, Alison left a message. 'Hi, sweetie. It's Mum. Call me, I'm getting worried.'

She went to the front room window and peered outside. Cars lined the street on both sides. A skinny woman was walking a dog that seemed big enough to eat her, and a man was struggling with a car seat in the back of a Toyota.

She phoned the two numbers in her contacts list where Jodie occasionally went for sleepovers and tea. Neither parent had seen her. Both assured her that Jodie would probably turn up with a perfectly good reason for not coming straight home. Alison wished she could believe them.

An idea. Not brilliant, but at least it was something. She grabbed her phone, slipped on her flip-flops, and hurried to Abbasi's.

Mr Abbasi was trying to tell a young man that it didn't matter how old he was, he didn't *look* twenty-five.

'Why I gotta look twenty-five when it's legal to buy booze at eighteen?'

'Because it's the law.

'But it makes no sense.'

'I'm sorry. If you show me some ID, then I'll serve you.'

The guy turned around and stomped out of the shop. 'Twat.'

Abbasi shook his head. 'Nice lad.'

Alison skipped formalities. 'Has Jodie been in for milk?'

'About an hour ago.'

'Was she with anyone else?'

'No.'

'Did she say where she was going.'

'No. Why?'

'Because she was meant to come straight home.'

'Perhaps she's gone to a friend's house.'

Alison swallowed her heart. 'I hope so. I really hope so.'

'Maybe you should call the police.'

Alison nodded, her mind already out of the shop. 'If you see her, tell her to come straight home.'

'Of course.'

Alison took off her flip-flops and ran most of the way back along St John's Road. She stopped at Chloe Parson's house three doors away from hers and jammed her finger on the bell. Chloe had a daughter the same age as Jodie. They weren't friends, but they sometimes walked home from school together in term time from the primary school opposite Abbasi's.

Chloe opened the door, hair dripping wet and brushed back from her pale freckled face. 'Ali? What's wrong?'

'Is Jodie here?'

She shook her head, spraying water on the woodchip wall. 'Why?'

'I sent her for milk over an hour ago, and she hasn't come home.'

'Shit.'

'I just wondered if she might be with Hannah.'

'Hannah's at her nan's in Brighton. Do you want me to help you look for her?'

Feelham suddenly felt the size of London. Jodie could be anywhere. With anyone. You saw stories on the news. Kids that never returned home. The frantic searches. TV appeals. 'I don't know what to do. My head's all over the place.'

'I'm sure she'll turn up looking sheepish and—'

'I'm scared, Chloe. It's really out of character.'

'Do you want to come in?'

Alison nodded. She didn't want to go home and be on her own.

Chloe offered her a seat in the lounge. The bland magnolia walls were daubed with crayon. No prizes for guessing the artist: Chloe's three-year-old son, Haydon. Pictures of wild cats decorated the top half of the walls, as if Chloe was trying to bring an African safari into her lounge.

Chloe lit a cigarette. 'Where's Terry?'

'He's on his way home.'

'Do you want me to call the cops?'

'No. I'll do it.' Alison punched in 999 and told the female call handler that her daughter was missing.

'Can I have your name and address, please?'

'Alison Willis. 97, St John's Road, Feelham.'

'And your daughter's name?'

'Jodie. Jodie Willis.'

'How old is she?'

'Eleven.'

'Her date of birth?'

'July 1st 2009.'

'Approximate height?'

'Four-foot-two.'

'Weight?'

Jesus Christ, what is this? 'Not sure. She's thin.'

'Any identifying marks?'

'Only a mole on her left cheek.'

'Eye colour?'

'Green.'

'Hair?'

'Light-brown.'

'What she was wearing when you last saw her?'

'Red tee-shirt and pink shorts. She also had a small purple purse.'

'Has Jodie any medical conditions such as asthma or diabetes?'

'No.'

'Have you contacted all her known friends and associates?'

'Yes.'

'Has Jodie got a mobile phone?'

Don't all kids these days? 'Yes.'

'Could you give me the number, please?'

'I'm gonna have to look it up on my phone. Hold on a minute.' Alison brought up the menu and read out Jodie's number to the call handler.

'How long has she been absent?'

'Nearly two hours. I sent her to the shops to buy some milk, and she hasn't come back.'

'Has she ever gone missing before?'

'No.'

'Been in any trouble?'

'No.'

'What about drug use?'

'No.'

'Other than contacting her friends, have you done anything else to locate your daughter?'

'I've been to the shop. Mr Abbasi said she came in for milk just after six, and that was the last he saw of her.'

'Mr Abbasi?'

'The local shopkeeper.'

'And you've not fallen out with her?'

'No.'

'Okay. I'll send someone out to see you shortly. In the meantime, if your daughter turns up, please let us know.'

Alison disconnected the call, thanked her neighbour, and headed home. Her stomach felt as if it was playing host to a nest of hornets, and a headache pulsed behind her eyes.

CHAPTER THREE

9 p.m. Mathew sat at the dining table. He was much happier now he'd showered and changed into a tee-shirt and shorts. A ceiling fan whirred, swishing warm air around. It felt good on the top of his head, cooling his thoughts and helping him to forget about Jim Bentley.

His mother, Sonia, walked in and put a glass bowl of salad in the middle of the table. 'How was your walk, love?'

'Okay.'

'You were gone a long time.'

Mathew crossed his fingers behind his back. 'I felt sick.' (The truth.) 'So I went down the river for a while.' (A lie.) 'It's nice and cool in the evening.' He didn't dare tell her he'd gone along the Bunky Line to the derelict farmhouse just to make sure Jim Bentley hadn't taken the little girl there to murder her. He also neglected to explain that he'd had another one of his emotional blackouts and couldn't account for most of the time he'd been gone.

'It would be a lot cooler if you didn't go everywhere in that daft coat.'

He dreaded to think what she might say if she ever found out he wore a stab vest beneath it when he went out. 'It's not daft. It's just a coat. Mrs Halliday's dog is daft when it chases its tail and scrapes its bum along the grass.'

'Thank you, Mathew, you've just put me off my tea talking about the dog like that.'

'But he does scrape it on the grass. And he licks himself.'

'Yuck!'

'I suppose he can't help it, because he hasn't got hands to scratch with.'

'I don't like dogs.'

'I don't like Mrs Halliday. She's always in a grumpy mood. And she shouts at the children when they get near Fester.'

Sonia went back to the kitchen and returned a few seconds later. She put a plate in front of Mathew with three slices of ham, a chicken leg, and half a dozen sweet potatoes. 'Fester?'

'Her dog.'

'Maybe she doesn't want anyone fussing around him in case he bites.'

'Then he should have a muzzle on.'

'True. Do you want to watch something on TV later?'

'I'm gonna talk to Tortilla and then get an early night.'

'I swear to God you think more of that tortoise than you do of me.'

Mathew's heart stuttered. 'That's not true. I love you more than anyone.'

'Just kidding. What do you think of the new cappuccino machine in the bookshop?'

Mathew helped himself to salad. 'I love it. The Book Café's my favourite place in the whole world.'

Sonia smiled. 'Mine, too.'

Mathew had worked at his mother's bookshop since leaving school. It wasn't like having a real job; more like getting paid to do the best thing ever. He loved helping the customers. Relished that wonderful aroma of a brand-new book while he studied the front cover for clues to the story within. Imagined himself as the hero of the story, marrying the pretty woman he'd rescued from a burning building and living happily ever after in a country cottage with roses wrapped around the front porch.

He ate in silence, mulling over the events of the day. Or, more precisely, the events during his trip to the shop. Every time he told himself he was just being silly, a pessimistic voice popped up in his head reminding him that terrible things happened to people all the time.

His mother banged and clanked in the kitchen. She was an amazing lady. Nothing was ever too much trouble for her, and she let nothing get her down in the grumps. Apart from Cory Wainwright's dog when it was barking in the yard at night.

Mathew took his plate and the salad bowl into the kitchen and put them on the worktop near the drainer. 'Do you want me to dry?'

'Thanks.'

Mathew concentrated hard as he dried the dishes. Partly because he didn't want to break anything, but also because it helped to take his mind off the little girl. As he put the salad bowl back in the cupboard above the fridge, he suddenly blurted, 'Someone's going to die.'

Sonia frowned. 'Pardon me?'

He cursed his careless mouth and busied himself putting away the dishes.

'Mathew?'

'What?'

'Did you say someone is going to die?'

His cheeks flushed. He nodded and stared at the marble worktop.

'Why would you say something like that?'

'The bird told me.'

'What bird?'

'The one on the back of the chair when I came in from feeding Tortilla this morning.'

'What exactly did it say?'

'Nothing.'

Sonia shook her head. 'Now you're confusing me.'

'I read in a book once that if you see a bird in the house, it means someone is going to die.'

24

'That's just a silly superstition. Like the one about rabbits being witches in disguise. I mean, has anyone ever seen a rabbit with a cauldron?'

Mathew grinned. 'No.'

'Do you remember Sunny?'

He searched the database in his head. He was hopeless with names. And dates. And times. 'Who?'

'Sunny. The lop-eared rabbit we had when you were ten. You used to spend hours playing with him in the garden.'

'Oh.'

'We buried him near the back gate when he died.'

'How did he die?'

'He just got old.'

'That's sad.'

'I know.'

'I hope you never get old.'

'Me, too.'

'I don't want you to die.'

'Don't worry about me,' Sonia said. 'I'm as fit as a fiddle.'

'Fiddles can't be fit; they don't even go to the gym.'

'It's just a saying.'

'But it's daft. Why do people say daft things?'

'Because people are daft.'

Mathew thought of Jim Bentley and nodded. 'True.'

Finished with the chores, Sonia poured her son a glass of lemonade. They sat at the small kitchen table listening to the grandfather clock in the hall marking time.

Mathew's mouth had another involuntary spasm and said, 'I'm really worried about the young girl.'

'What young girl?'

'The one at the shop.'

'Why are you worried about her? Because of the bird?'

'Yes.'

'But people die every day, Mathew. You don't see birds in everyone's houses, do you?'

Mathew considered this for a moment and then conceded his mother was probably right. He was just being silly again. Too sensitive. *Losing his thoughts in the fog*, as Gareth would say. Gareth was the coolest brother in the world. He worked as an estate agent and sold houses for millions of pounds. He also drove a brand-new black BMW. Mathew felt like a king when they rode through town in it with the music booming out and all the girls looking at them.

'You've got to stop imagining things, Mathew. I'm sure the girl is fine.'

Mathew thought he heard someone scream, but that was probably just his mind playing tricks and making stuff up. Like when he could still hear Cory Wainwright's dog barking long after Cory had called it in at night.

'Mathew?'

He rested his chin on his chest. 'You're right; I'm just being silly.'

'You're not. You just get in a bit of a muddle sometimes.'

'I'm gonna see Tortilla for a while then go to bed.'

'Don't stay out in that shed too late; I want to lock up before it gets dark.'

Mathew nodded. He knew only too well the importance of making sure all the doors were locked at night. Especially in Feelham.

CHAPTER FOUR

It was just after eight thirty when Terry walked through the door. Alison introduced him to a young female PC sitting at a small dining table pushed against the wall.

The officer stood and held out a hand. 'I'm PC Hughes. The Initial Investigating Office.'

'Pleased to meet you,' Terry said, his eyes contradicting the words.

'Alison tells me you've been to the pub.'

Terry nodded. 'I usually go for a pint or two after work to unwind.'

'Which pub?'

'Cross Keys.'

'Did you walk or drive home?'

'Walked.'

The officer nodded. 'Which way did you come?'

'Down Croft Road and along St John's.'

'Did you see anyone suspicious hanging around?'

'Not really. Just a gang of kids near Saxon's Green. For what it's worth, I reckon she's probably gone to a mate's house.'

'I've called all her friends,' Alison said. 'No one's seen her. Anyway, she wouldn't just go off like that without telling me first.'

'Have you had any trouble with Jodie recently?' Hughes asked. 'Drugs. Skipping school. That type of thing.'

Alison shook her head.

'Any rows?'

'She got a bit uppity the other day when I caught her prancing about in front of my bedroom mirror with makeup all over her face. But that was just something and nothing.'

Hughes wrote something in her notebook, then said, 'Would you describe your daughter as happy?'

'Pretty much. Apart from when her father shows up and spoils her rotten.'

Hughes looked at Terry. 'So you're not the father?'

'No.'

'He buggered off when Jodie was two,' Alison said. 'Good riddance to bad rubbish.'

'Does the father have much to do with Jodie?'

'Only when it suits him.'

'Is there any chance Jodie might have gone to see him?'

'She wouldn't walk all the way to Chorley. It's over three miles to his house.'

'Unless she arranged to meet him,' Terry said. 'I wouldn't put it past Colin to pull a stunt like that.'

'Have you tried ringing him?' Hughes asked.

Alison shook her head.

'Perhaps you ought to,' Hughes said. 'Just to rule it out.'

Alison brought up her contacts menu and reluctantly called her ex-husband. No answer. Straight to voicemail. No surprise there; he wouldn't speak to Alison if his life depended on it.

Hughes tapped her pencil against the edge of her notebook. 'If you can give me his address, I'll go and pay him a visit.'

'Nine Wellington Drive, Chorley. It's up near the railway station.'

Hughes wrote it down, then asked Alison what her relationship was like with Colin.

Alison laughed. 'Non-existent.'

'Okay. Would you say that Jodie's easily led?'

'Not really. She's just a typical kid. Obviously I don't watch her twenty-four hours a day, so I don't know what she's like when she's with her friends.'

'Do you think she would talk to strangers?'

Alison shrugged. 'She's always been taught not to.'

'They don't always listen, though, do they?' Terry said. 'As my old mum used to say, "Words go east, and deeds go west".'

Alison looked at him as if he'd just sprouted another head. 'What the hell's that supposed to mean?'

Terry didn't answer.

PC Hughes closed her notebook and put it in her pocket. 'Would you mind if I had a quick look around the house and garden?'

'Shouldn't you be out searching for her?' Terry said. 'She's not gonna be hiding in the laundry basket, is she?'

'Ignore him,' Alison said. 'Just do what you have to do.'

'I'd like to start in Jodie's bedroom, if that's all right?'

Alison nodded. 'Up the stairs, second door on the left.'

'Thanks.'

She waited for the copper to leave the room, then said, 'I feel like there's a bloody boa constrictor wrapped around my chest squeezing all the air out of me.'

'Try not to worry. I'm sure she'll turn up.'

'It's been two and a half hours, Terry. Something's wrong.' She thumped her chest. 'I can feel it right in here.'

'Was she all right before she left the house?'

'Yes.'

'Not narky about something?'

'She seemed fine. Said she'd come straight home because she wanted to watch something on telly. Oh

Christ, Terry, what if she's been snatched by a paedophile? Or had an accident? Been hit by a car?'

'Maybe I could go have a look round town,' Terry offered as Alison started sobbing. 'Ask around the pubs.'

She glanced up, eyes red. 'How much have you had to drink?'

'Not much.'

'How much?'

'Couple of pints.'

'For God's sake, be careful. The last thing I need is you getting nicked for drunk driving.'

He walked to her and put his hands on her shoulders. 'I'll be fine. I promise. Any news, ring me straight away.'

Alison nodded and sniffed.

He kissed her on top of the head. 'Love you.'

By the time PC Hughes returned to the lounge, Alison was drinking a second glass of wine.

'Where's Mr Stevens?' she asked, standing near an ironing board laden with laundered clothes.

'Gone to look for her.'

Hughes didn't seem impressed but said nothing. 'Have you got an up-to-date photo of Jodie I can have?'

Alison pointed to a school picture sitting amongst a jumble of other photos on top of a pine sideboard. 'That one was taken just before they broke up for the summer holidays.'

Hughes picked up the picture and tucked it inside her notebook. 'Thank you.'

'What happens now?'

'I'm going to have a quick check around the garden and the outbuildings. Then I'll report my findings and we can begin a search of the local area. For what it's worth, try not to worry too much. Kids go missing all the time, and they usually turn up safe. They have a lot to deal with these days, what with social media, bullying, and peer pressure. Sometimes they just need a bit of headspace.'

'Don't we all.'

'Any other relatives Jodie might have gone to?'

'There's only my mum, and she would've been straight on the phone if Jodie had turned up there.'

'What about Mr Stevens' family?'

'They're all in Portsmouth. He's got a few mates around here, but no one Jodie would know.'

'Okay. As I said, I'll have a quick scan around outside then report back to the station.'

Alison showed her out, then called her mother and told her what had happened.

'Why didn't you phone me earlier? Jesus, Alison, she's been missing for over three hours.'

'Because I kept thinking she'd come home. Then I went looking for her and phoned the police.'

'What did they say?'

'They're gonna do a local search.'

'Where's Terry?'

'Out looking for her.'

'Okay. I'll be round as soon as I can.'

Alison disconnected the call. She finished her wine and gazed out the window. It was still light enough to see part of the way along the Bunky Line. Overgrown weeds and brambles littered the disused railway track that ran for three miles from Feelham to Chorley. The neglected fields were waist-high with wild grass, making them the perfect place for predators to hide. The once thriving farmland that used to harvest barley, and the accompanying factory where the crop was processed to make malt were long gone. Just another ghost of an industry slaughtered in the name of progress. The perfect setting to find a little girl who'd gone missing after walking to the shops to buy some milk.

Alison would never forgive herself if anything had happened to her daughter. She should have gone to the shop herself. Or gone with her. Made sure she was safe.

She thought of Jodie outside wearing nothing but shorts and a tee-shirt. She'd be cold, scared, and vulnerable. And there was nothing Alison could do about it. Nothing at all.

CHAPTER FIVE

Mathew was glad it was Saturday because he didn't have to go to work at the weekend. He'd not slept much, thanks to thoughts of birds and death, and now he was in a bad mood because he was too tired to do the chores. He'd promised to hoover the house while his mother was at the Book Café, but he'd barely enough energy to go to the shed and feed Tortilla.

He sat at the kitchen table with a mug of coffee. The local radio station was playing country music. He liked the tunes, but the lyrics sometimes saddened him. Still, there were worse things going on in the world than Lucille leaving her husband and Ruby taking her love to town.

As the music faded out, the station delivered the local news bulletin:

'Police have today said they are concerned for the safety of eleven-year-old Jodie Willis, who was last seen buying milk from Abbasi's Convenience Store in Feelham at around 6 p.m. on Thursday evening. She is described as four feet, four inches tall, slim build with brown hair. She was wearing a red tee-shirt and pink shorts and white trainers. Police are appealing for anyone who has seen somebody matching Jodie's description to contact them immediately by calling 101 or their local police station.'

Mathew gawped at the radio as if it had just tapped into his mind and delivered the worst news possible. There was an intense pressure building inside his head, and his heart was thumping so hard he thought it would burst out of his chest.

He banged his fist on the table. Slowly. Rhythmically. 'I said this would happen. I said it would happen, but no one would listen.'

Maybe you should go to the police and tell them about the girl in Mr Abbasi's, and Jim Bentley following her along St John's Road.

Mathew considered this briefly but knew he'd only get in a muddle and make himself look suspicious with no one there to help him.

Get Mum to go with you, then.

But Mother had the shop to run. She couldn't just close up on a Saturday afternoon.

You don't want the coppers thinking you're trying to hide something, do you?

'I'm not!' Mathew said, as if the voice in his head was a prosecutor in a court of law. 'I'm not hiding nothing.'

You told Mum you went to the river after going to Abbasi's, but you really went to the Bunky Line.

Mathew's stomach tingled like it always did when he'd done something wrong. He'd only told his mother he'd been to the river because he'd not wanted to worry her about Jim Bentley and the little girl. Only she wasn't just the "little girl" anymore. She had a name, which somehow seemed to make her more real.

Jodie Willis.

The name swirled around his head and contaminated his thoughts with guilt.

Jodie Willis.

Eleven years old. Still at primary school. Her mum and dad would be worried sick.

So, go to the police.

Mathew went to the sink and splashed water on his face. He dabbed it dry on a tea towel, then poured a glass of water and took two paracetamol tablets. They got stuck in his throat, and he had to drink two glasses of water to wash them down properly.

Opening the back door, he stepped into the garden. It was just a small patch of baked earth with sporadic tufts of yellowing grass sprouting here and there. He'd set the mower too low the last time he'd cut it, and now it would need treating before the autumn.

Tortilla had told Mathew he wasn't to blame. That he wasn't responsible for the drought. True. But that still didn't stop him from blaming himself for not thinking ahead.

He walked into the shed and found the leopard tortoise lying in a large shallow dish filled with water. Sensible. Tortilla had belonged to a cousin who'd given him to Mathew six years ago. His cousin had told him that Tortilla was twenty-four and could live right up to a hundred if he was lucky. Mathew loved the idea of growing old with Tortilla. Sharing stories and caring for him for the rest of his life.

The wooden shed was six feet by eight. Large enough to stretch out on the floor and chat with Tortilla when the tortoise wasn't out foraging in the garden. Considering there wasn't anything to forage at the moment, thanks to the relentless heat, the reptile spent most of his time in the shed relying on Mathew to feed him with grasses and vegetation twice a day.

'How you doing, Tortilla?'

The tortoise stared glumly ahead, his poker face giving nothing away. He spoke in Mathew's mind. *Too hot.*

'I know how you feel. Said on the radio it's meant to rain on Monday.'

Good.

'Do you know much about the police?'

They catch criminals.

'I think someone's been killed.'

Who?

'A girl called Jodie Willis. She was in the shop last night, and Jim Bentley followed her along St John's Road.'

Have you told the police?

'I'm scared.'

Why?

'In case they think I've done something wrong.'

Why would they think that?

'Because I told Mr Abbasi someone was gonna die because there was a bird inside the house.'

Oh.

'And then I told Mum I went to the river after Abbasi's, but I didn't. I went along the Bunky Line to the derelict farmhouse to see if Jim Bentley had taken the girl there.' Mathew wiped a tear from the corner of his eye.

Why did you lie?

'Because I didn't want to tell Mum I was upset about Jim Bentley following her.'

You've got to tell her.

'But she's at work.'

Then go to the bookshop and explain everything to her. She'll know what to do.

'It's Saturday. I'm supposed to be doing chores.'

Chores, bores, snores. The house can wait.

'She'll be mad at me for lying.'

She won't. She loves you. She's on your side.

'I don't want to upset her.'

She'll be more upset if you don't tell her and the police come knocking on the door asking awkward questions.

Mathew considered Tortilla's words. Or thoughts. Or whatever the heck they were. 'Do you think I should tell her about going along the Bunky Line?'

Definitely.

'Even though I told her I went to the river?'

She won't be angry with you just because you were worried about a kid. I'm sure she'd have done the same.

'I wish I was a tortoise sometimes.'

It's not all it's cracked up to be!

'At least you don't have to do stuff you don't want to.'

Tortilla's head disappeared into its shell. Conversation over.

Mathew wished he had a shell that he could hide away in. It was hard being a person. Too many things to think about. Too many questions to answer. Sometimes he felt sorry for Tortilla because he didn't have much to do other than wander around the garden and sleep in the shed, but at least he didn't have to make massive decisions and prove anything to anyone.

He conjured up a mental picture of his mother in the bookshop. Her grey hair cropped short, spectacles perched on the end of her nose looking as if they might fall off any minute. 'I'm sorry I lied, Mum, but I never went to the river last night. I went to the Bunky Line to search for a little girl who's gone missing.'

No good. How would he know she'd gone missing last night when he'd only just heard it on the radio?

'Sorry, Mum, I went to the Bunky Line because I thought Jim Bentley might have taken Jodie to the farmhouse.'

Better. But it still sounded flimsy. He needed someone to help him get his words right before he let them out of his mouth. Someone who knew both him and his mum. Someone who could put some... what was the word... *perspective* on things.

He went back into the house, dressed in the stab-proof vest, black Nike tee-shirt, and black jeans. He donned his Burberry coat, checked all the electric sockets were switched off, grabbed his umbrella, and headed out the door.

Gareth would know what to do. Gareth always did.

CHAPTER SIX

Mathew walked along Wood Street, umbrella tucked under one arm, sweat dribbling down his face. He'd gone the long way around Saxon's Green to avoid passing Mr Abbasi's shop. He never wanted to see that place again. Not even in his dreams.

He was happier now he'd decided to confide in Gareth. Maybe his brother could accompany him to the Book Café to tell his mother what had happened. Give him some moral support. Help him articulate his thoughts without getting them lost in a pickle jar.

Gareth's flat was in the basement of a large house close to St Peter's Church. He rang the bell to flat 5C and glanced left and right, expecting the police to pull up at any minute and ask him to accompany them to the station. He'd watched enough TV programmes to know that the police sometimes got suspicious of people like him just because they were different to other folk.

Standing on the pavement outside the three-storey stone building, Mathew felt exposed. Almost as if his head was transparent, and anyone walking by could see all the thoughts running around inside his head like the chickens in Mrs Dawkins' garden. His mother said people shouldn't be allowed to keep chickens in residential areas, but Mathew didn't mind the birds as much as he did Cory Wainwright's barking dog.

After two minutes waiting for an answer, Mathew rang the bell again. Kept his finger pressed on the buzzer for a count of ten seconds. Gareth might be in the shower. Or the loo. Or eating breakfast.

Or at work.

Damn! He hadn't thought of that. Lassiter's Estate Agents was open on Saturdays just like the bookshop. Maybe Gareth was out selling another one of those posh houses that made him enough money to live like a king and drive a top-of-the-range car.

Maybe you should phone him.

But what if he was in the middle of doing the biggest deal of the summer? He might get mad and tell him he was old enough to make his own decisions. Which he was. He'd be twenty-one two days before Christmas.

The intercom crackled into life, and Gareth's mechanised voice asked who it was.

'Mathew.'

'Hello, mate. I've just got out of the shower. What do you want?'

'I need to talk to you about something.'

'Okay.' Hesitant. 'What's wrong?'

'The blackbird.'

'What blackbird?'

'The one that was in the kitchen yesterday.'

'You're not making any sense, Mattie. You been taking all your medicine?'

'Yes.'

'Okay. Two ticks.'

Mathew waited on the step, keeping a close eye out for any police cars that might be patrolling the area. His body felt as if it was about to burst into flames. To make matters worse, the stab vest had rubbed his nipples raw over the past few weeks, despite putting copious amounts of Vaseline on them.

Gareth buzzed him in a few minutes later, and he trudged down the concrete steps to the basement. Standing the umbrella up against the wall, he stepped through the open front door into the narrow hallway.

Gareth didn't let him bring the umbrella inside; he said it was bad luck. Mathew wasn't sure if that was right, because he'd looked it up on the internet and it had said it was bad luck to *open* an umbrella indoors. Which was daft; why would anyone want to do that unless they had a hole in the roof? And then it would be best to fetch a bucket and place it under the leak.

He called out and asked his brother where he was.

'In the kitchen.'

'Where's Snowy?'

'Don't worry. He's locked away in the Gaming Room.'

Thank God. Snowy was Gareth's cat. He only had three legs, thanks to getting hit by a car. Although his coat was pure white, Snowy had a dark soul and a tendency to attack anyone who wasn't Gareth.

Relaxing slightly, he headed into the kitchen.

Gareth grinned. 'Hey, bro! Good to see you. Take a pew.'

He sat at a large glass-and-chrome table. It was shinier than the shoes Mathew wore for special occasions.

'Why have you got that coat on? It's at least thirty degrees.'

'They said on the radio it's gonna rain.'

'Today?'

'Monday.'

'But it's Saturday.'

'I know. But the weather forecast isn't always right.'

'I suppose you've got the umbrella, too?'

Mathew nodded. The corner of the stab vest poked his tummy as if reminding him of the real reason he wore the coat everywhere.

'You'll dehydrate.'

Better than getting stabbed. 'I drink plenty of lemonade.'

'Water's far better for you than fizzy drinks.'

'That's what Mum says, but the water tastes yuck out of the tap, and Mum thinks bottled water's a waste of money.'

'Why don't you buy your own water?'

'I'm saving up.'

'What for?'

'In case I ever meet a nice girl.'

'Sensible.'

Mathew sighed. 'I doubt it'll ever happen, though.'

'Course it will. There're loads of girls who'd be lucky to have you as a boyfriend.'

'Do you reckon?'

'Definitely. You just have to be patient and wait for the right one to come along. Do you want a glass of water?'

'Okay.'

Gareth poured a bottle of Perrier into a glass. He added ice from a dispenser built into the large, silver American-style fridge, and placed it on the table in front of his brother. 'So, what's all this stuff about birds?'

Mathew told him everything. From seeing the bird in the house after feeding Tortilla, to walking along the Bunky Line to the farmhouse to look for the little girl. 'And now the girl with the startled eyes has gone missing.'

'Whoa there, Mattie. You're setting off before the starting pistol again. How do you know she's missing?'

'It said so on the radio.'

'You sure it's the same kid?'

49

Mathew bobbed his head. 'Double sure. They even said what clothes she was wearing and everything.'

'And you think Jim Bentley has got something to do with it?'

'Yes.'

'Just because he walked off in the same direction?'

Mathew nodded.

'But he could have been going anywhere, Mattie. Meeting his girlfriend to take her home for tea. It doesn't mean he's done anything bad.'

'He called me a retard. Said how come you're normal and I'm stupid.'

'Ignore him. He doesn't know you like I do. Do you want me to have a word with him?'

Mathew considered the offer for a moment, then shook his head. It would only make matters worse. 'I'd like to see him locked up in prison.'

'Even if he's done nothing wrong? You've got to be careful what you say in case it comes back on you.'

'Like a boomerang?'

'Exactly.'

'Tortilla told me to tell Mum.'

'Is that tortoise still alive? He must be at least a hundred by now.'

'He's thirty.'

'Wow!'

'Do you think I should tell Mum?'

'I don't see why not.'

Mathew tapped his leg. 'What if the police ask me about the girl?'

'Why would they?'

'Because I was in the shop the same time as she was, and I told Mr Abbasi someone was going to die.'

'Why the… why did you tell him that?'

'Because of the blackbird.'

'But the blackbird means nothing, mate. It's just an old wives' tale. Like throwing salt over your shoulder or not walking underneath ladders.'

'That's what Mum said. But now Jodie's gone missing, and it's all come true.'

'It's probably just a coincidence.'

'Do you think so?'

Gareth nodded. 'Absolutely. You go home and have a rest. Order a pizza for tea later to save Mum cooking. Then have a chat with her about it.'

'Can't I stay here until she comes home?'

Gareth shook his head. 'Sorry, mate, I'm too busy today. If I get time tomorrow, I'll come round and see you.'

'Really?'

'Scout's honour. Now get outta here before I call the police.'

Mathew walked home in a slightly better mood than he'd left. For the first time since he'd seen the girl with the startled eyes being followed along St John's Road by Jim Bentley, he felt everything would work out okay. All he had to do was tell the truth.

Or so he thought.

CHAPTER SEVEN

A lison hadn't slept. Not even a five-minute doze in the chair. Her hair stuck out in wild clumps as if it was an extension of her mind. She opened the front door to a tall thin man who introduced himself as DS Palmer. Judging by the creases in his black suit, he looked as if he might have slept in it.

She invited him in. Asked if there was any news.

Palmer followed her into the lounge and folded himself into a dining chair. 'Not as such. We've tried to contact Jodie by phone, but it was switched off at 6:47 p.m.'

Alison's heart stalled. 'Whereabouts?'

'Somewhere on the Milton Park Industrial Site in Didcot.'

Alison's eyebrows shot up. 'How the hell did she get all the way out there?'

'That's what we're trying to find out.'

'But she wouldn't just go off for no reason. She only went a few hundred yards up the road for milk.'

'We think it's possible she may have caught a bus.'

'But why would she do that?'

Palmer had no answer to that. 'We're checking the CCTV footage from Thames Travel. And talking to local cabbies.'

Alison's hands clutched at her top. 'Someone's snatched her. Someone's taken by baby.'

'I know why you might think that, Mrs Willis, but—'

'I'm not married anymore. Willis is my maiden name.'

Palmer nodded. 'Apologies. Does Jodie have a computer?'

'No. Just her phone. We can't afford more than the bare essentials at the moment.'

'Do you own a computer?'

'I've got a laptop. Why?'

'It might be worth taking a look at it.'

'What for?'

'In case Jodie's been using it.'

'She doesn't know the password.'

Palmer gave a weak smile. 'Don't underestimate kids. They can be a lot smarter than you think.'

'But she wouldn't do that. Not without my permission.'

'Would you mind if I took the laptop away just to make sure?'

Alison shrugged. 'I don't care what you do as long as you find my daughter.'

'Thank you. Have you had any fallouts with Jodie in the last few weeks?'

'I already told the other copper I scolded Jodie for using my makeup, but it was something and nothing. There's no way she'd have run off for something as trivial as that.'

'Where's Mr Stevens?'

'Out looking for her.'

'How long has he been living with you?'

'Three years.'

'Get on all right?'

'Mostly.'

'What about him and Jodie?'

'To be honest, he doesn't have that much to do with her. He lets me deal with her most of the time.'

'We've been to your ex-husband's house, but there appears to be no one home. Have you any idea where he might be?'

'No.'

'How do you get on with your ex?'

'No offence, but I keep getting asked the same questions over and over. Shouldn't you be out searching for my daughter?'

'Believe me, we're doing all we can to find her. We're conducting house-to-house enquiries and doing land and air searches. Going through CCTV coverage. We've also checked all local hospital admissions.'

A chain flushed in the downstairs loo, then Alison's mum, Christine, bristled into the room and sat on the sofa. She was a short dumpy woman with a large hooked nose and a tight blonde perm.

Alison introduced her to DS Palmer.

Christine didn't seem interested in formalities. 'How can a child just vanish like that? It's a ten-minute walk along a busy road. Someone must have seen something.'

Palmer nodded. 'I agree. DI Prendergast's making an appeal on the local news tonight. We're also going to release pictures and a description to the local media.'

'You hear about this sort of thing on the news,' Christine said. 'But it never seems real. It's always some other poor sod. I feel as if someone's ripped out my heart and thrown it to a pack of wolves.'

'I know it offers little comfort to you at such a distressing time, but a lot of the locals are busy assisting in the search.'

Christine lit a cigarette. 'They say the first twenty-four hours are vital. If you don't find them by then...' The missing words hung in the air like a pungent smell.

Palmer nodded. 'But there have been plenty of cases where children have turned up weeks later, unharmed.'

Alison wanted to lock those words away in her heart forever. Keep them safe. An antidote to the dozens of tragic scenarios playing out in her mind.

'Does Jodie's father have regular access?'

'No. He takes her out sometimes when he can be bothered. Sends a few quid at birthdays and Christmas, but he doesn't have much else to do with her.'

'Does he pay maintenance?'

'When he feels like it. He's self-employed. Does a lot of cash jobs. Claims he's as poor as a church mouse. But he's a liar. He was always doing cash jobs when he lived with me, and I've got no reason to believe he's any different now.'

Christine shook her head. 'He needs investigating. Driving around in a fancy car and leaving Alison to struggle to make ends meet all these years.'

'How well would you say Jodie gets on with her father?'

Christine puffed on her cigarette. 'She thinks he's a bloody hero. Just because he sometimes puts credit on her phone or treats her to a McDonald's. It's easy to come wading in throwing the cash around for a few hours then vanish back to his tart without a care in the world.'

Palmer wrote in his notebook for a short while, then looked up. 'What about Mr Stevens and Mr Pitman? Any bother between them?'

'Colin always waits up the road when he picks Jodie up. They never cross paths.'

'How would you describe your ex-husband?'

'A total shit,' Christine interrupted. 'A total shit who belongs in a sewer.'

Palmer ignored the older woman and focussed his attention on Alison. 'Does he have a temper?'

'Not really.'

'Has he ever been violent towards you or Jodie?'

'No.'

'Threatened you?'

'No.'

'Done anything you would consider inappropriate?'

'Yeah,' Christine said. 'Left his wife and kid in the lurch.'

Palmer scraped the tip of his pencil across his bottom lip. 'Other than that?'

'Nothing I can think of,' Alison said. 'It's a long time since I had anything to do with him.'

'Do you think Colin's got anything to do with this?' Christine asked Palmer.

'We have to consider all possibilities at this juncture.'

Alison shook her head. 'I can't see Colin doing anything like that.'

Christine perched on the edge of a dining chair. 'That's because you're too trusting. You always see the good in people.'

'I'm not going to say anything that's not true just because I don't like someone.'

Palmer wrote something else in his book, then sucked on the tip of the pencil. 'What about Mr Stevens? Has he ever given you any cause for concern regarding Jodie?'

'No.'

'Does Jodie like him?'

'I don't think she's too bothered about him one way or another.'

'She's never complained or shown any signs of being afraid of him?'

'No.'

DS Palmer stood. He put his notebook away and ran a hand through his slicked-back hair. 'Okay. That's all for now. The liaison officer will be with you shortly. In the meantime, if you've got any questions regarding the case, don't hesitate to contact me or one of my colleagues.'

'Thanks,' Alison said, feeling anything but grateful.

As he was walking back to his car, she asked him whether he thought Jodie was still alive.

'I have no reason to believe she isn't.'

His eyes told a very different story.

CHAPTER EIGHT

Jim was not having a good day. After falling out with his girlfriend, Shona, (casual shag when she was pissed enough or stoned enough to let him have his way with her) he now had the coppers at his door. To make matters worse, if they could be any worse, Shona had nicked his bag of weed to spite him. He had no idea why she'd got so uppity when he'd tried to shave her pubes with a Bic razor to play out a schoolgirl fantasy. Maybe it was the Irish blood in her. Or maybe it was because he'd cut the inside of her thigh while trying to negotiate the blade with two spliffs and three cans of strong cider impairing his vision.

Bentley peered through the peephole again. He didn't need an official ID badge to know that the tall guy in the black suit was a copper; he could spot one at two hundred yards after being arrested four times for drug dealing. He'd also done three years dancing to Her Majesty's tune for something that bordered on the greatest miscarriage of justice of all time.

Prising open the letterbox, he said, 'Whaddaya want?'

The copper bent over. Flashed his ID. 'I'm DS Palmer. I want to have a chat with you.'

Bentley's heart quickened. 'What about?'

'It would be better if I could come in, Mr Bentley. Discuss it in private.'

'I ain't done nothing.'

'No one's saying you have. This is just an informal chat.'

Bentley straightened up. He took the door off the chain and allowed Palmer into the flat. Leading him into the kitchen, he offered him a seat at a battered teak table littered with dirty cups and an ashtray sporting a half-smoked spliff.

'Heavy night, Jim?'

Bentley thought of the amply proportioned Shona leaping up off the bed and threatening to call the coppers on him after slicing her thigh. 'Could say that.'

Palmer eyed the spliff as if it might be an informer ready to tell tales of debauchery. He took a notebook out of his pocket, opened it, and sat with a pencil poised above the paper. 'Where were you on Thursday evening between the hours of six and eight?'

'Here and there.'

'Don't play games, Mr Bentley. Just answer the question.'

'Why do you wanna know?'

'Because a little girl has gone missing, and Mr Abbasi says you were in his shop at the same time as she was.'

For the first time in a long time, Bentley cursed his addiction to booze and drugs. He had very little recollection of his movements (apart from up and down on Shona before the ill-fated attempt to act out one of his many fantasies with her). 'I was with Shona.'

'Shona?'

'My bird.'

'What time did you meet up with her?'

Bentley shrugged. 'Dunno. I don't keep a diary.'

'Where did you meet her?'

'Didcot.'

'How did you get there?'

'Drove.'

Palmer scribbled in his notebook, then fixed Bentley with a look to suggest he didn't think he could drive. 'Where's your car?'

'Down by the garages.'

'Make and registration?'

'Vauxhall Nova. X312 SBE.'

'I take it you have a current driving licence, tax, and insurance?'

Bentley nodded.

'And you wouldn't have any objection to us having a look inside the vehicle?'

Bentley tried to remember what incriminating evidence might be inside the car, but his mind was incapable of doing a snap inventory. 'Why?'

'Just to rule out any involvement on your part.'

'You don't think I had anything to do with that kid disappearing, do you?'

Palmer shrugged. 'I'm just making enquiries to establish a timeline and rule people out.'

Bentley tried to recall where he'd gone after seeing the kid, but there were massive chunks of life missing from his memory. He remembered going back to the flat at some point and smoking a spliff before driving to Sainsbury's carpark to pick up Shona. He also knew that they'd gone to the river and returned to Feelham sometime later that night. But all the in-between bits were blank. Wiped from his memory like files from a computer.

Maybe the kid's hiding somewhere in that doped-up head of yours, a voice whispered. The one closely related to paranoia.

'So, would you mind if we take a look in the car?'

An image of a blood-stained boot popped into his mind. The child lying inside with her hands and feet bound with rope. But that was just bollocks. His mind playing tricks on him. He'd never hurt a kid... would he?

'Jim?'

'Fill your boots. You won't find nothing in there.'

64

'Did Shona stay with you all day Friday?'

Easy one. 'Yeah.'

'Never left your side?'

Bentley shook his head. But there were some large slices of Friday missing as well. Right up to when she'd buggered off squawking as if he'd tried to cannibalise her. Booze and dope suddenly turned from allies into enemies. 'Not unless she went somewhere while I was asleep.'

'But you were here all day?'

'Yeah.'

'And you haven't left the flat for anything since you brought Shona back to the flat?'

'No. I don't know why you're wasting time with me. It's—'

'I'm trying to establish what's happened to Jodie Willis. After all, you do have a bit of form with underage girls.'

Bentley tried to snort but only hacked phlegm. 'I wondered when you'd bring that shit up. For a start, that vicious little bitch was almost sixteen. And she was begging for it.'

'According to your file, you raped and abused her because she owed you money for drugs.'

'Bollocks.'

'Beat her black and blue.'

'She got someone to do that to her. Fucking bitch set me up because I didn't want to see her again as soon as I found out her real age. She told me she was eighteen, and so did her tits and her makeup.'

Palmer scribbled in his notebook, lips compressed, brow furrowed.

A memory. Sudden and jolting. How the fuck had he forgotten? 'I'll tell you who you ought to be talking to.'

Palmer looked up, eyebrows raised. 'Who?'

'That retard, Mathew Hillock. He was in Abbasi's shop babbling a load of shit about killing someone. He's nuts. The whole family's fucking cuckoo.'

Palmer nodded. 'We're well aware of what Mr Hillock said.'

'No wonder you lot can't catch a cold. You should be arresting that sicko instead of pestering me.'

'Thanks for the advice, Jim. I'll be in touch if we need a psychiatric evaluation for Mr Hillock. Oh, by the way, Jodie's phone was switched off in Didcot.'

'So?'

'Just saying, seeing as you drove there to pick up your girlfriend.'

Jim's heart almost careered off the road. 'Hundreds of people drive to Didcot every day. There's no law against it, is there?'

'No. But we can rule out most people because of the timeline. Where does Shona live?'

'Milton Heights. Why?'

'What number?'

'Fifty-six.'

Palmer wrote it down. 'Does she live with her parents?'

'Just her mum.'

'How old is she?'

'Nineteen.'

'You sure about that, Jim?'

Bentley wasn't. 'That's what she told me. But I never asked to see her birth certificate.'

'Maybe you should have, what with your track record.'

'Maybe I should've done a lot of things.'

'Or not.'

'What's that supposed to mean?'

'Nothing. What's Shona's surname?'

'McGee.'

Palmer made a note of it. 'I think that'll do for now. I'll see myself out.'

Bentley watched him walk along the hallway and vanish out the door. He needed a spliff. Or a six-pack of Strongbow Super. Or both. Jesus Christ, this couldn't be happening. He didn't even know the bloody kid had gone missing. But he knew Mathew Hillock had been jabbering on about murdering someone, and now, hey presto, the girl was missing along with his memory.

Maybe you'd better call Shona. Go through the timeline between Thursday night and now. Get your stories straight. Fill in the missing blanks before the coppers do it for you.

And wasn't that the cock-sucking truth? They'd stitched up enough poor bastards to strip the cotton fields bare. It wasn't about what you'd done – it was about what they *thought* you'd done; and there was a whole Grand Canyon of a gap between the two.

Jim Bentley banged his head against the table several times. His brain bounced off the walls of his skull. Why did bad shit always happen to good people like him?

CHAPTER NINE

Mathew tried his best to keep still, but his feet and hands seemed to have other ideas. He tapped the dining table, and his feet scuffed against the laminate flooring with rhythmic squeaks. His mother was in the kitchen making sandwiches for lunch. Ham and pickle. His favourite, only today he wasn't hungry. Not while Jodie was still missing.

He'd dreamed about her last night, but the dream had been fragmented, like pieces of a puzzle that he couldn't quite piece together. He remembered dream-Jodie had been skipping along the Bunky Line, ponytail swishing behind her like a tail. But every time he'd called out to warn her something was wrong, the words had got stuck in his throat.

The doorbell rang, and Mathew jumped. His imagination treated him to an image of a policeman at the door, a pair of handcuffs dangling in one hand, an arrest warrant in the other.

'Get the door, Mathew,' his mother shouted.

Mathew didn't want to. Even though Gareth had told him to tell her everything about not going to the river and going to the Bunky Line instead, he couldn't bring himself to say something that would disappoint her. Fibbers were next to thieves on his mother's list of undesirables.

'Mathew?'

'I don't feel well.'

Appearing in the doorway brandishing a large bread knife, Sonia Hillock frowned. 'What's wrong?'

Mathew gawped at the knife as if the blade knew his innermost secrets. He tapped the table again. 'My tummy hurts.'

'What have you been eating?'

'Nothing.' The truth. Unlike the tummy ache. His feet scraped across the floor again as if preparing to run.

So great was his relief when Gareth walked into the lounge, he almost leapt up from the table and leapt into his brother's arms. Opting for a more reasonable form of greeting, he held up his right hand and waited for Gareth to high-five him.

Gareth obliged. 'How's it going, Mattie?'

'Okay.' Somewhere between a lie and wishful thinking.

Sonia asked Gareth if he would like anything to eat.

'No, ta. I've just had a coffee at Costa.'

'That's not food.'

'I had a boiled egg for breakfast.'

Sonia made a face to suggest her son was on the verge of extinction. 'Suit yourself.'

As soon as his mother was back in the kitchen, Gareth whispered, 'Have you said anything to her yet?'

'No.'

'Why not?'

'I don't want to upset her.'

'She's not gonna tell you off. She loves you.'

'She told me off when I left my shoes at school.'

'Not being funny, mate, but that was before you needed to shave.'

Sonia put a plate of ham and pickle sandwiches in front of Mathew. 'What's this about shoes?'

'Nothing. Nothing important.'

'Mattie said you told him off once for losing his shoes,' Gareth said.

Sonia frowned. 'When?'

'At school,' Mathew said. 'You were mad at me 'cos I walked home in my socks after someone hid them in the changing rooms.'

Sonia shrugged. 'Don't remember that. Would you like a glass of milk with your sandwiches?'

'Yes, please.'

Gareth followed his mother into the kitchen. 'There's something he wants to tell you, but he's worried you'll get mad at him.'

'What?'

'I think it's best if he tells you himself.'

Sonia poured a glass of milk and returned to the dining room. 'Gareth says you want to tell me something.'

Mathew's insides wobbled. 'Not really.'

Gareth sat opposite him. 'Just tell her, mate.'

'Don't want to.'

'Do you want me to tell her instead?'

Mathew looked at the table. 'No.'

'Come on, Mattie. It's not half as bad as you think it is.'

'Isn't it?'

Sonia laid a hand on her son's shoulder. 'Just tell me what it is. I promise I won't be mad at you.'

'You will.'

'I won't. I swear on the moon and the stars and the nears and the fars.'

'Promise?'

'Cross my heart and hope to die.'

'Don't say things like that. It scares me.'

'Sorry.'

Mathew drained his milk. 'It was all Jim Bentley's fault.'

'Who?'

'The local idiot,' Gareth explained. 'A legend in his own head.'

Sonia looked at Mathew. 'What's this Jim Bentley chap done?'

As he was about to tell her, the doorbell rang. Saved by the bell.

This time his mother returned with a tall man dressed in a dark-blue suit. He smiled and held out his hand. 'I'm DS Palmer. Thames Valley Police.'

Mathew thought he seemed like a wolf with bad intentions. He tapped his right hand on the table, fighting an urge to get up and run. He shook Palmer's outstretched hand. 'Mathew.'

'Pleased to meet you, Mathew.' He turned his attention to Gareth. 'And you are?'

'Gareth. Mathew's brother.'

Palmer shook the older brother's hand. 'Good to meet you.'

Gareth nodded. Shot Mathew an impatient glance. 'Would you stop tapping your hand, Mattie?'

Mathew grabbed the hand and stilled it. It pulsed beneath his palm, demanding to be let free. But that would be rude, and he didn't want to upset Gareth. He wanted his brother with him if the policeman started asking awkward questions such as where he went on Thursday night.

'Take a seat,' Sonia said.

Palmer sat next to Gareth. Mathew thought the detective still appeared tall enough to reach the ceiling without a ladder.

'Would you like a cup of tea?' Sonia asked. 'Or coffee?'

'A glass of water wouldn't go amiss. It's hot enough outside to fry eggs on the pavement.'

Mathew thought that was a really dumb thing to say, especially when everyone had cookers at home.

Plus, the ground was dirty where dogs went to the toilet and slugs slithered all over it.

Sonia returned with a glass of water.

Palmer took a few sips and placed the glass on a coaster. 'I'm investigating the disappearance of a little girl called Jodie Willis.'

Mathew's heart skidded to a halt.

'Is that the girl who went missing?' Sonia asked, joining the three men at the table.

Palmer nodded and stared at Mathew. 'A witness has informed me that you were in Abbasi's Convenience Store at the same time as Jodie Willis. Is that correct?'

Mathew stared at a picture of his father hanging above the oak sideboard. His kind blue eyes peered out from beneath a floppy sunhat. A faint smile played on his lips.

'Mathew?'

'He saw the girl,' Sonia said. 'But that's all. Then he went for a walk down the river, didn't you, love?'

Mathew nodded.

Palmer took another sip of water. 'The witness also stated you said someone was going to die. Is that correct?'

'That's because there was a bird in the house on Thursday morning,' Sonia said. 'It's meant to mean someone's going to die. It's just a silly old wives' tale.'

Palmer returned his attention to Mathew. 'Can you please tell me your exact movements between 6 p.m. and 9 p.m. on Thursday 6th of August?'

Mathew's hand, despite his best intentions, broke free and tapped the table.

'What time did you leave home to go to Abbasi's?'

'Six. I always get my paper at six.'

'And what time did you leave Abbasi's?'

Mathew shrugged. 'Probably about twenty-past six.'

'Then what did you do?'

'Sat on a bench at the corner of Croft Road.'

'For how long?'

'Don't know.'

'You need to tell the detective about Jim Bentley,' Gareth said. 'It's important.'

Palmer raised an eyebrow. 'Mathew?'

'He was in the shop. Calling me names. Then he came and sat next to me on the bench.'

'Did he speak to you?'

'Yes. He asked me how come I was a retard when Gareth was normal. His eyes were all red and weird like he was drunk or on drugs. I tried to ignore him. Gareth says Bentley's a loser, and Gareth's right. A loser with a tiny brain and a big mouth.'

'So, what happened next?'

'The little girl walked by, and Bentley asked her if she would make him a cup of tea.'

'Why would he say something like that?'

'Because she was carrying a carton of milk.'

'Did Jodie speak to him?'

'No. She just ignored him and carried on walking. Then he got up and followed her.'

'And that was the last you saw of her?'

'Yes.'

'Did you go home then?'

Mathew's fingers picked at a knot in the table.

75

'I already told you,' Sonia interrupted. 'He went for a walk down the river.'

Palmer nodded. 'Is that right, Mathew?'

Scraping back his chair with enough force to tip it over, Mathew said, 'I don't want to talk about it no more. I said someone was going to die, but no one would listen. And now she's dead.'

He stomped through the kitchen, opened the back door, and went into the garden. He didn't want to talk to the detective anymore. Not until he'd asked Tortilla what to do.

Even though DS Palmer appeared to be a reasonable man, Mathew knew the police were good at saying things to trap people. He'd watched enough programmes on TV to know that sometimes the police put the wrong people in jail.

CHAPTER TEN

Tortilla was in his customary position in the corner of the shed. He didn't acknowledge Mathew as he walked inside and closed the door behind him. He also seemed uninterested in a wasp buzzing around the window as if trying to cut a hole in the glass to let himself out.

The barometer on the shed wall informed Mathew it was thirty-three degrees. Hot enough to fry eggs on the pavement if you didn't care about hygiene like DS Palmer. He sat on the floor by Tortilla and laid a hand on the shell. He thought it was really clever how tortoises were born with their own ready-made homes. Somewhere they could hide when they didn't want to be disturbed by detectives looking for dead little girls.

'I'm in trouble.'

Why?

'Because of the lie I told about going to the river.'

Oh, that.

'Yes, that.'

I told you to tell your mum the truth.

'I chickened out.'

Why?

'Because I'm as dumb as everyone says.'

True.

'Thanks!'

Don't mention it.

'There's a detective in the house.'

What does he want?

'He's trying to find out what happened to Jodie.'

Jodie?

'The kid who went missing.'

So, how come you're in the shed talking to me?

'I don't want to speak to him anymore. I'm scared in case he thinks I killed her.'

But you didn't. The police need evidence to solve crimes. They can't just lock you up for no good reason.

Mathew wasn't sure if that was true. He tried to remember all the cases he'd watched on TV, but his mind refused to think of anything other than the girl with the startled eyes and the carton of milk.

The shed door opened. Gareth leaned around the corner. 'What you doing out here, Mattie?'

Mathew tapped Tortilla's leopard-print shell. 'Nothing.'

'You can't be doing "nothing". Everyone's doing "something".'

'I don't want to talk to the detective.'

'Why?'

'I don't like him.'

'Does it matter? He's only doing his job.'

Mathew tried to think of a reasonable response. Instead, he begged Gareth to go back inside and tell the DS he was too tired to answer any more questions.

'I can't do that, Mattie.'

'Why?'

'He's gonna get suspicious.'

Mathew's hand tapped harder against the shell. His feet jerked back and forth on the wooden floor. 'But I don't like the way he keeps looking at me as if he knows something I don't.'

'Don't worry about that. The police are always like that. They're suspicious by nature.'

'But I don't know what happened to her. All I know is she walked past us on the bench and then Jim Bentley followed her.'

'Then that's all you need to say.'

'But I told Mum I went to the river when I didn't.'

'Just tell the truth, Mattie. You know what they say about being honest?'

'What?'

'The truth can't lie.'

Mathew wasn't sure what Gareth meant by that, but it was probably true because Gareth was clever and he didn't tell lies. At least, not to him. 'Do you promise?'

Gareth saluted. 'Scout's honour.'

'I'm tired.'

Gareth held out a hand. 'Come on. Let's get this over and done with. Then I'll treat you to a pizza.'

'I've got sandwiches.'

Gareth hauled his brother up. 'They'll be stale by now.'

As they walked back into the dining room, DS Palmer smiled. Mathew wasn't fooled. The detective was only trying to make him feel comfortable and put him at ease so he could trick him with his questions.

Gareth gestured for Mathew to sit at the table, then took his own seat next to Palmer. 'Mathew's sorry he ran out. He's just feeling tired. We all are in this heat.'

'Okay. That's understandable. I promise this won't take long.'

Mathew fiddled with his plate of uneaten sandwiches. 'But I've already told you everything. Jodie walked past us on the bench, then Jim Bentley followed her.'

Palmer opened his notebook and sat with a pencil poised. 'Along St John's Road?'

'Yes.'

'How far did you watch them go?'

'As far as the bend near the Brooklands Estate.'

'And you didn't follow them?'

'No.'

'Then what did you do?'

'I sat on the bench for a while, then I went for a walk.'

'Where did you go?'

Mathew gawped at his mother, lower lip trembling. 'I'm sorry. I didn't go to the river. I went along the Bunky Line.'

Sonia seemed about to say something, then closed her mouth.

'Why did you go along the Bunky Line?' Palmer asked.

'To see if Bentley had taken Jodie there.'

'Why would you think that?'

'Because of the farmhouse.'

'What farmhouse?'

'The one where the girl died.'

'Are you referring to the Calum Sheppard case?'

Mathew nodded.

Sonia picked at a loose thread on her yellow tee-shirt. 'But why did you say you went to the river?'

'I... I didn't want to worry you.'

'And you think lying to me is the best way to achieve that?'

'I'm sorry.'

'He was only doing what he thought was best,' Gareth said. 'He wasn't trying to hurt you.'

'Did you see anything suspicious when you walked along the Bunky Line?' Palmer asked.

'No.'

'How far did you go?'

'Up to the farmhouse.'

'Did you look inside?'

'No. I was too scared. My imagination kept showing me stuff.'

'Like what?'

'Bentley with the little girl.'

'How do you mean?'

'Tying her up. Hurting her.'

'How long did you stay there?'

Mathew shrugged. 'Don't know.'

'What time did you get home?'

'About half eight.'

'And you saw Jodie in the shop around six?'

'Yes.'

'That's quite some time before you got back home. How long were you at the farmhouse?'

'I can't remember.'

'Did you see anyone else along the Bunky Line?'

'No.'

'So, no one can verify your whereabouts between half six and half eight?'

Mathew shrugged. 'I don't know what anyone else saw.'

'Prior to seeing Jodie in the shop, have you ever spoken to her or had contact with her before?'

'No.'

'Seen her before?'

Mathew dug his nails into the bare flesh of his leg. 'No.'

'Not even around town?'

'No.'

'In the bookshop?'

'No.'

'Do you know Terry Stevens?'

'Who?'

'Jodie's step-father.'

Mathew's nails drew blood, wet and sticky on his skin. Still, it was better than letting his hand loose on the table to wreak havoc. 'Never heard of him.'

'What about Alison Willis?'

Mathew shook his head.

'Mathew's told you everything he knows,' Gareth said. 'He clearly doesn't know any of these people.'

Palmer shrugged. 'Sometimes people forget. Even the minutest detail could be important in solving a case. I know it seems as if we're going round in circles sometimes, but I can assure you we have very good reason to ask these questions.'

Mathew stood before he gouged any more of his leg. He needed to cut his nails. 'I'm going to bed now.'

Palmer snapped his notebook shut and stood. 'Okay. That's all for now. If you remember anything, anything at all, get in touch.' He handed Mathew a card with his personal number printed on it.

Mathew took the card. 'Okay.'

Palmer glanced at the wound on his leg. 'You're bleeding. How did you do that?'

Mathew didn't answer. He stared at the floor.

'It's nothing,' Gareth said, filling the awkward silence. 'Mattie does things like that to himself when he gets agitated.'

Mathew watched Palmer's gaze fall upon his leg again. The detective's eyes looked full of suspicion. Mathew didn't like him. He didn't like him one little bit.

CHAPTER ELEVEN

Alison felt as if her small terraced home had become a prison. She'd already had three reporters banging on the door asking her for a comment. The Police Liaison Officer, a lovely woman called Michelle, had advised Alison to say nothing. Alison had gladly agreed. The press were like a pack of wolves, waiting to gorge on the misery of her family.

Christine sat by the window, a cigarette in one hand, the other holding back the edge of the curtain so she could see what was going on outside. 'There's about half a dozen of them camped out there now.'

'Ignore them,' Michelle said. 'They're only doing their job.'

Christine puffed on her cigarette. 'Some job. Why do they keep taking pictures of the house?'

'I know it's annoying, and an invasion of your privacy, but they do have their uses. Especially concerning publicity for the case.'

The doorbell rang. Christine announced that it was DS Palmer with a 'fat dumpy guy' she didn't recognise.

Michelle went to the door and let the two men in. A flurry of reporters' questions, as if blown in on the wind, followed them inside the house. DS Palmer introduced the other man as DS Corrigan.

Michelle asked the two detectives if they wanted a drink. Both requested water and then sat on the battered green sofa like two awkward uncles at a family gathering.

'Have you got any news?' Christine asked.

Palmer shook his head. 'We're really not sure what's happened at this stage.'

Christine stubbed out her cigarette. 'It's been close on three days now, and you still haven't got a clue?'

'I wouldn't go quite that far. But—'

'All those cameras everywhere, and not one sighting?'

'We're still studying CCTV from Lassiter's Industrial Site.'

'What about Abbasi's?'

'There is footage of Jodie in the shop buying milk.'

'Who else was in the shop with her?' Christine asked.

'At the time Jodie left, there were two other men and the shopkeeper.'

'What men?'

'Two locals. Jim Bentley and Mathew Hillock. Do you know either of them?'

Alison shook her head. 'Never heard of them.'

'Isn't Hillock that simpleton who works in the Book Café with his mother?' Christine asked. 'The one who always wears a bloody great coat, even in the middle of summer?'

Palmer nodded. 'He suffered some sort of brain injury when he was a child.'

'Have you spoken to him yet?' Alison asked.

'Yes.'

'And?'

'He's confirmed that he was sitting on a bench at the end of Croft Road with Mr Bentley when Jodie walked by carrying a four-pint carton of milk.'

'Don't need to be Inspector Morse to work out who the prime suspect is, do you?' Christine said. 'I don't understand why people like him are even allowed to walk the streets.'

'Please don't jump to any conclusions,' Palmer said. 'Being odd doesn't necessarily make you guilty of anything.'

Corrigan took his drink from Michelle and drained it in one go. He put the glass on the coffee table. 'DS Palmer's right. If all offenders appeared at odds with the world, our job would be an awful lot easier.

Unfortunately, most criminals look normal. Plausible. Go unnoticed in a crowd. It's how they get away with things.'

Alison tucked a loose strand of hair behind her ear. 'Does Bentley know Hillock?'

'Only in passing.'

'What does Bentley have to say for himself?'

'That he picked up his girlfriend from Didcot and spent the rest of the evening with her.'

'Do you believe him?'

Corrigan stood. 'We have no reason not to at the moment. We'd like to have a look around the house and the garden, if that's all right with you.'

'One of your lot's already done that.'

'I know. But we'd like to see for ourselves. We'll start upstairs and work our way down.'

Alison flapped a hand. 'Do whatever you want if you think it'll help find my daughter.'

'Thanks. We'll try to make this as quick as possible.

As soon as the police went upstairs to begin their search, Christine resumed her vigil at the front window. 'There's a BBC news van out there now.'

Alison sighed. 'I don't care.'

'If I had my way, I'd shoot the lot of them.'

'Yes, Mother, because that would do us all the world of good, wouldn't it?'

'I'm just saying.'

'Then don't.'

'Pardon me for breathing.'

'Perhaps it would be better to come away from the window,' Michelle said, joining Alison at the table.

'It will only encourage them if they see the curtains moving.'

'They don't care about the likes of us,' Christine said. 'They wouldn't even give us the time of day if Jodie wasn't missing. I went to the *Feelham Herald* once to complain about the council ignoring potholes in the road, and they as good as told me to stop wasting their time.'

'I'm sure they've got better things than potholes to think about,' Alison snapped. Footsteps thudded above her in Jodie's bedroom. She hadn't even got around to making the bed yet. The room would be a tip. Jodie seemed to enjoy living in chaos. But stupid things like that no longer mattered. Alison would have given anything to have her beautiful little girl home again making all the mess she wanted.

Just over an hour later, the two detectives returned to the front room. Corrigan looked as if he'd just run a marathon. Under normal circumstances, the difference in the two men's size and stature might have made Alison smile, but these were not normal circumstances. Alison didn't think she'd ever smile again.

She watched them going through the cupboards and drawers in the Welsh dresser. Taking out paperwork. Bills, receipts, old photo albums – so dated compared to the storage facilities of the digital revolution.

'What are you looking in there for?' Christine asked. 'She's not gonna be hiding in a cupboard, is she?'

Palmer shook his head. 'I'm sorry. I know it doesn't seem relevant, but it's a necessary part of the investigation.'

After they'd finished rifling through the contents of the dresser and a matching sideboard, Alison followed them into the kitchen and watched them search the cupboards and base units. They even checked in the fridge-freezer and the washing machine.

Palmer stretched, hands almost reaching the spotlights on the ceiling. He looked out the window and asked Alison if the shed was locked.

'No. There's nothing in there except a knackered lawnmower and a load of junk.'

'I'm just going to check inside.'

As he headed out of the back door, she turned to Corrigan. 'She's dead, isn't she?'

Corrigan appeared thoughtful for a moment. 'From my experience, I'd say you should always expect the unexpected. We had a young girl around Jodie's age who went missing in Oxford three years ago. Four days later, a kid found her trapped in a garden shed when he kicked his football over the fence. Tired, cold, and hungry, but still very much alive.'

Alison wanted to hang on to that for all she was worth, but life had taught her optimism was only for those born on the other side of the tracks. The ones whose lives rolled along as smoothly as a brand-new car on a freshly tarmacked road.

CHAPTER TWELVE

Two hours after Corrigan and Palmer had left the house, there was a loud persistent knocking on the front door. It sounded to Alison as if someone was trying to break down the door. To make matters worse, Michelle had also gone back to the police station about half an hour ago, leaving the two women alone to fend for themselves.

'Who's that?' Christine asked. 'If it's one of them reporters, I'm gonna give him both barrels.'

Alison walked to the window and peered around the edge of the curtain. Her ex-husband, Colin, was standing on the doorstep. There was a small posse of reporters behind him, firing questions and jostling to get closer to him. Alison couldn't make out what they were saying, but she didn't need to; it would be the usual tripe which had little to do with facts and everything to do with sensationalism.

Alison let go of the curtain. 'It's Colin.'

Colin's deep gravelly voice boomed through the letterbox. 'I know you're in there, Alison. Open the door, or I swear to God I'm gonna knock it down.'

'Look, I'm the last one to take his side,' Christine said. 'But maybe it would be better to see what he has to say.'

'Why should I? He wouldn't answer the phone when I tried to ring him.'

'Because he *is* Jodie's father.'

'Only when it suits him. He's never once called and asked if she needs anything. How she's doing at school. He walked out on us and left us up shit creek without a teaspoon. The only reason he's here now is because he wants everyone to think he actually cares.'

'I know, sweetheart, but you two are gonna have to come together at some point. For Jodie's sake if nothing else.'

Alison paced back and forth in front of the window. 'I hate him.'

'Why won't you answer your phone?' Colin shouted. 'You got something to hide?'

Alison shook her head as if trying to empty his words from her brain.

'Bet that creep Stevens has got something to do with this,' Colin added.

Christine rubbed her daughter's shoulder. 'Come on, don't let him stand there feeding the press with his vile mouth.'

Alison reluctantly agreed. 'But if he threatens me, you call the police straight away.'

'Has he ever been violent in the past?'

'No.'

'You sure?'

'I think I'd remember if he had.'

Christine peered out the window, then went into the hallway. She returned a few seconds later with Colin in tow.

A large man, with a permanent scowl, Colin Pitman always reminded Alison of a bull with a wasp up its arse. He was barely in the front room before he launched a verbal attack on his ex-wife.

'What the fuck's happened? I only got back home from Southsea yesterday, and the old bill were at my door asking questions about Jodie and where I'd been for the last four days.'

Alison ground her teeth to stop her thoughts turning into words.

'Why didn't you answer your phone? It's a bloody good job Linda's been with me all week at the caravan park to give me an alibi. I dread to think what the coppers would have thought if I'd been somewhere on my own.'

'They're only doing their job,' Christine reminded him. 'But, as usual, you seem more concerned about yourself than your daughter.'

'You want to watch that mouth of yours, Christine. It's gonna get you into serious trouble one day.'

'Are you threatening me?'

Colin laughed. A chilling sound without humour. 'I'm just giving you some friendly advice.'

'I don't take advice from pigs. Especially ones who dip their snouts in other people's troughs.'

Colin's hair, bleached white by the sun, made his face look like an overripe tomato. 'I'm gonna ignore that on the grounds that you have the mental capacity of a frog.'

'Pack it in. Both of you.' Alison turned to her ex. 'Just say what you've come to say and leave. I've got enough on my plate without listening to you two exchanging insults.'

'I just want to know what's happened.'

Alison sighed. 'Jodie went to Abbasi's to get milk and didn't come home.'

'I bloody well know that already.'

'That's it. There's nothing else to tell.'

'What were you thinking of, sending Jodie to the shops on her own?'

'What the hell's that supposed to mean?'

'She's a child.'

'She's eleven years old. She walks to school on her own. Goes to dance class. What are you suggesting? I never let her out of my sight?'

'If that's what it takes to keep her safe, then yes.'

'Says the man who abandoned her when she was two years old. Didn't even have the decency to say goodbye.'

'That's got nothing to do with this.'

'Hasn't it! Maybe if you'd done your fair share towards caring for her, none of this would have happened.'

'Now you're talking crap. I'm not the one who moved a dodgy bloke in with me.'

'And how, exactly, is he "dodgy"? At least he's supported us. Hasn't gone sniffing around other women.'

'Don't listen to him, love. He's judging everyone by his own grubby standards.' Christine turned to Colin. 'Terry might not be perfect, but he's ten times the man you'll ever be.'

'Where is he?' Colin asked.

'At work,' Alison said. 'Not that it's any of your business.'

'You should have called me,' Colin said. 'Told me what was happening. I had a right to know.'

'I tried. It went to answerphone.'

'You obviously didn't try very hard. There was only one missed call all week on my phone from you.'

'So, why didn't you return it? Or didn't you want to ruin your nice little holiday in your nice little caravan with your nice little tart?'

Colin's face went a deeper shade of red. 'Linda's not a tart.'

'If you say so.'

'I'm gonna fight for custody when they find Jodie. You're obviously an unfit mother.'

'Good luck with that,' Christine said. 'No court in the land's gonna award you custody of a child when you're nothing but a selfish overgrown one yourself.'

'We'll see.'

'You'll get custody over my dead body,' Alison said.

'Don't fucking tempt me, Ali. Don't fucking tempt me.'

Christine took a few steps towards him. 'You think you're such a big man, don't you? Coming in here and throwing your weight around. Acting all concerned for your daughter for the first time in your life. But you're not fooling anyone. For all we know, you might have her stashed away in that caravan of yours.'

Colin glared at her. 'Don't you dare suggest that, you spiteful bitch. For your information, plenty of other people at the holiday park saw us. Me and Linda. No one else. Jesus Christ, you really do have a poison mind.'

'And I wonder who poisoned it.' Christine walked into the kitchen and poured herself a glass of water.

Colin wiped sweat from his brow with the back of his hand. He turned back to Alison. 'Anyway, the police asked for the keys to the caravan, so I'm sure they're gonna search it. And they won't find nothing in there because there ain't nothing to find.'

Alison sat at the table. She didn't believe Colin was capable of abducting his own daughter. 'I don't have a clue what's happened to her. Every time I manage to snatch a few hours' sleep, I wake up and forget she's missing. For a few seconds my life is normal again. The sun's streaming in through the curtains. Birds are singing outside. And then I remember she's missing. It's as if the bedroom ceiling collapses, and all my hopes and dreams come crashing down with it.'

'If you ask me, the old bill ought to take a closer look at Stevens. I've never trusted that idiot. Every day I have to hope and pray he's not molesting her. Bullying her. You hear all sorts of shit about blokes moving in with single women to target their kids. Disgusting predators.'

Alison banged a fist on the table. 'Terry might be a lot of things, but he's not a paedophile.'

'How do you *know*?'

'Because I do. It's called instinct.'

'Bullshit, more like.'

'Jodie would've said something to me if he'd been acting out of line.'

'Not if he'd threatened her.'

'Jodie's not scared to speak out.'

Christine walked back into the front room. 'I think you should leave now, Colin. Alison's told you everything she knows.'

He stood. 'You make sure you call me as soon as you hear anything.'

Alison nodded. She watched her mother escort him to the door. Things couldn't get any worse.

Could they?

CHAPTER THIRTEEN

Jim had often felt like committing murder. Bad drug deals, wankers who'd disrespected him, his dad for beating the crap out of him more times than he cared to remember, and his mum for giving birth to him in the first place. But that had all been fantasy stuff. Mind movies to ease the pain and humiliation that had accompanied him all his life.

It had been as much as he could do to stop himself dancing a jig and spitting on the grave when they'd lowered his old man into the ground three years ago. He'd even imagined he was responsible for his death. Killed him with his bare hands and popped out his eyes with a corkscrew.

But there was a vast difference between fantasy and reality. He wasn't a killer. Yes, he was a bit wayward at times. He'd even listen to arguments that he was a loser. A waster. So what? He liked to get high. Guilty as charged. You couldn't travel to amazing places when you hopped on a number forty-nine bus, could you? None of the funky stations were sitting along the railway line. Sobriety was for dumbed-down fools who wanted to spend their entire lives trapped in spiritual prisons.

But this evening, he really wanted to kill. Throttle Shona with his bare hands and bury her in Bentley Senior's grave. He speed-dialled her number for the twentieth time in as many minutes. Straight to voicemail. He'd left about six or seven messages, ranging from "Please call me", to "I'm gonna fucking kill you". Each had been met with silence. No return call. No lame excuses why the bitch wouldn't pick up.

For the first time in as long as he could remember, Jim regretted ever getting stoned. Or, more particularly, stoned the night that blasted kid went missing. Here was the thing eating away at him like a parasite on speed: he couldn't swear that he had nothing to do with her disappearance. The truth, stark and terrifying, was that he didn't know. There were too many chunks of his life missing between

Thursday evening and that stupid DS turning up on his doorstep.

He remembered being in Abbasi's, but not actually walking there. He remembered seeing that retard Hillock on a bench and sitting with him when the girl walked past. But everything else was a blur. Dope could do that to you. One minute you'd be watching TV, the next, you'd be sitting in the communal garden with nothing but blank spaces in between. But Shona could give him an alibi. Say she was with him all day when the kid went missing.

All well and good, Jimmy-boy, but you told that copper you picked Shona up from Didcot around half eight that night.

Shit! His stomach felt as if it was about to evacuate its contents and add soiled boxers to his list of troubles. His head pleaded for a spliff. Request denied. He was staying sober for the foreseeable future. And he was never touching skunk again. Bloody shit was way too strong. He didn't want to end up a paranoid schizophrenic like Archie Harper.

Maybe he could say he got his days mixed up. That he picked her up on Wednesday night instead. She was at the flat with him all day Thursday, apart from when he'd nipped to Abbasi's to get some Rizla papers.

Good idea. If only the stupid little mare would answer her phone!

He dialled again. Same result. Definition of stupid: to continually repeat something and expect different results. He was left with no choice but to drive to Didcot and risk the wrath of Shona's manic mother, Trish.

After rummaging in the kitchen cupboards and emerging triumphant with a packet of Imodium, he swallowed two, brushed his teeth for the first time in a week, combed his dark matted hair, and left the flat.

Half an hour later, he was parked outside Shona's house with the engine running. He didn't dare switch it off in case he had to beat a hasty retreat. Trish McGee had two dominant traits: moody and psychopathic. At least Shona's brutal Irish father was no longer in residence. Thank heavens for small mercies.

He tried to call Shona again. No answer. He gripped the steering wheel to steady his hands. Not because he was afraid, but because he needed drugs. He tried to swallow, but there was no saliva in his mouth. And, as always at times of great stress, he needed to take a leak.

He walked to the door and rang the bell. He didn't have to wait long before Trish opened the door. It was as if she'd been standing guard behind a dirty veil of net curtain, ready to pounce if he came within a hundred yards of her precious daughter.

He tried to calm his nerves by telling himself he knew things about Shona that would make Trish's hairs stand on end, and there were plenty of those black buggers adorning her arms and top lip.

'What do you want?'

Bentley skipped formalities and cut to the chase. 'Is Shona home?'

'Why?'

'I wanna talk to her.'

'What about?'

'It's private.'

Trish laughed. A throaty sound that bubbled like a witch's cauldron. 'Well, she doesn't wanna talk to you.'

'It's important.'

'We've had the police round.'

'Huh?'

'Talking about that kid who went missing.'

Bentley's heart dropped a stitch.

'I told 'em you attacked Shona with a razor blade. If I had my way, I'd have you charged with assault. But Shona, God help her, doesn't wanna press charges. She's softer than a pig's underbelly, that one.'

'Assault?' Bentley squawked. 'I ain't done nothing to her.' But his mind begged to differ. What if it was true? What if he'd done more than just try to shave her pubes? Jesus Christ and Mary, why were there so many holes in his life? All of them offering him a free burial.

'And you think I'm gonna believe you ahead of my daughter, do you?'

'Please, Mrs McGee, I need to see her.'

'It's all right, Mum. I'll talk to him.'

To Jim's tortured mind, Shona's words sounded as if an angel had just descended from Heaven and spoken of enlightenment.

Trish turned to face her daughter. 'After what you told me? Have you taken leave of your bloody senses?'

'I just want to hear what he has to say.'

Trish turned back to Jim. 'You say one wrong word, and I'll have the coppers on you. Do you understand?'

Jim nodded.

'You pressurise my daughter in any way, and I'll have you locked up for intimidating a witness.'

The holes in Jim's mind grew deeper. He cautioned himself to stay calm in the face of provocation. 'I just want to talk. That's all.'

'Words can be as dangerous as a weapon in the wrong mouth,' Trish warned, stepping aside to let Shona pass. 'You need me, I'll be right here.'

'Can we go for a walk?' Jim asked. 'Just around the block or something. I need to clear my head.'

'I don't wanna walk. I'd rather stay here.'

'At least come and sit in the car.'

'Are you stoned?'

'No.' Possibly the first time he'd ever been completely straight with Shona.

'Pissed?'

'I'm clean. I swear.'

After a slight standoff, Shona agreed to sit in the car, as long as he switched off the engine and she could leave the passenger door open. Jim was in no position to argue. If he wanted Shona to lie for him, he would have to make sure he buttered her toast first.

Seated in the car, Jim switched off the engine and tried to order his thoughts into a coherent sentence. It was like trying to command puppies to sit still and behave.

'Why do the police think you've got something to do with that missing kid?'

'Because I saw her in Abbasi's, and I saw her when I was sitting on a bench with Mathew Hillock. But that's it.'

Are you sure, Jimmy? Are you one hundred and fifty percent sure you didn't follow her along St John's Road and take her back to the flat? Do things that only usually happen in your worst nightmares?

'I don't get it,' Shona said. 'They asked me to confirm that I was with you on Thursday.'

'What did you tell them?'

'The truth. You picked me up around half eight, then we went back to yours.'

'Shit!'

'What?'

'Nothing. I just need an alibi from six until eight on Thursday, or I'm gonna end up doing time for something I ain't done.'

'I don't understand.'

Bentley grabbed her arm. 'You don't know the coppers like I do.'

'And I don't fucking want to. Let go of my arm.'

Bentley gawped at her as if she'd just grown a second, far more defiant head. 'None of this would've happened if you hadn't got the hump and buggered off home the other night.'

'I "buggered off" because you tried to mutilate me,' Shona hissed. 'Now let go of my arm.'

'All I wanted to do was shave your pubes.'

Shona yanked her wrist free. 'Why?'

Bentley shrugged. He had no answer to that, other than it had seemed like a good idea at the time.

'Do you have fantasies about schoolkids?'

'No.'

'I think it's best you go home, Jim. I don't want to see you no more.'

Bentley tried a different tack. 'If you don't give me an alibi, I'm gonna tell your old lady what a nice girl you ain't.'

'Fuck off.'

'Tell her about the abortion you had when you was fourteen.'

'She won't believe you.'

'Maybe she will and maybe she won't, but I'm sure she'll have a good time wondering whether her own brother had it away with her daughter. Good job he paid for the abortion, otherwise the poor kid wouldn't have known whether to call him "Great Uncle Tommy" or "Daddy".'

After a few seconds silence, Shona said, 'But I was at home until I walked down the park on Thursday to meet you. My mum's gonna know I'm lying.'

'You were at Rachel Sedgewick's before I picked you up. Don't start messing with my head. All I'm asking you to do is give me two hours. Two lousy hours. Then we can go our separate ways.'

'But I'm crap at lying.'

'Then go back indoors and practise in the mirror if you don't want the world to know who got you up the spout five years ago.'

Shona hoisted her frame out of the car. 'I told you that in confidence.'

'And now I'm telling you this in confidence – tell the coppers you were with me from six o'clock on Thursday, or I'm gonna tell the whole fucking word your dirty little secret.' He switched on the engine, revved it several times, and lurched away from the kerb.

106

Confidence, that fickle friend who never failed to abandon you in desperate times, was once again absent by the time he returned to the flat. He couldn't rely on Shona. Not unless he killed her and removed her ability to contradict him. But if he did that, he would also have to remove anyone else who'd seen Shona before he'd picked her up that night. Especially Rachel Sedgwick.

He sat in his kitchen chugging on a can of Tenants Super. By the time he'd popped the tab on the second one, his mind felt like a car careering downhill with no brakes. He was up shit creek no matter what he did. Unless he could find some way of stitching up that overgrown retard, Mathew Hillock.

CHAPTER FOURTEEN

Monday morning. Day four of Jodie's disappearance.

Mathew sat opposite his mother at the dining table. He watched her nibble on a slice of toast and wished for the thousandth time he was anywhere in the world but Bluebell Cottage. He felt sorry for his mum. None of this was her fault, but he could tell by the dark shadows beneath her eyes she'd not been sleeping well.

'Aren't you going to get ready for work?' Sonia asked. 'We need to leave in half an hour.'

'I don't feel well,' Mathew lied. Truth was, he couldn't stand the thought of facing people when they were probably all gossiping behind his back.

'What's wrong with you?'

'Bad head.'

'Do you want some paracetamol?'

'I'll get some in a minute.'

'I'll pop home at lunchtime to see you.'

'You don't need to do that.'

'I *want* to. Is there anything you need from town?'

'No.'

'Magazines?'

'It's all right, Mum. I just want to sleep.' He almost added *forever*.

'How about some chicken soup?'

Mathew relented. 'Okay. Thanks.'

Sonia stood. 'I'm going to get ready.'

Mathew watched her scurry away. She looked so much older than her fifty-three years, especially without her makeup. He wished he could treat her to a luxury cruise. Something just for her. She deserved it after all the nice things she'd done for him.

He pushed his half-eaten bowl of cornflakes away, stretched, and yawned. He didn't want to face another day. His mood was slipping dangerously close to depression. He hated the dark days. They could appear out of nowhere, triggered by nothing more than a memory or a certain phrase. Sometimes he couldn't even get out of bed. His mother did her best to help him lift his mood, but ultimately, like bad weather, the dark days passed all by themselves.

He was tempted to go back along the Bunky Line and force his way inside the farmhouse. Check the basement for signs of Jodie. But he was too afraid to venture outside when there were people out hunting for the girl all over town. He'd seen it on the news. They were checking the fields, gardens, and all along the river. He'd wanted to shout at the screen and tell them to search the farmhouse.

He went to the sink, poured a glass of water, and took two paracetamol tablets to settle a headache pulsing behind his eyes. He hated headaches, especially the ones that preceded his blackouts. The doctor called them fugues and explained they were reasonably common, but that didn't make them any less scary.

Once, about six months ago, he'd found himself sitting by the river with no idea of how he'd got there. To add to his confusion, he'd only been wearing a tee-shirt and shorts in the freezing cold weather. He'd also found himself in the shed several times with no recollection of going there.

His mother walked into the kitchen twenty minutes later, transformed by eye makeup and foundation. 'I'm going to get off now. Give me a ring if you need me for anything.'

'I'll be fine,' Mathew lied. 'I'm gonna take a shower and go to bed after I've fed Tortilla.'

'Why don't you give your brother a call?'

'He'll be at work.'

Sonia winked. 'Contrary to popular belief, estate agents sit on their bums half the day drinking tea and gossiping.'

'Really?'

'Yes. And don't let anyone tell you otherwise.'

'But he sells million pound houses.'

She smiled. 'I know. But it's not like that all the time. Maybe he could pop round to see you during his lunch break.'

Mathew couldn't think of anything he'd like better, but he didn't want to commit to anything. 'I'll think about it.'

She kissed him on the cheek. 'And don't forget, I'm only a phone call away.'

He waited for her to go before rubbing a smudge of lipstick off his face. His reflection in the small kitchen mirror looked like a cross between a werewolf and a zombie. And little wonder. He'd barely slept since Jodie's disappearance, and when he had, terrifying images of mutilated corpses with startled eyes had dominated his dreams.

He took a large Tupperware bowl of kale and chopped apple from the fridge, opened the lid, and treated the snack to a light dusting of calcium powder. Tortilla's breakfast. As he was about to go outside, the doorbell rang. Thinking his mother had forgotten something, he put the plastic bowl down on the table, rushed into the hall and opened the door.

Mathew's breath caught in his throat. It wasn't his mother. It was Jim Bentley.

'Hello, Mathew.'

'What do you want?'

'Just a chat.'

112

'How do you know where I live?'

'Google knows everything. Especially when it comes to retards.'

'I'm not a retard. Anyway, I can't talk to you. I've got a bad head and I'm going back to bed as soon as I've fed Tortilla.'

'Who the fuck's "Tortilla"?'

'My tortoise.'

Bentley laughed. 'Trust you to pick a pet as slow as your wits.'

Mathew started to close the door.

Bentley jammed his foot in the way. 'Whoa there, Mr Slow Boat. We need to talk.'

'Why?'

'Ain't you gonna ask me in and make me a nice cup of tea?'

Mathew's heart thumped. 'No.'

'Don't you know how to make tea?'

'My mum's here.'

'Don't tell porkies. I just watched her drive off in her car. That's the big metal shiny thing with headlights, in case you're wondering.'

'She's only going to the garage to get petrol, then she's coming back.'

Bentley didn't look so sure of himself. 'All right. I'll keep it simple. I want you to go to the coppers and tell them that you killed that kid.'

'But I didn't.'

'I think you did.'

'You were the one who followed her along St John's Road.'

'I went back to my flat. Where did you go?'

Mathew didn't answer. There was no way he could tell Bentley he went along the Bunky Line.

'I'm waiting.'

'I went for a walk.'

'Bollocks. You took that kid somewhere and murdered her, didn't you?'

'No.'

'What did you do to her, pervert?'

Beads of sweat hatched on Mathew's forehead. 'Nothing. I—'

'Can't get a girlfriend, so you pick on a little kid who can't fight back?'

'I never touched her.'

'Is she still alive?'

Mathew's head felt as if it was about to explode. 'Go away.'

'They ought to castrate perverts like you at birth.'

Mathew pushed against the door. 'If you don't go away, I'm gonna call the police.'

'When you do, make sure you tell 'em what you've done.'

'I haven't done nothing.'

'If you don't admit it, I'm gonna set that fucking stupid bookshop on fire and kill your mummy. Is that clear?'

'Go away!'

Maybe it was something in Mathew's eyes that finally persuaded Bentley to remove his foot from the jamb, but when he did, the door slammed shut with enough force to shake the glass panel in its frame.

Mathew slid a large brass bolt across the top of the door. His legs felt wobbly enough to tip him over. He sat on the stairs and rested his head on his knees.

Are you sure you didn't have one of your fugues again? a voice whispered amongst the gathering storm in his head. *Didn't take that little girl along the Bunky Line and hide her in the farmhouse?*

Mathew didn't have an answer to that.

CHAPTER FIFTEEN

Mathew pulled himself up off the stairs using the banister rail to support his weight. He couldn't remember the last time he'd cried. It was probably just before Gareth had left home and moved into his flat eight years ago.

Mathew, twelve at the time, had held his emotions in check throughout dinner that evening. He'd just sat there fiddling with his food while his mother bombarded Gareth with a million questions. But

Gareth had answered every one with his usual calm assurance. He was doing well at the estate agent's. Decent salary. The rent on the basement flat was cheap enough for him to afford. Yes, it needed a bit of work, but he'd never been afraid to get his hands dirty. Anyway, he knew a few people who could help him get things done. No, he didn't have a girlfriend. His only ambition was to make his way up the ladder at Lassiter's and complete the work on the flat before he went looking to share his life with someone else.

But after dinner, as Mathew had sat in his room staring at the fading light outside the window, Gareth had knocked on the door and asked to come in.

'What do you want?' Mathew had asked, terrified that his brother was about to deliver even more terrible news.

'Just to have a chat.'

'What about?'

'Are you mad with me, Mattie?'

'No.' The truth. He could never be mad with Gareth. He was the best brother in the world. He was just scared by the prospect of living at Bluebell Cottage without him.

'Can I come in, then?'

'I suppose.'

Gareth sat on the edge of the bed. 'You okay?'

'Not really.'

'Is it because I'm moving out?'

'I just don't want you to go.'

'I'm only moving into a flat in Feelham. I'm not going to Australia.'

'But you're the only one who listens to me. Mum's always busy at the bookshop, and I don't like Karen.'

'Karen's all right. Anyway, she only picks you up from school and looks after you until Mum comes home.'

'But I like to tell you about her. Especially the stuff like her smelly armpits and the daft things she says.'

'I've got an idea.'

'What?'

'Why don't you write it all down in a diary, then, say, every couple of weeks you can come round to my flat and read it to me.'

Mathew brightened. 'Promise?'

'Cross my tummy and hope to eat pie.'

Mathew giggled. 'I like your rhymes.'

Gareth saluted. 'Why, thank you, sir.'

'Can I visit you loads?'

'Course. You're my best brother ever.'

'I'm your only brother.'

'Oh yeah, silly me. You can even come to dinner once I've learned how to cook.'

'Can we have sausages and mash? It's my favourite.'

'I'd never have guessed.'

'But I don't like the beef ones.'

Gareth screwed up his face. 'Me neither. They smell like cow dung.'

'Taste like it, too.'

'You ever tasted cow dung?'

Mathew's stomach flipped over. 'That's gross.'

'Dung burgers, fresh from the field.'

Despite feeling sick, Mathew giggled. 'I'm gonna miss you.'

'Me, too. But I'm only gonna be half a mile away. And, we're gonna have a lot more to talk about when we don't see each other every day, aren't we?'

'I suppose.'

Gareth stood and reached into his pocket. He held out a penny. 'I want you to have this.'

'What is it?'

'I found it on the pavement outside the front gate. It was made the same year Dad died.'

'I don't understand.'

'You ever heard the phrase, *Pennies from Heaven*?'

'No.'

'I think Dad dropped it.'

'Why would he do that?'

'To let us know he's watching over us.'

'Really?'

Gareth nodded. 'Think about it, Mattie. It's right outside the gate, and it was made the same year he died. It has to be from him.'

Mathew took the coin and examined it. Just a regular old penny. No golden halo of light around it. 'Thanks.'

'Keep it with you. It'll help you stay safe and look out for you when I'm not around.'

Mathew clutched it in his right hand and closed his eyes. Pictured his father's face in his mind's eye. The kind blue eyes. The hint of a smile. The slight tilt of his head, as if always listening intently.

'I've gotta go, buddy. Sort a few things out. Anything you need, anything at all, just call me, okay?'

Mathew opened his eyes, releasing the image like a helium balloon to the wind. 'Okay.'

He waited for Gareth's footfall on the stairs, then closed the door and threw himself on the bed. He cried until there was nothing left inside him.

Recovering his mind from memory lane, Mathew trudged upstairs to his room. He rummaged in the bottom drawer of his pine dresser and fished out the penny. Kissed it and slipped it into his pocket. He would keep it with him from now on.

As he went back downstairs, hand wrapped around the coin, he felt better about Jim Bentley's threat. Bentley was just an ignorant bully who didn't know the first thing about him. A druggie loser who wasn't worth wasting his energy on.

He walked into the kitchen, grabbed Tortilla's bowl of food, and headed into the garden. Mathew's heart jolted. The shed door was open, swinging back and forth in the breeze. Which was impossible, because he always closed it at night. It was part of his evening routine. Just like brushing his teeth for three minutes. Flossing. Washing his face before going to bed and thanking God for everything he had. Promising to be good, even when the darker days were upon him and he didn't feel like being good.

At least the back gate was still closed. The bolt slid across the top.

Maybe you didn't latch it properly, what with all this bad stuff happening.

Mathew wanted to believe that, but he knew, even at his lowest ebb, he always made sure Tortilla was safe before going to bed. He would never get to sleep otherwise.

The shed door creaked. Mathew crept forward. The baked earth felt as hard as rock beneath his bare feet. A shiver rolled down his spine. He called Tortilla's name.

Silence. Except for some piece of machinery running somewhere up the road. He stopped a few feet away from the door, watching it swing back and forth on its rusty hinges.

He spoke in his mind to the tortoise, asking him if he was all right. Tortilla was unusually silent. Ten feet away, something white was lying on the shed floor. For a moment, he thought it was a fish. But that couldn't be right. The river was over a mile away, and even when it burst its banks, the water never got anywhere near the Brooklands Estate.

Seven feet away. It wasn't a fish. It was a bare leg. For one crazy moment, Mathew thought a homeless person had taken up residency in the shed. But the leg was too small for an adult. Way too small. And as smooth and white as polished alabaster.

Three feet away. He didn't need to see her face to know it was Jodie Willis. His heart seemed to drop into his stomach. He wanted to run, to scream. He rested one hand on the shed wall and peered inside. With a mouth as dry as the weather, he gawped at the lifeless naked body.

He dropped Tortilla's bowl of food on the shed floor. 'Oh no. Oh no. Oh no.' Tortilla was in the corner of the shed, virtually obscured by the body.

Call the police!

Mathew wasn't sure if that was his own thought or an instruction from the tortoise.

Run!

The girl with the startled eyes was lying on her back staring at the roof. Perhaps looking for the angels to take her to Heaven.

Dead, Mattie! She's dead. Dead as the dinosaurs.

His phone was on the kitchen table. Ten seconds away. All he had to do was walk into the house, pick it up, and call the police.

He suddenly realised that Jodie's hair had been cut off. There wasn't even a speck of stubble on her head. Why hadn't he noticed that straight away?

Maybe you had another fugue and cut it off yourself.

He looked at his hands. No. It couldn't have been him. He didn't have any scissors.

Unless you did it earlier.

Mathew thumped the side of his head to shut the voice up. It wasn't helping matters making scary suggestions. He would never hurt anyone, especially a child.

'Why is this happening to me?' he whispered. 'Oh God, why?'

Jodie's mouth hung open, exposing a set of wonky front teeth. It was as if she was trying to tell Mathew who did this to her. But then he already knew the answer to that question: Jim Bentley.

He stepped a little closer to the body. His imagination treated him to an image of the Book Café engulfed in a ball of flame. His mother trapped inside. Burning to death with her beloved books.

'Did Jim Bentley do this to you?' he asked.

Jodie wasn't saying. The freckles on her face moved, as if they wanted to leave her skin before she was buried. But then Mathew realised that the "freckles" were red ants. He wanted to sweep them off, but he knew not to touch the body.

In his mind, he entered the cave. His secret place. A sanctuary where he could seek refuge when he was unable to cope with reality. Without being consciously aware of doing so, he walked into the shed, stepped over the body and sat next to Tortilla. He drew his knees up to his chest and closed his eyes. No more body. No more terror. Just an empty, dark, safe place.

For the time being.

CHAPTER SIXTEEN

Sonia arrived home at just after six. It had been a quiet day with very few customers at the Book Café. Most people who'd come into the shop had seemed more interested in talking about the missing girl. Sonia thought it was terrible that a child could just vanish on her way home from the shop, but she'd elected not to talk about Mathew seeing her, or fibbing about going to the river afterwards. She didn't understand why her son had lied, but it made little difference to her opinion of him. He was a good lad with a good heart.

She called up the stairs to tell him she was home and that she'd stopped at Waitrose and bought some frozen burgers. 'Do you want them with chips?'

No answer. Maybe he was asleep. She put the bag of shopping on the floor, walked upstairs, and knocked on his bedroom door. No answer. She knocked again, this time opening the door a few feet and peering inside. 'Mathew?'

The room was empty, the bed unmade. Sonia's heart jumped. He never left his bed like that; it was one of his many golden rules. Along with putting his clothes away and making sure his bookshelves were tidy and the books all lined up in alphabetical order.

She checked the bathroom and the other two bedrooms before going back downstairs and looking in the lounge. Empty. Despite the humidity, she shivered. Mathew never went anywhere without telling her where he was going. Even if it was only a brief text message.

'Mathew? You home?'

Nothing. Just the ticking of the clock. She checked the downstairs loo, grabbed her bag of shopping and went back into the kitchen. The back door was open, and Mathew's phone was lying on the table. Relief. He was probably in the shed with Tortilla.

She put her shopping away, then ventured outside. The shed door was closed. It had to be roasting inside that wooden box. How Mathew could spend so much time shut away in there with that tortoise was beyond comprehension.

Sonia opened the door. At first her brain refused to process the horrific scene. She stood with her hand clamped over her mouth, gagging at the stench emanating from the baking-hot shed. She gawped at the naked child lying next to her son, Tortilla's food scattered across the floor next to her.

'Mathew?'

He didn't answer. He stared straight ahead as if in a catatonic state. His right hand tapped slowly against Tortilla's shell, and his bare feet thumped the wooden floor. It sounded to Sonia like the rhythm of death.

She looked back at the child. 'What have you done, Mathew? What the hell have you done?'

Tap, tap, thump! Tap, tap, thump!

'Mathew? Speak to me.'

Tap, tap, thump! Tap, tap, thump.

As if seeing clearly for the first time, Sonia noticed the child was bald. And there were several patches of red on her skin that seemed as if someone had scrubbed her clean with something abrasive. 'Oh... my... dear... God.'

Sonia backed out of the shed. She needed to call the police. Or maybe she should call Gareth first and get him to come over. Calm Mathew down and coax him out of the shed before the police arrived.

She stumbled into the kitchen. The heat was unbearable, and there was hardly enough air to breathe. The kitchen walls seemed to close in around her. She staggered into the hall, intoxicated with shock. She fished her phone out of her handbag and sat on the stairs.

Bringing up the menu, she dialled Gareth's number. A female voice informed her that Gareth was busy with a client.

'I need to speak to him. It's urgent.'

'Can I take a message?'

'Tell him it's his mother and I need to speak to him right now.'

'Please hold the line.'

Seconds ticked by disguised as minutes. Mathew's rhythmic tapping drummed in her head. She tried to tell herself that her son would never harm a child. He even took ants and spiders out of the house and set them free. He'd once nursed a bird with an injured wing and cried for hours when it had died.

'What is it, Mum? I'm really busy.'

'You need to come home.'

'Why? What's happened?'

'It's… Mathew.'

'What about him?'

'I think he's killed someone.'

There was a silence on the other end of the phone that seemed to stretch on for hours. Then Gareth said, 'I don't think I heard you right.'

'I think Mathew's killed that child who went missing. He's in the shed with her, and she's dead.'

'Fuck.'

'She's naked, and all her hair's been shaved off.'

'Have you called the police?'

'Not yet. I want you to come home and try to get him out of the shed first.'

'What has he said?'

'Nothing. He just keeps banging his feet on the floor and staring into space.'

'I'm on my way.'

The phone went dead, leaving Sonia alone with only her terrifying thoughts for company.

Fifteen minutes later, Gareth let himself in the front door. His face was red, and beads of sweat glistened on his forehead. 'Tell me this isn't true. Please tell me this isn't true, Mum.'

Sonia hauled herself up on legs that felt barely able to support her eight-stone frame. 'Oh God, Gareth, I can't get my head around this.'

'Is he still in the shed?'

'Yes.'

'How long's he been in there?'

'I don't know. He didn't come to work with me this morning because he said he had a bad head. I only got home ten minutes ago, and that's when I found him.'

'Are you certain the kid's dead?'

'It stinks to high heaven in there, and she's not moving.'

'Have you checked her pulse?'

'I didn't want to touch her.'

'I can't believe this,' Gareth said as they stepped into the garden. 'Mattie even gets upset when the birds catch worms.'

'He has his dark days, though,' Sonia said, the words settling like blisters on her lips. 'And his blank moments.'

Gareth approached the shed, hands held out in front of him as if to ward off an attack. He stopped in the open doorway and turned to his mother. 'You call the police. I'll talk to Mattie and see if I can get him out of there.'

'She is dead, isn't she?'

'I think so. You go back inside.'

Sonia walked back to the house. *Welcome to Hell,* a voice whispered inside her head. *How does it feel to be back where you belong?*

CHAPTER SEVENTEEN

Mathew had no concept of time in the cave. He sat with his back against the cold stone wall listening to bats screeching and rustling on their perches. He didn't mind them, except when they wanted to drink his blood. At least he now had his father's penny from Heaven to protect him. His own special crucifix.

Occasionally, a small orb of light visited the cave and silently observed him reciting poetry. These were the words he would never share with anyone else. Not even Gareth or his mother. Verses of love and unfulfilled ambition.

He sat deep within the cave, a tiny pinprick of light at the entrance. A large rock guarded against predators. As if conjured from thought, the orb appeared. A pure, white light surrounded by a golden aura. Love poured from it, filling his heart with peace. And then, for the first time in all the times the orb had visited the cave, it spoke in his mind the same way Tortilla did.

Hello, Mathew. How are you feeling?

He stared at the orb, dumbfounded by its ability to communicate with him. 'I'm tired.'

That's understandable. The soul has to endure a long arduous journey to reach the truth.

Mathew didn't have a clue what that meant. It sounded religious.

I want you to know that you're loved.

'I know.'

And I want you to listen. Can you do that for me?

Mathew nodded.

You must leave the cave now and go back into the light.

'Why?'

Because you need to put things right.

'What things?'

You'll know when the time comes. Do you know what courage is, Mathew?

'Fighting lions?'

Having the strength to do something, even when you don't want to do it.

'Like working late at the Book Café when I want to write in my journal?'

Not exactly.

'I've upset my mum.'

You haven't. She loves you.

'I love Tortilla, but he still annoys me when I can't find him.'

That's different.

'How?'

There's no time to explain. Please get out of the cave now.

'But…'

The orb vanished, leaving Mathew alone in the darkness once again. Time no longer existed. Minutes could be hours. Hours could be days. The unrelenting darkness allowed no access to the sun in this private universe.

Another voice broke the silence, words straining on a leash, bouncing off the walls of the cave. 'Mattie? What are you doin' in there? Hey, come on, speak to me.'

Dozens of caterpillars crawled across his tummy.

'Who did this, Mattie?'

Don't let him in. He might be trying to trick you.

Good advice.

'Come on, Mattie, let's get you back inside before the police come.'

The word *police* sent a chill through his heart.

'It's me. Gareth.'

Mathew suddenly found his voice. 'Gareth?'

'I'm right here.'

'You can come into the cave if you move the boulder out of the way.'

'Boulder?'

'I put it in the entrance to keep the predators out.'

'Oh. Yeah. Right. Maybe it's best if you move it yourself. I've got a bad back.'

Mathew frowned. 'Why are the police coming?'

'Just to talk.'

'What about?'

'Let's just get you inside first.'

'Is it about the girl?'

Gareth sighed. 'Why don't you get that boulder out of the way so we can see each other?'

'Okay. But you have to be careful.'

'Why?'

'Because there're bats in the cave.'

'Oh.'

'I've got Dad's penny to protect me.'

'Good idea.'

'Is the orb with you?' Gareth asked.

'What orb?'

'The one who visits the cave.'

'No… I'm on my own.'

'Where's Mum?'

'In the house waiting for you. She's made a nice pot of tea.'

'I'd prefer lemonade.'

'I'm sure that can be arranged.'

'Good. I'm thirsty.'

'I'll bet your hungry, too?'

Mathew's stomach rumbled. Like a grumpy bear as his mum used to say when he was a kid. 'I'm starving.'

'How does hot dogs and mustard sound?'

'Yummy to my tummy.'

'How long have you been in the… cave?'

'I don't know.'

'What's he done?' His mother's voice this time. Thin and shrill, as if delivered on a breath of nitrous oxide. 'Oh my God, Gareth, what's he done?'

'It's all right. He's coming out now, aren't you, Mattie?'

Mathew crawled towards the mouth of the cave. 'I want my hot dogs and lemonade.'

'They're on the table waiting for you,' Gareth said. 'Do you need any help to move that boulder?'

'What boulder?' Sonia asked. 'What the heck is he talking about?'

Gareth didn't answer her. He asked Mathew again if he needed any help.

'It's all right; I can move it myself.'

'Have you seen his eyes?' Sonia asked. 'He looks like a zombie.'

'Why don't you go back inside and let me handle this, Mum.'

His mother cried as Mathew removed the boulder from the cave. High-pitched squeaks that reminded him of a mouse. Why was she so upset when he was only in the cave? Maybe it had something to do with the police.

He shoved with all his strength and rolled the rock out of the way. Bright light burned through his eyelids. Leaving the cave was like being born again. It took him a few minutes to adjust to the light and get his bearings. Focus on Gareth. Feel the unbearable heat. Smell the awful stench emanating from the body next to him and hear the flies buzzing around him like dozens of tiny spitfires.

Gareth reached out a hand. 'You want me to help you up?'

Mathew was about to take his brother's hand when he caught sight of Jodie's naked body. Saw the flies. The ants crawling across her face. Eyes staring at the ceiling.

'Mattie?'

Mathew wanted to scream. Go back into the cave and hide with the bats.

'Come on, mate, let's get you out of there.'

He banged the floor. 'She's dead!'

'Don't think about that. Just give me your hand and let me help you up.'

'I want to talk to the orb.'

'You can later.'

'Does the orb know who killed her?'

'Come on, Mattie. Don't upset yourself.'

'The orb told me I need to put things right.'

'Don't worry about that for now. We'll think about that later.'

Mathew's brow furrowed, as if trying to underline his thoughts. 'I didn't kill her, did I Gareth?'

'No.'

'Do you know who did?'

'No.'

'I feel sick.'

'Then let's get inside. You don't wanna puke and contaminate the crime scene, do you?'

'No. But I want to kill those pesky flies.'

'Me, too.'

Mathew's chest swelled. There was a sudden pressure behind his eyes, pulsing down through his nose. And then the tears came. Hot and salty. He banged the back of his head against the shed wall, trying to make everything go away. Several pots lined up on the shelves danced to the rhythm of his heartache.

'She's only a little kid,' he wailed, banging his head harder. 'Dead. Dead. Dead.'

Gareth grabbed his wrists and tried to haul him up. He only succeeded in dragging his brother closer to Jodie's corpse. 'Come on, Mattie, help me out here. I can't lift you up on my own.'

'Mathew? Mathew Hillock?' A new voice. Deep. Male. Breaking through the barrier of his grief.

'He's had one of his blackouts again.' Gareth this time. Familiar. Kind.

'We need to get him out of there and seal the shed off as a crime scene.'

'I know. But please don't do anything to hurt him. He's got enough to deal with as it is.'

'Mathew? My name is PC Harlow. Can you come out of the shed, please?'

'I said someone would die,' Mathew shouted, 'but no one would listen. Now she's dead.'

'It's okay, Mattie,' Gareth said. 'We're listening now.'

'I want to go back in the cave.'

'What's he talking about now?' Deep voice again. PC Harlow.

'It's nothing,' Gareth said. 'It's just where he goes when he's having a blackout.'

Mathew's mother and a plainclothes detective appeared behind Gareth and Harlow.

'Am I in trouble?' Mathew asked. 'Am I in trouble, Mum?'

Sonia shook her head, but her eyes said otherwise.

He allowed Gareth to help him up. His whole body felt numb, but his mind was still full of screeching bats.

CHAPTER EIGHTEEN

DS Palmer agreed to let Gareth accompany Mathew to the police station. Gareth assured his brother that everything would be okay, but Mathew knew it wouldn't. He'd been arrested on suspicion of kidnap and murder, and that meant he was going to get a one-way ticket to a police cell.

Palmer was being nice to him, even telling him to mind his head as he climbed into the back of the police car with his brother, but they had stern faces and spoke in an official language that seemed designed by robots.

Mathew just wanted to go back to his house and lock himself in his bedroom. Maybe forever. The world was too dangerous, and he didn't want to be in it anymore.

Palmer told Gareth to wait outside and led Mathew into a small white-walled room. There were two plastic orange seats either side of a teak desk with a tape recorder sitting in the middle. A middle-aged woman sat in one chair. She was introduced to Mathew as a responsible adult.

'What's that?'

'Just someone who sits in to make sure everything is carried out appropriately.'

Mathew chewed his lip. 'I wanna go home.'

'Take a seat, Mathew.'

'Please! I just wanna go home.'

'You can. Just as soon as you've answered some questions.'

'I don't like answering questions.'

'I know. But these ones are really important. You do understand that, don't you?'

'Why can't Gareth be with me?'

'It's just the rules. Don't worry, though, he's right outside.'

'I'm scared.'

'Why?'

'Because…'

'You've got nothing to be afraid of, just as long as you tell us the truth, okay?'

Mathew sat and wiped sweat from his forehead with the back of his arm. He felt naked without his stab vest and Burberry coat.

'Do you understand why you're here, Mathew?'

'Because of the girl with the startled eyes.'

'I'm sorry?'

'Jodie.'

'That's right.'

'I'm hot. Can I have a glass of lemonade?'

'We've only got water, I'm afraid.'

'Okay.'

Palmer smiled. Mathew didn't think it looked very friendly. More like the way Jim Bentley grinned when he was talking to you.

'I'll see what I can do.' Palmer left the room.

There was a large black clock with a white face on the wall opposite. Twenty past seven. Where had the day gone? One minute he'd been talking to Bentley at the front door, the next he'd been in the shed and Gareth and the police were there trying to get him to come outside. He had no idea why he'd gone into the shed, and no recollection of seeing Jodie's body before Gareth had arrived. It was as if he'd lost a whole chunk of his life, and now he was in the biggest trouble ever.

He wanted to go back into the cave and ask the orb what had happened. Who'd killed Jodie. Why he'd been sitting in the shed with her body. But he could never get into the cave by willing himself there. It mostly just happened. He could be reading a book, or gazing out the window at the people passing by, imagining who they were and where they were going, and BAM! He'd be in the cave, rolling the boulder into place.

Although the day was lost, and he had no recollection of what had happened after his altercation with Jim Bentley, other than preparing Tortilla's food, he was certain this was all Bentley's fault – he was the one responsible for killing Jodie and putting her in the shed.

Palmer returned ten minutes later and interrupted his thoughts. He put a glass of water on the desk in front of Mathew, sat opposite him, and introduced a female detective with short blonde hair. 'This is DC Halliwell.'

Halliwell sat beside Palmer and brushed crumbs from the front of her jacket. A fan whirred on the ceiling, swirling warm air and dust around. She pressed a button on the tape recorder. 'The time is nineteen thirty-two. I'm DC Halliwell.'

Palmer leaned closer to the machine. 'And I'm DS Palmer. We are interviewing…'

Halliwell asked Mathew to state his name for the tape.

'Mathew Hillock.'

'And your address, please?'

'Bluebell Cottage. Brooklands Estate. Feelham.'

Palmer leaned back in his chair. 'Okay, Mathew. First of all, I'd like you to tell us how you came to be in the garden shed with the dead body of a child?'

'I don't know. I was in the cave, and when I came out, she was just there.'

'By the *cave*, do you mean the shed?' Halliwell asked.

'No.'

'Can you explain what the *cave* is?'

'It's my secret place inside my head.'

'What's in the cave?'

'Just bats.'

'Do the bats do anything?'

'No. But I have my dad's penny to protect me.' He reached inside his pocket and exhibited the coin. 'He sent it from Heaven.'

Palmer frowned. 'You are aware this sounds... strange?'

Mathew shrugged. 'It's true.'

'Anything else in the cave, Mathew?'

'Just an orb.'

'Like a spiritual ball of light?' Halliwell asked.

A surge of relief flooded through Mathew. At least she knew about orbs. 'Yes. It spoke to me for the first time today.'

'What did it say?'

'It told me to put things right.'

'What things?'

'I don't know. Then it told me to leave the cave.'

Palmer jumped into the conversation. 'When was the last time you saw Jodie Willis?'

'Today.'

'Before today?'

'Thursday evening.'

'When you were sitting on the bench with Mr Bentley?'

'Yes.'

'You told us you went along the Bunky Line after seeing her. Is that correct?'

'Yes.'

'Why?'

'To make sure Jim Bentley hadn't taken her there.'

'Why would you think that?'

'Because he's a bad man.'

'Is there anything else you want to tell us about Mr Bentley?'

'He came to see me before I went into the cave.'

'What did he want?'

'He told me I had to confess to killing Jodie.'

Halliwell coughed and glanced at her colleague. 'Why on earth would he tell you to do that?'

'I don't know.'

'How well do you know Mr Bentley?'

'Enough to know he's evil.'

'Do you have any idea how Jodie Willis ended up in your shed?'

'No.'

'You do realise it looks suspicious when a young girl goes missing and turns up dead at your property?'

'Yes.'

'Especially when you were one of the last people to see her,' Palmer said. 'Is there something you're not telling us, Mathew?'

'No.'

'Did you take Jodie Willis to the farmhouse along the Bunky Line?'

Mathew tapped his hand against his leg. 'No.'

'Did you keep her there against her will?'

The tapping grew louder. 'No.'

'Do you know who did?'

'Jim Bentley.'

'Do you know that for certain, or are you just saying that to get yourself off the hook?'

'I know he's capable of hurting someone.'

'That could apply to most people given the right circumstances.'

Mathew didn't agree. Most people were decent, hard-working folk who only ever wanted to get on with their lives and be left alone. But he didn't want to argue with the police and upset them.

'It only takes one second to lose control,' Halliwell said. 'One moment of madness, and that's it. No going back. Why did you say someone was going to die when you were in Mr Abbasi's shop?'

'Because a bird was in the house.'

'Did this bird talk to you like the orb?'

'No.'

'Then how did you know?'

'Because that's what a bird in the house means.'

'Like a superstition?'

'Yes.'

'Don't you think it's a bit odd that you're telling people someone is going to die right before a child goes missing?'

'I only said it because it was true.'

'And then, hey presto!' She thumped the desk. 'Jodie Willis is found in your shed four days later. How do you explain that, Mathew? Coincidence?'

'I want to go home now.'

'Did you kill Jodie Willis?'

Mathew wiped sweat from forehead with the back of his arm. 'No.'

'The truth, Mathew. Just tell us the truth and it will be all over for you.'

'I didn't do it.'

'Where did you keep Jodie before taking her to the shed?'

'I want to see Gareth.'

'In the farmhouse?'

'No.'

'The Book Café?'

'No.'

Halliwell stood and announced to the tape that she was leaving the room. It was 8 p.m.

'I didn't do anything,' Mathew said as the door closed behind her. 'It was Jim Bentley. He killed her and put her in the shed.'

Palmer nodded. 'The truth will come out in due course, Mathew. It always does.'

'I don't want to go to prison.'

Palmer ignored him.

'Can I phone my mum?'

'Soon.' Palmer leaned back in his chair and focussed on the clock.

Without being aware of doing so, Mathew smashed his head against the desk.

By the time the detective leapt into action and restrained him, Mathew Hillock was already back in the cave. Only this time the bats wanted to drink his blood and gorge on his flesh, and no amount of pennies from Heaven could stop them.

CHAPTER NINETEEN

Alison opened the door to DS Palmer and a young female PC who introduced herself as Katie Booth. Alison knew from the look in Palmer's eyes that it was bad news. Her stomach seemed to fold in on itself as the detective asked to come in. Behind him, a cluster of reporters, salivating and ready to feed off Alison's grief, shouted questions and bayed for blood.

Alison led the coppers into the front room. Her mother was sitting at the table surrounded by an aura of blue-grey smoke. She was cradling a half-empty glass of red wine. The colour of the alcohol matched her eyes.

'Sit down, please, Alison,' Palmer said.

The young PC, a good foot shorter than the detective, seemed as if she was about to burst into tears at any minute.

'Have you found her?' Alison asked. 'Have you found my baby?'

'Please sit down.'

'I don't want to sit down. And before you ask, I don't want a cup of tea either.'

Palmer nodded. 'I'm afraid we have found someone who matches Jodie's description.'

Alison's body shook as if an earthquake was spreading out from the epicentre of her heart. 'Is she dead?'

'I'm afraid so. But we still need the body to be formally identified.'

The words smashed into Alison's brain. Her heart felt as if a giant hand was squeezing all the love out of it.

'Where did you find her?' Christine this time, wine glass clutched dangerously close to breaking point.

'At a property in Feelham. On the Brooklands Estate.'

Christine put down the glass. 'Who owns the house?'

'All I can tell you at the moment is we've taken a man to Oxford Police Station for questioning.'

'How… did… she… die?' Alison asked.

'Tests are still being carried out to determine the cause of death.'

Terry ambled into the room, hair splayed out in greasy spikes. 'What's this?'

'They've found Jodie,' Christine said.

Terry rubbed his eyes. 'Found her? Where?'

'Some house on the Brooklands Estate.'

'Is she all right?'

'A member of the public alerted us to a child's body,' Palmer said.

Terry frowned. 'What do you mean, *body*?'

'Is that all she is now?' Alison said. 'A body? No name? No identity?'

'Dead?' Terry said, the colour draining from his face. 'Jodie's dead?'

Palmer nodded. 'I'm afraid it appears so. I'm really sorry to have to ask this, but we need someone to formally identify the deceased.'

With no reply forthcoming, Palmer said, 'I know this is an extremely difficult time for everyone, but—'

'Difficult?' Alison screeched. 'You think my daughter being murdered is *difficult*?'

Palmer shook his head. 'No. Of course not. Poor choice of words. Please accept my apologies.'

Alison sat at the table. It felt as if the room temperature had plummeted to zero. 'I'll do it. I'll identify her.'

Terry rested a hand on her shoulder. 'Are you sure, Ali?'

'She's my child.'

'I know, love. But you don't—'

'It's my fault she's dead.'

Terry squeezed her shoulder. 'It's no one's fault but the bastard who murdered her.'

'I should've gone to the shop myself.'

'But you weren't to know what was gonna happen,' Terry said. 'How could you?'

'It was my job to protect her. Look after her. Make sure she doesn't come to harm.'

'You can't start thinking like that,' Christine said. 'No one can watch their kids twenty-four-seven. You sent her to get some milk ten minutes up the road in broad daylight.'

Alison shook her head. 'No, Mum. I sent her out to get snatched by a killer.'

Christine asked Terry to get Alison a stiff drink.

'I don't want a drink.'

'It'll help take the edge off it,' Terry said.

Alison leaned forward and clawed at her hair as if searching for thoughts. 'And that will make it all go away, will it?'

'Of course not, love.'

'Maybe I could have one of those disgusting fags to go with it. Disappear behind a cloud of smoke like Mum does every time she can't cope.'

'No one's suggesting—'

'All I want is my daughter back home where she belongs.'

Palmer nodded. 'I'm so sorry to have to deliver such terrible news. I'll arrange for a Family Liaison Officer to visit. I'll call you in the morning and arrange for a car to come and pick you up. Please believe me, we'll do everything we can to make sure the person responsible for this horrendous crime faces justice.'

'What exactly is justice?' Christine asked. 'Twenty years in jail and out in half the time for good behaviour?'

'I—'

'It's a bloody joke. It's as if the system forgets what they're inside for in the first place. Of course they're gonna behave to get out early.'

'I understand your frustration, but let's just take this one step at a time and try not to look too far ahead.'

'That's easy for you to say,' Christine said. 'It's not you who's gonna be stuck in this moment forever. Who's gonna be lying awake night after night asking why this had to happen.'

Alison looked up, tears blurring her vision. 'Have you got kids?'

Palmer shook his head.

'Then you'll never understand how I feel, will you?'

He had no answer to that. 'I'm sorry. All I can do is promise to do my very best to put whoever's responsible behind bars.'

Alison stood holding the back of the chair for support. Terry tried to put his arm around her, but she brushed it away. She wanted to be alone. Her baby was dead. So cruelly taken in the blink of an eye. It felt as if her heart was a black hole, and she had absolutely nothing left to live for. She'd failed the one person who'd completely depended on her, and she was going to have to take that failure to the grave with her.

Overhead, the first rain for eight weeks fell from a darkening sky. Thunder rolled across the hills to the west of Feelham, as if heralding the beginning of the end for Alison and her family.

CHAPTER TWENTY

Wednesday morning found Sonia barely able to function. She hadn't slept since her son's arrest on Monday night. Gareth had helped her to move some essential belongings to her parents' house at the top of Heritage Road while Bluebell Cottage was sealed off as a crime scene. She'd packed some of Mathew's clothes and put Tortilla in his vivarium, but she didn't think Mathew would be joining them any time soon.

Bernard Halsey, her father, sat in a cream leather chair puffing away on a pipe. 'There's no way on earth that lad could hurt anyone. It's not in his nature.'

'They found him sitting next to that girl's body,' Sonia said. 'Sometimes the truth doesn't matter when the police have already made up their minds.'

'If Mathew didn't do it,' Bernard said, 'then they'll have no evidence against him.'

'What if he touched her? Tried to resuscitate her?'

'I don't think trying to administer first aid is reason enough to convict someone of murder.'

Her mother didn't agree. 'I've seen plenty of programmes where people are sent to jail for crimes they didn't commit. Look at that Steven Avery case in America.'

'This isn't America,' Bernard reminded her.

'What about Timothy Evans, then?'

'Who's he?' Sonia asked.

'He got hanged for murder.'

Bernard puffed on his pipe. 'Good God, woman, that was in the last century.'

'It was still a British court and a British jury that hanged him.'

Bernard pushed his glasses onto the bridge of his nose. 'Next you'll be quoting injustices from the Victorian era.'

'I'm only saying.'

Sonia plucked at a thread on her yellow blouse. 'I know he's not been right since... well, you know...

but I never dreamt anything dreadful like this could happen.'

'The lad's as docile as a spring lamb,' Bernard said. 'Let's have no more talk like that. How long's it been since his arrest?'

'They took him away at about half seven Monday night.'

Bernard looked at his watch. 'Well, it's almost ten o'clock. That's a good thirty-six hours by my reckoning. I thought they had to let him go after twenty-four hours if they haven't charged him with anything.'

Sonia shook her head. 'Gareth said it's different for murder. The police can apply to keep questioning a suspect for up to ninety-six hours. It breaks my heart to think of him all alone in that police station.'

'At least Gareth's with him,' Pam Halsey said. 'And the solicitor. I'm sure—'

Sonia's phone rang and displayed Gareth's name on the screen. 'Hello?'

'Hi, Mum. It's Gareth.'

Sonia tried to speak, but her voice was as lost as her mind.

'What is it?' Bernard asked. 'Has something happened?'

'Mum?' Gareth repeated. 'Are you there?'

Sonia couldn't speak. Tears glistened in her eyes.

'Mum?'

Bernard asked his daughter who it was. When she didn't answer, he took the phone from her. 'Hello? Bernard Halsey speaking.'

'Hi, Granddad, it's Gareth. They're gonna release Mattie around midday.'

'Hey! That's great news. Have they charged him with anything?'

'No. But he has to surrender his passport and remain at a fixed address while the investigation is ongoing.'

'How's he bearing up?'

'He's not saying much. They had to restrain him because he kept banging his head against the desk. I don't think he really understands what's happening to him.'

'Poor lad. Does he remember anything at all about being in the shed?'

'Only that he was sitting by Jodie's body when we got him out of there.'

'What a mess.'

'For what it's worth, I reckon someone drugged him, then put Mattie and the girl together in the shed.'

'But who on earth would do such a thing?'

'I've got my suspicions. But I don't think this is the time or the place to be talking about it.'

'Quite. Let's just concentrate on getting the lad home safe. Then we'll take it from there.'

'How's Mum taking it?'

'As well as can be expected. I think she'll feel a bit better once Mathew's here.'

'Okay. I'd better go. Give my love to Mum and Nan.'

'Will do.' Bernard disconnected the call.

'Have they charged him with anything?' Sonia asked, heart thumping.

Bernard shook his head. 'They're letting him come home at midday.'

'Really?'

156

'That's what Gareth said.'

Clapping as if in receipt of the news directly from Heaven, Sonia smiled for the first time since she'd said goodbye to Mathew on Monday morning.

'I think we should have a special lunch,' Bernard said. 'Do something to celebrate the good news.'

Pam shook her head. 'I don't think we should get too carried away with ourselves just yet. This might only be a temporary reprieve.'

'As far as I'm concerned, the lad's innocent,' Bernard said. 'It might take the police a while to realise it, but I'm confident the truth will come out in the end.'

'Let's have a fish and chip supper,' Sonia said. 'Mathew would like that. Oh, and a nice cold glass of lemonade to go with it.'

Pam stood. 'I'll make up his room up and check on Tortilla.'

Sonia forced a smile. 'Thanks.'

'Everything will be fine,' Bernard told his daughter. 'You just have to stay strong for the lad.'

Sonia wished she could believe that, hang on to it for all she was worth, but it was like being thrown a lifeline, only to find someone had greased the rope.

Gareth accompanied Mathew into the front room. The big guy stood just inside the doorway, head bowed, hands clasped in front of him, hair glued to his forehead in sweaty strands. He begged his mind to take him back into the cave where he could roll the boulder over the entrance and sit alone in the dark.

Bernard strode towards his grandson, stopped just in front of him, and held out his hand. 'Good to see you back.'

Mathew didn't acknowledge him. He stared at the floor as if entranced by the patterns in the carpet.

'I think we need to give Mattie a bit of space,' Gareth said. 'He's exhausted.'

Bernard nodded and stepped back. 'Of course.'

'I need a shower first,' Mathew mumbled. 'They took my fingerprints and put a big cotton wool bud in my mouth. Then they took my blood.'

'I'll set the temperature on the shower,' Sonia said. 'How warm do you want it?'

Mathew didn't respond.

Gareth stepped alongside his brother. 'I think it's best to just give him some space, Mum. I'll take him up and get him settled.'

'And they asked me lots of questions.'

Gareth nodded. 'I know, mate. Come on, let's get you sorted out.'

'I kept telling them I didn't know the answers to their questions. That I'd been in the cave all day, but they wouldn't listen. They kept telling me I had to know something because I was in the shed with her body. But I don't. Why won't they believe me?'

'Because they're daft,' Bernard said. 'The truth will come out in the wash. It always does.'

Mathew shook his head and allowed Gareth to lead him upstairs to his temporary bedroom. He didn't trust the police anymore. They were sneaky. Trying to trip him up with their trick questions. He'd decided not to talk to them again, even if they drove him back to the station and made him sit in that

158

horrible room again with the tape recorder and the big clock on the wall.

Walking into the small box room, Mathew saw Tortilla's vivarium on top of the pine dressing table. He wanted to get him out and talk to him. Tell him how much he'd missed him and promise to never go away and leave him again. But that would be a lie, and he hated telling lies, especially to the tortoise.

Gareth opened the single pine wardrobe. 'Looks like Mum's brought most of your stuff from the house.'

Mathew sat on the single bed. 'Why can't we go home?'

'You know why, Mattie. They're gathering evidence.'

'Tortilla needs to be in the shed during summer. He could get Runny Nose Syndrome if I keep him in the house for too long.'

'But it's not gonna be forever, is it? Just a few more days at the most.'

'What if they arrest me again?'

'They won't.'

'How do you know?'

'Because I know *you*. And so will the police once they've gathered all the evidence.'

'What if the killer planted evidence to make it look like I did it?'

Gareth shook his head. 'You have to stop thinking like that. Killers always make mistakes. Leave clues, no matter how careful they are.'

'This one might not.'

'Do me a favour, Mattie. Have a shower and grab some sleep. You'll feel much better for it. Then we can have a proper chat when you're not so tired.

'I just want to go to sleep and never wake up.'

'I know. But it *will* get better. I promise.'

Mathew stripped out of his tee-shirt and shorts. 'It can hardly get any worse, can it?'

He would soon learn that it could.

CHAPTER TWENTY-ONE

Jim studied the plainclothes policewoman through the spyhole. She didn't need to identify herself; he had an inbuilt radar regarding plod. Her blonde hair curled around her delicate chin. Unlike most female coppers around these parts, this one was a looker. Not a trace of a butch lesbian about her. She even had pretty blue eyes.

'Who is it?' Shona called from the front room. 'I'm only in a towel.'

Bentley strode back into the lounge. 'It's the filth. Go back in the bedroom and make yourself decent.'

'Do you think they're here about the murder?'

'No, Shona, I reckon it's about the unusual number of fucking mosquitos down the river at this time of year.'

Shona uncurled herself from the sofa and tossed her *Take a Break* magazine onto the coffee table. It clipped the edge of a beer can and caused it to teeter and wobble.

'And put some make up on. You look like a lump of pastry that's sprouted a nose and a pair of eyes.'

'Thanks!' She headed off towards the bedroom, a small tattoo of a rose just above her right arse cheek the only sign of anything blooming in Shona.

Bentley returned to the door, took a deep breath, and opened it.

'Hello, Mr Bentley. I'm DC Halliwell. May I come in?'

Jim flashed her his best grin, which might have been a little more appealing if he'd had a full set of front teeth. 'What can I do for you?'

'There's been a development in the Jodie Willis case,' Halliwell said. 'Quite a major one. I'd like to ask you a few questions.'

'Come on in,' Jim said, in a voice cheerier than his mood.

He watched Halliwell's gaze roam all over the flat. The empty beer cans sitting on the table suddenly looked like informants. Bentley gestured to the space on the sofa Shona had just vacated. 'Take a seat. Can I get you anything?'

She declined his hospitality and stood by the TV. 'Can you tell me where you were on Monday morning, August 10th.'

Bentley stalled for time as his mind wandered over the bleak landscape of his memory. Despite his best intentions to stay away from booze and drugs, he'd succumbed to the unbearable pressure in his head.

'That's two days ago, Jim. Not last year,' she prompted.

'I was here with Shona.' A partial truth. 'You can ask her if you like. She's in the bedroom getting ready.'

'Thank you. I will. So, you didn't leave the flat at all on Monday morning?'

'No.'

'Because we have reliable information that you did.'

'From who?'

'Several witnesses have reported seeing a man who meets your description on the Brooklands Estate around eight thirty on Monday morning.'

'That's bullshit.'

Shona appeared from the bedroom dressed in a yellow crop top and matching cotton shorts. Jim thought the transformation was nothing short of miraculous. Even her eyes had changed from bleary to seductive in the stroke of a mascara brush.

'Hey, babe, the police want to know where I was on Monday morning.'

Shona gawped at Halliwell as if she was a love rival. 'He was here at the flat with me.'

'All morning?'

Shona nodded. 'We never left the bedroom.'

'And you've been with him ever since?'

'The only time I wasn't was when he went to Abbasi's on Thursday to get some fag papers. And he was only gone fifteen, twenty minutes tops.'

Bentley almost gave his girlfriend a round of applause for delivering a word-perfect script.

'And you're willing to give a statement to that effect?'

'I'd swear to it on my sister's life.'

Bentley almost lost control and brayed laughter. Shona didn't even have a sister. Just three brothers and a mother all suffering varying degrees of mental illness.

Halliwell turned her attention back to Jim. 'Did you go to Bluebell Cottage on Monday August 10th and threaten Mathew Hillock?'

Bentley's brain stalled. 'Hillock?'

'Yes. Mathew Hillock.'

'Why would I want to threaten that freak?'

'I don't know. You tell me.'

'I didn't. He's lying.'

'As I said, there are several witnesses who put you on the Brooklands Estate at that time. Are they all lying, too?'

'Maybe it was just someone who looks like me.'

'We also have CCTV footage of you entering the estate at eight twenty-seven.'

'You're yanking my chain. There ain't no cameras on the estate.'

'On the contrary. There are several houses fitted with security cameras. So, I'll ask you again, did you go to Bluebell Cottage and threaten Mathew Hillock?'

Bentley glared at Shona, hoping for help. With none forthcoming, he admitted going to Mathew's house. 'But I never threatened him.'

'Why did you go there?'

'To tell him to go to the police and tell them the truth.'

'Which is?'

'It's obvious, ain't it? He was with me on the bench when she walked past. And now she's dead. Said on the news they found her in his shed. No offence, love, 'cos I know you lot are a bit slow off the mark, but how much evidence do you need?'

'Why did you tell Mr Hillock to confess? Do you have any proof that he abducted her?'

'No. But it's bloody obvious. You see a dead bird by a cat, you don't blame the squirrel sitting on the fence. Hillock's a retard. He walks around in that bloody coat with an umbrella in the middle of a heatwave. He says someone's gonna die. I mean, come on, how much more do you need?'

'Did you go inside Bluebell Cottage on Monday morning?'

'No.'

'Did you go into the garden?'

'No.'

'Do you have any idea how Jodie Willis ended up in the shed?'

'Are you serious?'

'Yes, Mr Bentley, I am.'

'Hillock must have killed her and put her in there.'

'Did you threaten Mr Hillock if he didn't help you to conceal the body?'

'He's already told you,' Shona interrupted. 'He was with me Thursday night, and he's been with me all weekend.'

'I need to search the flat,' Halliwell said. 'If that's all right with you?'

'Have you got a warrant?'

'No. But I can get one if you'd rather make it seem as if you've got something to hide.'

Bentley sighed. The nosy bitch could look all she liked; she wouldn't find anything because there was nothing to find. Apart from drugs, and he was certain she wouldn't be interested in such trivialities when she was investigating the murder of a child. 'Be my guest.'

'Thank you.'

'Would you like a guided tour? I could show you around the bedroom.'

'I think I'm capable of finding my way around your flat, Mr Bentley.'

He watched her walk along a narrow corridor towards the two bedrooms and the bathroom. When she was out of earshot, he motioned for Shona to follow him into the kitchen.

Shutting the door, he put his hands around her neck and slammed her head against the wall. 'You say one word out of turn, and I'm gonna bury you in Grundon's Pit. Alive. Is that clear?'

With her breathing restricted, Shona could only manage a slight nod.

'If she asks you anything else, don't answer. And just stick to what I told you to say if they take us in for questioning.'

'Okay.' The word sounded as if it was being fed through a mincer. 'You're hurting me.'

Bentley let go of her throat. 'Not half as much as I will if you fuck this up, Shona. Trust me.'

Shona massaged her neck. 'Why are you being so nasty to me? I'm doing everything you asked.'

'So, keep it that way and you'll be all right, won't you?'

'I ought to call my mum and let her know I'm okay.'

'For fuck's sake, Shona, you're not a kid.'

'I'm scared.'

'Of what?'

'What's gonna happen.'

'Nothing's gonna happen as long as you do as I tell you.'

'Why did you threaten Hillock?'

'Because he's an arse, and I don't want to end up getting blamed for something he's done.'

'Do you swear you had nothing to do with it?'

'I'm not even gonna answer that. I've had it up to here with coppers accusing me of all sorts.' He smacked his forehead with the heel of his hand. 'So if you don't wanna lose that tongue of yours, keep your stupid questions to yourself.'

'What if they find out I'm lying?'

'They won't if you stick to our story.'

'And if Rachel blabs?'

'You told her not to say she saw you on Thursday, right?'

'Yeah.'

'Then we've got nothing to worry about.'

'But she might tell someone else I was there.'

Bentley thought about it for a few seconds, then said, 'Do you believe in God?'

Shona smirked. 'No.'

'Then you'd better start, because if she so much as breathes a word about you being at her house on Thursday, you're gonna need to say your prayers before I kill the pair of you.'

'But I can't control what she says,' Shona whined.

'Then you'd better call her and remind her not to be a silly girl.'

'Now?'

Bentley slammed her head against the wall again. 'Are you really as stupid as you look?'

'No. I—'

'Wait for the copper to go first. And don't look at me like that. You're ugly enough without pulling stupid faces.'

Shona turned away, rubbing the back of her head.

'And sort yourself out before that bitch pokes her nose around the kitchen. You look like you've just been told someone's died.'

CHAPTER TWENTY-TWO

Friday morning found Mathew lying on the bed facing Tortilla's vivarium. The police had told his mother they could move back to Bluebell Cottage on Monday, but Mathew didn't want to live there anymore. He wanted to stay at his granddad's forever. Didn't anyone understand he could never look at the garden again without thinking of Jodie Willis's dead body lying in the shed? Her startled eyes staring up at the ceiling?

It was so unfair that nasty people like Bentley got to live, and good girls like Jodie never even made it to be a teenager. She would never get married. Have children. A job. Live in a nice house.

There was a knock on the door. Twice, in quick succession. Gareth's knock.

'Come in.'

His brother walked in and sat on the end of the bed. The mattress springs creaked beneath his weight. 'How you doing, Mattie?'

'Okay,' he lied.

'Mum wants to know if you'd like some toast and marmalade.'

'I'm not hungry.'

'You've gotta eat, mate. You'll waste away and slip down the drain if you don't.'

This comment would normally make him laugh, but it no longer seemed right to do so when Jodie was dead. 'Don't care.'

'Maybe you don't, but I do. So, eat something for me instead.'

'Why don't you eat something for yourself?'

'Now we're going round in circles.'

'Why does it have to be circles? Why not squares or triangles?'

'Good point.'

'Jodie was only eleven.'

'I know.'

'Not much older than Amy when she died.'

'Three years.'

170

Mathew jammed his thumb into his mouth. 'Amy's always going to be eight, isn't she?'

Gareth shrugged. 'I'm not sure how it all works up in Heaven.'

'She would be twenty now?'

'I know.'

Mathew sniffed and rubbed his eyes. 'It's as if I lost a part of my heart when she died.'

'We all did, Mattie.'

'Sometimes I could tell what she was thinking.'

'Really?'

Mathew nodded. 'Not like I could hear her thoughts or anything, but I knew if she was upset or wanted something.'

'I've heard twins can do that.'

'But I didn't know anything was going to happen on the night she died.'

'I know.'

Mathew thumped his hand against the bedside table. 'How come she died, and I didn't?'

'I don't know, Mattie. Maybe God wanted her to go to Heaven.'

'That can't be right, because that would mean God told Paul Whittacker to attack us, and He wouldn't do that if He was as good as everyone says He is.'

'They say He works in mysterious ways.'

'Stupid ways, more like.'

Gareth nodded. 'Not gonna argue with that.'

'Why did Paul Whittacker kill Dad and Amy?'

'He was a drug addict. His sort will do anything when they're desperate for money.'

'But we were asleep. He didn't have to hurt us.'

'Some people are just evil.'

'He would've killed Mum as well if you hadn't stopped him.'

'I just wish I'd got to the bastard before *any* of you got hurt.'

'I think you're really brave.'

Gareth shook his head. 'To tell the truth, I was shit scared. I don't even remember stabbing him.'

'You're still brave.'

'If you say so.'

Mathew knew his brother didn't like praise; he seemed embarrassed by it. But he shouldn't. He was a hero for saving Mum. Saving him, too, because if Gareth hadn't called the ambulance, the paramedics wouldn't have been able to take him to the hospital.

'Maybe we could go for a walk this afternoon,' Gareth said. 'Get out of here and get some fresh air.'

'I don't want to.'

'How about we go into town and buy some flowers for Amy's grave? Tidy it up a bit before the winter comes.'

Mathew brightened. 'Can we buy some purple stones as well? Amy liked purple, didn't she?'

'Her favourite colour.'

'Do you think she's an angel now?'

'Definitely.'

'Maybe she'll be able to help Jodie when she gets to Heaven.'

'You can bank on it.'

'I miss Amy.'

'So do I.'

'She was pretty, wasn't she, Gareth?'

'Pretty as a peach.'

Mathew frowned. 'Peaches aren't pretty – they're all furry.'

'It's just a saying.'

'Sayings are daft. They make no sense.'

'Not a lot of things do.'

After a short silence, Mathew said, 'I wish I'd died instead of Amy.'

'Don't talk like that.'

'I mean it.'

'It's no good wanting to change things that have already happened. It's pointless and impossible.'

'If I was a superhero, I'd change the whole world so there weren't any bad people in it.'

'You and me both, mate. You and me both. Come on. Let's get some fresh air.'

The walk from the top of Heritage Road into town took half an hour. Mathew felt naked without his coat and stab vest but reassured by Gareth's presence alongside him. No one would hurt him while he had his big brother to protect him. Especially Jim Bentley.

One or two people waiting for a bus at the end of Heritage Road gawped at him, but he was used to that. People always stared at him because he looked *different*. Sometimes, he pretended he was a film star, and they were staring at him because they wanted his autograph. He was the leading man in all the best romantic comedies – Hugh Grant in a Burberry.

But when they got into the town centre, people were pointing at him as if he was the Monster of Feelham. Whispering as they scurried past him on the narrow footpath. Nudging one another and talking with their hands held over their mouths.

'Just ignore them,' Gareth said as they stopped outside Say It With Flowers to look at the roses and carnations.

'They all hate me.'

'They're just ignorant because they don't know the truth.'

An elderly woman walked past them. 'You should be locked up.'

'I didn't—'

Gareth grabbed Mathew's arm. 'Ignore her. You'll only make it worse if you argue.'

'But I didn't do anything.'

'I know. But it's all over the news. People just make up what they don't know.'

'Why?'

'Because they're sad. It makes them feel better about themselves. It's like saying, *Hey, I'm not perfect, but at least I'm not as bad as him.*'

'Maybe we should go back to Granddad's.'

'Who's more important? Amy or stupid strangers who don't know the first thing about you?'

'Amy.'

'Then let's hear no more nonsense about going home. I think a nice bunch of pink carnations would look nice on the grave. What about you?'

'Amy liked Daffodils.'

'Daffodils it is, then.'

After buying the flowers, Mathew followed his brother along St Mary's Street and across the road at the traffic lights to Castle Street. At least there was no one to stare at him as they neared the cemetery.

Upon reaching Amy's grave, his nerves had settled down slightly. The blue-grey marble headstone had a streak of bird poo running through Amy's date of birth, but he needed no inscription to know when she was born: one hour after him, three days before the new millennium.

'We need to clean the headstone,' Gareth said. 'I'll get some water while you do the flowers.'

'What am I going to cut them with?'

Gareth produced a small pair of scissors from his jeans pocket. 'These might help.'

Mathew took the scissors. He wished he could remember things like his brother could. Sometimes, he couldn't even remember his own name or what he'd had for breakfast. He knew it was only because of the fractured skull he'd suffered thanks to Paul Whittacker's drug addiction, but that didn't make it any better when the Dark Days came.

Gareth returned with a watering can. He pulled a cloth out of his pocket, poured some water over the headstone, and rubbed it to remove the bird poo. By the time he'd finished, the headstone was almost as clean as the day it had been erected twelve years earlier.

Gareth straightened up and stretched. 'Fit for a queen.'

'Amy was a princess.'

'True. But she'll probably be a queen by now.'

'Do you think so?'

'I know so.'

'I love you, Gareth.'

'Love you, too, buddy.'

'Do you think I'll go to prison?'

'Not if I have anything to do with it.'

Mathew wished he could believe him, but he knew no one could protect him. He was at the mercy of the police, and that was just about the scariest place in the world to be.

CHAPTER TWENTY-THREE

Alison sat on the bed in Jodie's bedroom. Terry and her mother talked downstairs, but the floorboards and the threadbare carpet muted the words. They'd been planning to give the room a makeover when Jodie went back to school. Alison had saved enough money from her part-time job at the school, and Terry had promised to chip in with the rest. They'd ordered a new burgundy carpet, a pine bed and a bright-yellow duvet set from Bedland. Yellow had been Jodie's favourite colour, thanks to her love of daffodils and buttercups.

The duvet was screwed up and hanging over the end of the bed. Dirty washing littered the floor. Alison needed to tidy the room, but she didn't want to do anything to erase that final Thursday from the history of the house.

On a white dressing table with a heart-shaped mirror, a notebook sat open and facedown. She went to the dresser and picked it up. Turned it over and walked back to the bed. The springs creaked as she sat back down on the lumpy mattress.

Her child's writing was so contradictory to the messy room. There was a drawing of a smiling yellow sun in the top right-hand corner of the page. Then Alison read what may have been the last thing Jodie had ever written.

I wish I was a flower,
Sitting in the sun,
Watching all the children play,
Having lots of fun,
Hoping I'll be picked,
To be a special friend,
Someone to depend upon,
Until the very end.

By the time she reached the end of the poem, tears were streaming down her face and spilling onto the page. Her hands trembled as the poignancy of the words filled her heart. The simple wishes of a child. The simple wishes of most people on the planet, captured in one simple verse.

Alison laid the book on the bed. Wiped her eyes. Replayed that fateful Thursday in her mind. Waking Jodie at eleven. Beans on toast for lunch. Telling Jodie to tidy her room, and Jodie rolling her eyes in that way only young girls can. Both defiant and dismissive.

Thursday. A normal day on a normal street. The school holidays starting to drag. Jodie's initial excitement at breaking up for the summer turning into boredom. A lot of the other kids were away on holiday with their parents at this time of year. Some abroad, others at the coast. Alison always felt guilty they didn't have enough money to take Jodie away. Terry's wages at the supermarket kept the wolf from the door, and this year they'd paid off the catalogue, but they'd spent all the spare money on the upcoming bedroom makeover.

So much for plans. So much for hope. She stared at the ceiling. 'Do you really hate me that much?'

God didn't seem to be available for comment. Maybe He was busy plotting the next miserable chapter in someone else's life. The next poor sod to wake up on a warm summer's day and have their heart turned to ice.

Jodie was dead. And all for the sake of a stupid carton of milk so they could have cornflakes for breakfast. Seeing her lying on that cold mortuary slab, dressed in a plain white gown, the strangulation marks around her neck looking like a devil's necklace, had proved heartbreaking beyond anything Alison could have ever imagined. Jodie had seemed so peaceful, yet so violated. Her mouth, once so vociferous, now silent forever. What sort of sick human being could take an innocent child and do something so terrible to her?

There were no words to describe the hatred she felt for the monster who'd taken the life of her beautiful daughter for his own depraved pleasure. Reduced her to nothing but a shell. Jesus Christ, she didn't even know what she wanted to do with Jodie's body. They'd never talked about cremation or burial before. Why would you when your child was only eleven years old?

A knock on the door. If that was her mother come to offer her another cup of tea, she wouldn't be held responsible for her actions. Alison knew she only meant well, and that Jodie's loss had ripped a chunk out of her heart. too, but it seemed the more she tried to help, the more Alison wanted her to go away.

The door creaked open. It was Terry. He looked whiter than the ceiling. Stubble peppered his cheeks and chin. 'I'm gonna nip into town. Is there anything you need, love?'

Alison sniffed and folded the poem in half. 'To change places with Jodie.'

'I know. Me, too.'

'I keep thinking she's gonna walk in any minute. Then we're gonna have a row about the state of her room.'

Terry nodded, eyes downcast.

'I'd give anything to have her back.'

'I know, love.'

'How can she be dead, Terry? How the hell can she be dead? She left here full of life on Thursday. Said she wouldn't be long. Then she never came back.'

'Try not to torture yourself, Ali.'

'How can life be so cruel? What have we done to deserve this?'

'Nothing.'

'She was a child. I should've called you and asked you to pick up the milk on your way home.'

'You can't change what's happened, Ali. None of us can.'

'Or gone myself. Why didn't I do that?'

'You weren't to know what was gonna happen. Jodie's been to the shop loads of times and nothing's happened.'

'I prayed last night. Begged God to send her back to me. Told him I'd do anything if He would make this right and give me back my daughter.'

'I'm so sorry, Ali. I don't know what to say.'

'You know what hurts me the most? Seeing other kids out enjoying the holidays. Wondering why it had to be Jodie. I know it's selfish, and I hate myself for saying it, but I wish it had been one of them instead.'

'That's only natural, love.'

'It's so unfair.'

'I know.'

'I feel so weak and powerless, Terry. I know Jodie's gone. I know she's never coming back. And there isn't a damn thing I can do about it.'

Terry sat on the bed beside her. Wrapped an arm around her shoulder. 'We've just gotta try to stay strong. Hold on to each other for all we're worth. And hope to God they find the bastard responsible.'

Alison unfolded the poem. Handed it to him without speaking. After he'd finished reading it, they collapsed into each other's arms, sobbing.

CHAPTER TWENTY-FOUR

J im sat with his back leaning against the town centre war memorial, chugging his way through a third can of Special Brew. There were five others sitting in a carrier bag beside him. Enough to take his mind on a temporary vacation to the Island of Don't Give a Fuck. He'd also had a line of coke in the flat to celebrate the news that his car had turned up clean. So that meant there wasn't one shred of evidence linking him to Jodie Willis's murder. Along with Shona's alibi, he was cleaner than a lobster in a cooking pot.

But the law didn't care about things like the truth when they had the scent of blood in their snouts. Especially that prick Palmer. Jim would have paid good money to have that cocky smirk wiped off his face.

Shona was currently nursing a black eye and tied to the bed with leather restraints. Jim thought she might also have a few cracked ribs by the way she was struggling to breathe, but it was no more than she deserved after threatening to squeal to the filth if he didn't let her phone her mum. Who the fuck did she think she was? He'd also stomped on her phone and left it to drown in the toilet cistern, just in case she was tempted to tell tales.

He tried to convince himself that everything would be fine as long as they stuck to their story, but the large chunks of life missing from his faulty memory banks kept dragging him down.

In Abbasi's. Click. Talking to the retard on the bench. Click. Waking up in the flat two hours later. Click. Picking Shona up from Didcot. Click. Trying to shave her pubes with a razor. Click. Shona running out on him and nicking his dope. Click. A whole heap of shit falling on him from a great height. Click. You have now reached the end of the tape. Rewind to listen again, or press stop by drinking eight cans of Special Brew.

'I ain't no child killer,' he said as an old lady walked past with a shopping trolley.

She glanced at him as if he might be contagious and hurried on her way.

His mind roamed to DC Halliwell. Or, more precisely, what he'd like to do to her. He'd never fancied a copper before, and for good reason, but she was different. Made Shona look like a scraggy mongrel in an animal rescue centre. Jim was realistic enough to know that his thoughts regarding Halliwell would have to stay locked in his head and kept for private pleasures, but it didn't hurt to have the occasional forage into fantasy land.

'How's it going, Jim?'

Bentley watched Curtis Pollock dump his skinny frame next to him on the memorial steps. 'Are you taking the piss?'

Curtis frowned and ran a hand through a mop of curly dark hair. 'No. Why?'

'Then why are you asking me how I am? Surely even you know what happened to that kid.'

'Jodie Willis?'

Bentley finished his third can and popped the tab on another. 'Ten out of ten.'

'I know she got murdered and they found her in a garden shed somewhere. Arrested the bloke who lives there, didn't they?'

'And then they let him go again.'

'Why?'

'Because they're stupid. But here's the good bit: the filth think I had something to do with it.'

'Why?'

'Because me and Hillock were the last ones to see her alive.'

'Is that the dude with the shed?'

Bentley nodded. 'They've been crawling all over my flat. They even took my car away to search it.'

'Did they find anything?'

'Of course they didn't. I ain't done nothing wrong. Anyway, I was with my bird when the kid went missing. Been with her ever since.'

'Then you ain't got nothing to worry about... have you?'

'Coppers don't give a fuck about the truth. They'd love to see me locked up for something I ain't done.'

'They can't do that without proof, Jim.'

'Wish it were that simple.'

After a short silence, Curtis asked him if he had any gear.

'No. I ain't giving them bastards any excuse to nick me.'

Curtis eyed the crumpled cans littering the step. 'I thought they'd banned drinking in public places?'

'Yeah, well, I ain't staying here. I'm going down the river.'

'I'll come with you, if you want. I ain't got nothing to do.'

'You've never got nothing to do.'

'True. Can I come, then?'

'Okay. At least it'll make a change from Shona's constant whinging.'

'Shona your bird?'

'One of 'em.' Jim didn't see any harm in bending the truth for a dickwit like Curtis. 'Not for much longer, though. Why do women get hysterical all the time? Turn everything into a bloody drama?'

'I reckon it's 'cos they watch all them soap operas,' Curtis offered. 'My mum does. *Emmerdale.*

Corrie. EastEnders. Then she jumps down my throat because I haven't put the bog lid down. Or picked me socks up from the bathroom floor. I mean, fucking hell, what does it matter? Anyone'd think I'd sparked World War Three by the way she goes on.'

'I'll tell you this for nothing: Shona better buck her ideas up or she'll wind up feeding the fish at the bottom of the river.'

'That bad?'

'Worse. Much fucking worse.'

They stopped off at Waitrose so Curtis could buy some cans. Jim treated himself to a scotch egg to fill a grumbling hole in his belly. He could feel people staring at him as if he had no right to be in their nice clean supermarket buying stuff from their nice clean shelves. Fuck 'em. He had nothing to be ashamed of. His money was as good as theirs. All right, he could do with a shower and a change of clothes, and maybe his eyes were sore from a lack of sleep, but that didn't give them any right to look at him as if he was a turd on toast.

As they passed through the checkout and headed towards the exit, a tall security guard in a black jumper and matching trousers asked Bentley what was in his carrier bag.

'Cans. Why?'

'Have you paid for them?'

'I bought them in Abbasi's.'

'Would you please open the bag, sir.'

'I just told you, I didn't buy 'em here.'

'Then you won't mind showing me, will you?'

Jim pointed at a man in a business suit. 'What about him? You gonna check his bag? Or don't you bother with the posh nobs?'

'It's got nothing to do with that. Just let me check your bag, and you can be on your way.'

Jim turned around and addressed the businessman. 'Bet you live on the Brooklands Estate, don't you? Nice posh house, fancy fucking car in the drive, yeah?'

The man ignored him and carried on loading his shopping into a trolley.

'Think you're better than me, do you?'

Showing no signs of acknowledging Bentley, the man paid for his goods.

'Hillock's from the Brooklands Estate. Funny that, considering they all think their shit don't stink.'

'If you don't open the bag,' the guard said, 'I'll have to escort you to the office.'

'Just show him, Jim,' Curtis said. 'Then we can go to the river.'

'Mathew Hillock murdered Jodie Willis,' Bentley shouted, his voice rising several octaves. 'And he lives on the Brooklands Estate. The retard is one of you. One of the posh people. How d'ya like that, eh?'

Several people stared as Jim continued his rant for another thirty seconds. He concluded by pointing in the vague direction of the checkouts. 'Not so fucking perfect now, are ya?'

'Do you want me to call the police?' the guard asked. 'It's up to you.'

At the sound of the word "police", something tripped in Jim's brain. 'All right. All right. I'll show you.' He opened the bag, fished out the receipt, and handed it to the guard.

After studying the contents of the bag and matching them to the receipt, he told Jim to leave.

'Ain't you gonna say sorry?'

'I'm just doing my job, sir.'

Bentley snorted. 'That's what the guards used to say in the concentration camps.'

Curtis grabbed Jim's arm. 'Come on. Let's go. We don't want no trouble.'

'I'd listen to your friend, if I were you,' the guard agreed.

Bentley saluted. 'Okay, sir. Right away, sir. Quick march!' He strode out of the shop, arms swinging by his sides, bag thumping against his hip.

When they reached the river, Bentley's head was pounding. Maybe it was the heat. Or drug withdrawal. Or an overbearing urge to kill Mathew Hillock. Probably all three. And you could throw Shona into that mix if you really wanted to know what was boiling his pot.

They walked along the narrow path towards the weir. It was more private on this side of the water. No campsite and swimming pool. Just a few folk fishing, and the occasional dog walker.

They sat on a bench opposite the old boathouse and drank their cans in silence for a while, just gazing at the water, lost in their own private thoughts. Then Bentley asked Curtis if he'd ever done anything terrible.

'Like what?'

'I dunno. Hurt someone. Ran over a cat on your pushbike.'

'I ain't got a pushbike. I used to have a scooter, but I totalled it one night riding around the industrial site when I was pissed as a pudding.'

Jim laughed for the first time in what felt like forever. 'How many pissed puddings do you know?'

'Huh?'

'Never mind. So, have you ever done anything really bad?'

'I robbed my old lady once. Nicked her rent money to buy some weed. And stole our Johnny's iPad and swapped it with Davey Harper for a joint and six cans of Tennent's Super.'

'Proper little gangster, ain't you?'

Curtis necked the rest of his can in one go and tossed it into the river. 'Not really. I just do daft stuff sometimes.'

'How would you like to earn two hundred quid?'

'Me?'

'No, that fucking duck over there!'

'You serious?'

'Deadly.'

'What is it?'

'I'll tell you later if you're interested?'

'Too right.'

'If you do a good job, I'll pay you five hundred for a second job.'

Curtis popped the tab on another can. 'Sounds good to me.'

Jim touched his tin to Curtis's. 'To the future.'

'To the future.'

Within an hour, they were both asleep in a field backing onto the river, Jim Bentley's plan to murder his girlfriend temporarily forgotten.

CHAPTER TWENTY-FIVE

Ten days after Jodie had been found in the Hillocks' shed, Alison and her mother sat in the front room with DS Palmer and DC Halliwell. Every day seemed to bring fresh torment. The police had confirmed that Jodie had been manually strangled and sexually assaulted. Alison tried hard not to imagine the violation of her daughter's body. How alone and terrified Jodie must have felt being at the mercy of that monster. She should have been there to protect her daughter. Keep her safe. Not send her on errands because she couldn't be bothered to go herself. She'd failed as a mother, and she would never forgive herself for that.

The only blessing, if you could call it that, was at least the press were no longer camped on the doorstep. They'd got their stupid stories, written their sensationalist headlines, and gone on their merry way. Back to their families, safe in the knowledge that it wasn't their daughter lying dead on a mortuary slab. They could move on to the next big story. Forget about Alison and Jodie until the killer was caught. Then begin the process all over again.

'Whoever did this thoroughly cleansed Jodie,' Palmer said. 'There wasn't a single trace of any other human DNA on her body.'

Christine stubbed out her cigarette and lit another. 'I thought you'd arrested Mathew Hillock?'

'We did. But we haven't got enough evidence to charge him.'

'How much evidence do you need? He was in the bloody shed with her.'

'I know, but we've found no physical evidence to suggest he's responsible.'

Christine shook her head. 'Jesus Christ! I don't bloody well believe this. How else do you think Jodie ended up in his shed?'

'The biggest problem we have is finding out where Jodie was between Thursday evening and Monday evening. We know she wasn't at Bluebell Cottage because there isn't any evidence of her presence in the house. Only in the shed. The forensic guys have been all over the place with a fine-tooth comb. Nothing. Not even a stray hair or a fingerprint.'

'Doesn't mean to say Hillock couldn't have cleaned up after himself.'

'That's true. But Mr Hillock's mother has confirmed her son was at home every evening following Jodie's disappearance because he was too distraught to go anywhere apart from the Book Café.'

'She could be covering for him,' Alison said. 'It wouldn't be the first time.'

Palmer nodded. 'It is possible, but we don't have any reason to believe Mrs Hillock has done anything improper. She called the police the minute she discovered Mathew and Jodie in the shed.'

'And as far as we know,' Halliwell added, 'he doesn't have access to anywhere else.'

'What about the bookshop?'

'We've conducted a thorough search of the premises. There's no evidence to suggest Jodie was ever kept there. Again, it would be unlikely Mathew could abduct your daughter and keep her hidden right under his mother's nose.'

'So what are you saying?' Christine asked. 'That's it? Let him off the hook just because you don't have any proof?'

'Not at all. But we need a lot more evidence than we've got to take the case to the CPS. Our biggest problem is a lack of physical evidence. And the manual strangulation marks around Jodie's neck suggest the perpetrator had much smaller hands than Mr Hillock.'

'You've got fingerprints?' Alison asked.

Palmer shook his head. 'The perpetrator wore gloves. But the gloves themselves leave prints just as unique as fingerprints. We can tell what size they were and identify them by distinguishing marks such as stitching and so forth.'

'Fat lot of use that is, then,' Christine said. 'Unless you test every pair of gloves in Oxfordshire.'

'On the contrary. It could prove to be a useful piece of evidence when the case goes to court.'

'*If* it goes to court,' Alison said.

Christine took a sip of water. 'Even my bloody cat could tell you Hillock's guilty.'

'I understand how it looks. But we believe Jodie was killed and placed in the shed by someone else. Mathew Hillock found her and went into an emotional blackout.'

'He'll go into a bloody blackout if I ever get my hands on him,' Christine promised. 'I'll wring his bloody neck.'

'What do you mean, "emotional blackout"?' Alison asked.

'Mr Hillock suffered a serious head trauma when he was eight years old. An intruder broke into his home and beat his sister and father to death with a baseball bat. Mathew survived the attack, but he's suffered some degree of mental impairment since. He sometimes goes into what they call a fugue.'

'What the hell's that when it's at home?'

'It's a kind of trance. I don't know much about it, but he describes it as his cave.'

'Sounds like a load of old fish hooks to me,' Christine said. 'A bloody excuse 'cos he doesn't wanna face up to what he's done.'

'I understand how you feel,' Palmer said. 'But I have to stress that it's important not to jump to conclusions. Believe me, we're doing everything we can to find out who committed this dreadful crime.'

'Not enough from where I'm standing,' Christine said. 'It's been two weeks since Jodie was found, and all you can say is the man sitting next to her dead body doesn't have anything to do with it because he was suffering a mental breakdown. Not good enough, Detective. Not good enough at all.'

Palmer stood. 'I'm sorry we've got nothing more positive to tell you.'

Alison rubbed her eyes with the heel of her hand. 'Do you know what it's like to look at your only child lying dead on a mortuary slab?'

Palmer shook his head. 'I can't imagine—'

'Knowing she's never gonna grow up and have kids. Get married. Come round for Sunday lunch. I had to say goodbye to my baby before she even got to be a teenager.'

DC Halliwell nodded. 'You've been put through hell, Alison. No one wants to see the monster who did this get away with it. If Mathew Hillock is involved, believe me, he will be brought to justice.'

'And what exactly is justice?' Christine asked. 'A nice cushy life in prison for a few years before some idiot psychiatrist deems him fit to be released?'

'Unfortunately, we have no say in sentencing policy, but I can promise you we'll continue to do everything in our power to catch the person responsible. Have you any questions before we leave?'

'Do you have any other suspects apart from Hillock?'

'Not at this time. Sorry.'

Halliwell stood and joined her colleague in the doorway. 'Anything you need, anything at all, please don't hesitate to call.'

'I need you to catch the filthy bastard who did this to my daughter,' Alison said. 'That's it! Nothing else.'

Alison watched them walk into the hall. She had no faith in the police. Maybe they were doing their best, but it wasn't good enough. If Mathew Hillock wasn't responsible for Jodie's murder, then the real killer would get away with it. Be free to kill again. Put another family through hell.

The front door banged shut. Christine shook her head. 'Well, that was a fat lot of good.'

Alison felt the room closing in around her. 'Tell me something I don't know.'

'Do you want me to run a hoover round?'

'No.'

'But the house needs a clean, love. Let me at least do a bit of washing.'

Alison sighed and shook her head. 'I want to be on my own.'

'You know that's not a good idea.'

'Isn't it? Tell me what is, because I'd love to know?'

'Time, Ali. That's the only thing that will help.'

'Bugger time. I've had enough of time. First Colin does the dirty on me, and now I lose Jodie. I can't take any more of this shit.'

'I'm gonna ring the doctor.'

'What for?'

'He'll be able to give you something to help you sleep.'

'I don't want pills. I just want Jodie back.'

'I know you do, love.'

'Then stop rattling on about time and pills. Go home. I don't want you here.'

'I'm not going anywhere while you're like this.'

Alison stood. 'Then I'll stay in my room.' She walked into the hall and ran upstairs. There was no point in living anymore. Her life was over. All she wanted was to be with her beautiful little angel. Take care of her and never leave her side again.

CHAPTER TWENTY-SIX

Thursday morning found Mathew sitting on his bed talking to Tortilla. His mother had gone back to Bluebell Cottage on Monday afternoon. She'd tried to persuade him to go with her, but he'd refused. He never wanted to see Bluebell Cottage again, let alone live there. Granddad had said he could stay with him for as long as he wanted, which was forever, unless the police arrested him again and put him in jail.

'I hate my stupid life,' Mathew told the tortoise.

Try not to get upset. The police said the glove prints around Jodie's neck were too small to be yours, remember?

'I don't trust the police.'

And there wasn't any of your DNA on the body.

'Why can't I remember what happened after Bentley threatened me?'

Because you went into the cave.

'Do you remember me coming into the shed?'

No.

'Did you see who put Jodie in the shed?'

I was asleep.

There was a gentle tap on the door, followed by his granddad peering around the corner. 'Your mum's here to see you, Mathew.'

He tapped his leg. 'I'm not going home.'

'She's not here for that, lad.'

'What does she want?'

'I think it's best if she tells you herself. Why don't you come downstairs and see her? I've just made a nice pot of tea.'

Mathew wondered why his granddad always seemed to think a cup of tea was the answer to everything. *World War Three. Don't worry, I've made a nice pot of tea.*

'Nan's bought some scones from Waitrose. And some proper strawberry jam.'

Mathew would have normally leapt off the bed and bounded downstairs before his granddad had finished the sentence. But he wasn't hungry. Not even for something as nice as scones and strawberry jam.

'You do love your mum, don't you?'

What sort of question was that? He loved his mum more than anyone else in the world. 'Yes.'

'So, just give her a few minutes of your time. I promise she won't take you home if you don't want to go.'

Mathew reluctantly agreed and trundled downstairs still wrapped in his blue-and-green dressing gown.

His mother's appearance shocked him. Her glasses magnified the bags beneath her eyes, and she was dressed in a loose-fitting red tee-shirt and black jogging bottoms instead of the usual smart clothes she wore at the bookshop.

'Mum? What's wrong?'

'Sit down, Mathew.'

He folded himself into a chair at the kitchen table and stretched his legs underneath. 'What's happened?'

'There's no easy way to say this, so I'm just going to say it. The Book Café's gone.'

Mathew tapped the table. 'What do you mean, *gone*? Where?'

'It's been destroyed by a fire.'

He heard the words. Was dimly aware of his granddad sitting at the table with them. His nan flushing the toilet upstairs. But nothing made any sense. How could the bookshop be gone? It had fire alarms.

His mother rested a hand on his arm. 'Mathew?'

'But it can't catch fire.'

'The police think someone set it deliberately.'

Mathew thumped the table. The Book Café was his favourite place in the world. One of the few places he felt comfortable. Where no one poked fun at him. 'But how?'

'By pouring petrol through the letterbox and setting fire to it with a lighted rag,' his granddad said.

'How do they know that?'

'Because the fire brigade have found evidence at the scene.'

'What evidence?'

'I don't know, lad. We'll have to wait and see what the report says.'

Mathew stopped tapping and glanced at his mother. 'Are the books okay?'

She shook her head. 'I'm sorry, love. Everything's been destroyed.'

The tears in her eyes stung his heart. 'But didn't the firemen put the fire out?'

'By the time they got there it was already burning out of control.'

'When did it happen?'

'In the early hours of the morning.'

'Do you think someone did this to get back at me?'

Sonia looked away. 'Who knows.'

'What have the police said?'

'That they're treating it as arson.'

After a short silence, Mathew said, 'I know who did it.'

'Who?'

'Jim Bentley. He killed Jodie *and* set fire to the shop.'

'Well, if he did,' Bernard said, 'he'll get what's coming to him.'

Mathew tapped the table again. 'I hate him. He's a bad man. And a drug dealer.'

'It could've just been a random act of vandalism,' Bernard said. 'I don't think it's wise to jump to conclusions about who might be responsible.'

'I still think we should tell the police about him.'

'I'm sure the police are well aware of Jim Bentley,' Sonia said. 'Like Granddad says, he'll get what's coming to him.'

'When are you going to open the Book Café again?' Mathew asked.

'I don't think we'll be able to. It'll cost a fortune to replace all the books and get all the damage repaired.'

'I thought the insurance company paid for all that stuff.'

'Not all of it. Anyway, I don't think I've got the energy to start over again. I just want to move out of Feelham and never come back.'

'That's because it's still raw,' Bernard said. 'Give it time before you make any big decisions.'

Sonia sighed. 'The way I'm feeling, I don't even want to go back to Bluebell Cottage.'

'Me neither,' Mathew said. 'What if someone sets fire to that as well?'

'You're more than welcome to stay here, Sonia,' Bernard offered.

'We should've moved out of that house years ago, Sonia said. 'It's as if the bloody place is cursed.'

It shocked Mathew to hear his mother swear. She had what Gareth called a *sterile tongue*. 'I'd like you to stay here with us, too, Mum.'

'I don't know. There's so much to do. So much up in the air. I can't even think straight.'

'Why don't we go down to the caravan for a while?' Bernard suggested. 'Get away from all the mayhem.'

Pam Halsey walked into the kitchen and poured herself a glass of water. 'Bournemouth beach is packed in the summer. Sardines have got more room in a bloody tin.'

'There's more than just the beach to enjoy,' Bernard said. 'There are the Winter Gardens. The aquarium. Not to mention all the shows they put on at this time of year.'

'I don't fancy watching a load of second-rate celebrities masquerading as talent, thank you very much. I think we've got far too much to do here, without running off to the seaside to play happy families. Anyway, Sonia needs to be here for the investigation.'

'Mum's right,' Sonia agreed. 'I need to be around to sign things and talk to the police.'

Bernard held up his hands. 'Okay, it was only a suggestion. You do what you think's best. I'm only trying to help.'

'I know, Dad. And I'm grateful.'

'So, what do you want to do, love?' Bernard asked. 'Stay with us or tough it out at home?'

'I think I'll stay with you for a while. Just until I can get my head straight.'

Bernard clapped. 'That's fantastic news.'

Pam, never one to display emotions, treated her daughter to a rare smile. 'Would you like me to go with you and help you pack?'

'It's all right,' Mathew said. 'I'll go with Mum. I want to get the rest of my stuff.'

Sonia nodded. 'Thanks, Mathew. I'd like that.'

'Have the police gone yet?'

'Yes.'

'Do you know if they found anything?'

'Only in the shed.'

'Is it all right if I have a look around the garden while we're there?'

'Why?'

'To see if the police missed anything.'

'I don't think they would, lad,' Bernard said. 'They had a forensic team going over the place with a fine-tooth comb.'

'I still want to look.'

Sonia touched his arm. 'Of course you can.'

Mathew knew the chances of finding something incriminating were somewhere between slim and zero, but it was better to try and fail than to never try at all.

He would later come to wish that he'd never gone back to Bluebell Cottage.

CHAPTER TWENTY-SEVEN

Jim sat in his flat smoking a spliff and adding fuel to the fire with a can of Strongbow Super. He was in a good mood, partly because of the drugs, and partly because events at the Book Café had gone much better than expected. Curtis, who had all the intelligence of a doormat, had surpassed expectations. Not only had he set fire to the place without getting caught, he'd turned the building into a burnt-out shell.

After examining Curtis's handiwork from the safe distance of the pub opposite, Bentley believed the building would never see a day's business again.

'When am I going to get my money?' Curtis asked, stretching out like a cat lazing in the sun.

'As soon as I've got it. But I want you to do something else first.'

'Oh shit, man, I need the dough now.'

'You threatening me, Curtis?'

'No. I just—'

Bentley threw an empty can at him. ''Cos if you are, I'm gonna rearrange your ugly mug so your own mother won't recognise you.'

'It's just I owe the Chisel Twins.'

'How much?'

'A grand.'

'Tell you what, as soon as you complete this next job, I'll settle up your bill with the Chisel Twins myself. Okay?'

'You mean it, Jim?'

'On my life.'

'So, what do you want me to do?'

'Fuck Shona.'

Curtis's lips curled into a lopsided grin. 'Very funny.'

'Am I laughing?'

Curtis took a swig of his lager. 'I can't shag your bird, Jim.'

'Course you can. She's strapped to the bed and gagging for it. Well, she's *gagged* to be exact.'

'I don't wanna fuck your bird, Jim. It don't seem right.'

'You turning up your nose at the offer of a free ride?'

'No. But—'

'Don't you fancy her or something?'

Curtis stared at his beer can as if it might offer him advice. 'It's not that. I just don't know if you're being serious.'

'Never been more serious in my life.'

'I ain't got a condom.'

'So?'

'What if I get her up the gut?'

'Don't worry about that. There's always the morning-after pill.'

'What if she doesn't want me to do it?'

'She's a slag, Curtis. She'll be well up for it.'

'Are you sure?'

'Yep. Now go fill your boots before I change my mind.'

Bentley watched Curtis head off towards the bedroom. He glanced at Jim one last time before opening the door.

'Go on. Give her one for me.'

Half an hour later, Curtis reappeared in the front room. His face had a waxy sheen of sweat glistening on the skin, and his eyes appeared as if they were still in the bedroom.

Bentley popped the tab on another can. His last. He needed an alert mind to carry out the rest of his plan. 'How was it?'

'Good, thanks.'

'Did the bed move for you?'

Curtis brayed laughter. 'Nice one.' He sat on the sofa and finished his can. 'What's happened to her face? It's covered in bruises.'

'She got lippy, so I had to put her in her place.'

'Cool.'

'That's the thing with women, Curtis – they need to know the boundaries. If you let them step over the line, then that's it! You're in for a whole heap of trouble.'

'What did she do wrong?'

'Talked too much.'

Curtis nodded, as if that made perfect sense. 'How long you gonna keep her strapped to the bed?'

'As long as it takes for her to realise she needs to keep her big mouth shut.'

'You might wanna give her some water, Jim. It's roasting in that bedroom.'

'And you might wanna keep your nose out of my affairs if you don't want it broken.'

Curtis recoiled as if the words had physically assaulted him. 'Is there anything else you want me to do?'

Bentley didn't answer. He walked into the kitchen and returned with a large carving knife. 'This baby could carve the meat right off the bone just by showing it the blade.'

Curtis's eyes looked as if he didn't doubt that for one moment.

'Wassamatta, don't you like knives?'

'I do when they're in a drawer.'

Bentley flipped the knife around and held it by the blade. Offered the handle to Curtis. 'You feel the weight of that. It's perfectly balanced.'

He took the knife and held it out in front of him. 'Cool.'

'You ever stabbed anyone, Curtis?'

He shook his head. 'I don't like blood.'

'Why?'

'It gives me the willies.'

'Like you just did to Shona?'

'Huh?'

'Gave her the willies.'

Curtis tried to laugh but only emitted a strange noise somewhere between a cackle and a whine.

'Do you think I've ever killed anyone?'

Curtis's eyes widened. 'I don't know. Have you?'

'Twice. The first one was an accident. I strangled some tart I picked up on a one-night stand.'

'How was it an accident?'

'Because she was into all that choking bollocks, and it went too far.'

'Jesus.'

'But I meant to do the second one. He owed me money and kept fobbing me off with a load of crap about needing more time to pay.'

'So you killed him?'

Bentley nodded. 'Took the fucker round the back of the old Waitrose and slit his throat. Could say I bled him dry.'

This horrific news drained all the colour from Curtis's face. He looked like a wannabe ghost. 'And you got away with it?'

211

Course I did. I just made it up to keep you in your place. 'Murder's easy when it's just a random act. The filth don't have nothing to go on. As long as you wear gloves and don't leave any DNA at the scene, they've got no chance of tracing you.'

'I've never really thought about it. I used to watch some of those crime programmes on the telly, but...'

'It's different in real life.'

'How?'

'Hard to explain. It gives you a better rush than drugs.'

'Even speed?'

'Makes speed look like a fucking snail.'

'My uncle worked in an abattoir. But I don't suppose it's the same killing animals 'cos they're for eating, anyway.'

'And it's legal.'

'I wouldn't wanna work in an abattoir.'

Bentley frowned. 'Why?'

'It'd put me off meat.'

Bentley laughed. 'You're fucking priceless.'

'I'd better get going soon.'

'You're not finished yet.'

Curtis spread his arms. 'But I've shagged Shona.'

'That was pleasure, Curtis, not business.'

'But I've got to run some errands for my mum.'

'How old are you?'

'Twenty-two.'

'Then grow a pair of balls and tell your mummy to run her own errands.'

Curtis tried to hand the knife back to Bentley.

'I don't want it.'

'Neither do I.'

'But you're gonna need it, Curtis.'

'What for?'

Bentley stood. 'Come with me.' He led Curtis back to the bedroom. 'Doesn't she look a picture?'

Curtis didn't answer.

'What's the matter?'

'Nothing.'

'If you're feeling guilty about raping her, don't. She ain't gonna tell no one.'

Shona gawked at her two assailants, one eye hidden beneath a purple-black swelling. Her breathing was shallow, and sweat soaked her naked body. Bruises covered her arms and chest like a map of abuse.

'Don't you think you ought to let her go, Jim? She ain't looking too clever, is she?'

Bentley stroked Shona's hair. 'She's all right. Just a bit washed out, ain't you, love?'

Shona tried to say something, but the duct tape covering her mouth stifled the words.

'You ready to do the next thing on the list?'

'I don't wanna shag her again. I'm—'

'You're not going to.'

'What then?'

Bentley pulled an air pistol out of the waistband of his jeans and aimed it at Curtis's head. 'I want you to kill her.'

'Kill her?'

'That's what I said, Curtis. Kill the stupid bitch.'

'I can't do that.'

'Course you can. It's easy. Just stab her in the chest half a dozen times, and Shona will be a gonna.' He bent the vowels to make the words rhyme.

Curtis shook his head. 'No way.'

'D'you want me to go to the filth and tell them you torched the bookshop?'

'No.'

'Caught you beating and raping my girlfriend?'

'No.'

'Or maybe you want me to call the Chisel Twins and tell them you're round my flat?'

'Please, Jim, don't make me do this. I ain't no killer.'

'Or maybe you want a bullet between your eyes?'

Curtis's eyes widened. 'But why do you want to kill her?'

'Because she needs silencing.'

'Why?'

'Because she knows too much.'

'About what?'

'Never you mind. The least you know, the better. I'm gonna lock you in here for ten minutes, then I'm coming back. Do a good job, and you'll get your money. And a bonus.'

'I can't do this. I already told you I hate the sight of blood.'

'You know something, Curtis?'

'What?'

'It's a good job the likes of you weren't all we had to rely on to defend this country from Hitler. No wonder England's in decline with spineless wankers like you making up half the population.'

'I can't help the way I am.'

'You've got ten minutes, then it's goodnight Vienna. And don't think I won't plug a hole in your head, 'cos I will. Gladly.'

He closed the door and locked it before the wimp responded. If this went as planned, he would get Curtis done for Shona's rape and murder and silence the bitch once and for all. Pollock's DNA was already waiting in Shona's love tunnel for the forensic dudes to discover. The cops would have him bang to rights, so to speak. And serves the dirty little rapist right. If anyone deserved to be locked up for life, it was Curtis Pollock.

CHAPTER TWENTY-EIGHT

They pulled into the driveway at Bluebell Cottage. Mathew's demeanour changed from apprehensive to withdrawn. His hand tapped against the side of the car and his foot pressed down on an imaginary brake pedal in the foot well. He gawped at the front door and imagined Jim Bentley standing there, telling him to confess to Jodie's murder.

Sonia applied the handbrake. 'Are you okay?'

He didn't answer.

'You don't have to come in if you don't want to.'

'I never did it.'

'I know you didn't.'

'Jim Bentley killed her.'

'Just let the police worry about that, Mathew.'

'If they know my hands are too big to match the marks around her neck, why don't they check Bentley's?'

Sonia rested a hand on his arm. 'I'm sure they will.'

'Or search his flat for the gloves?'

'Come on. Don't upset yourself.'

'It's not fair that Jodie's dead.'

'I know.'

'I'll bet it was Bentley who burned down the bookshop.'

Sonia opened the driver's door. 'He'll have made mistakes. Idiots like him always do.'

Mathew didn't think the house seemed like his home anymore. It was just a building with a lot of terrible memories locked up inside.

'Do you want to come in or not?'

Mathew nodded. He had to do this. Try to find one of Jim Bentley's mistakes.

The house felt cool inside, almost as if it had been frozen in time. His Burberry coat hung on the stand at the foot of the stairs. He would need to take it to Granddad's with him. And his stab vest along with the rest of his clothes and the umbrella. Not that he had any intention of going outside again unless it was absolutely necessary. Now the Book Café was gone, Mum would have a lot more time to run errands. Pick up Tortilla's food and get the daily paper from Abbasi's.

'Are you okay?' Sonia asked.

'I'm gonna go to my room and pack the rest of my belongings before I look in the garden.'

'Do you need a hand?'

'No.' The last thing he wanted to do was set his mother's tongue on fire with a thousand questions about the stab vest.

Although his bedroom appeared the same, it didn't *feel* the same. It was as if he was visiting a museum. All his romance novels and poetry books were still lined up in alphabetical order on the shelves. His favourite pale-green duvet cover and matching pillowcase remained on the bed, squared off with military precision. The old wooden chair that his father had made at a woodwork class still sat at a perfect right angle to his wardrobe. Several framed school certificates adorned the wall. One was for winning a writing competition when he was fourteen. Another for outstanding good behaviour. A third for gaining a bronze Duke of Edinburgh award.

He sat on the bed. His room was next to Amy's. Her bedroom had been stripped and redecorated a few months after the attack. All traces of the murder removed. A new divan bed had replaced the bunkbed. His mother had bought a new duvet, pink, with tiny red roses and a matching pink headboard. But Amy would never get to sleep in it. Her vast collection of dolls and soft toys now sat on the bed as if awaiting the return of the little girl who loved to read them all stories and teach them their sums and spellings.

It was a good job Gareth's bedroom was in the basement, otherwise they would have all been dead. Mathew remembered nothing about the attack. He'd gone from asleep to unconscious to comatose in a matter of seconds. He had no recollection of the two months he'd spent in the hospital, or the rehabilitation programme which had followed. There was almost a two-year gap in his memory.

Paul Whittacker would never know how much pain and misery he'd caused. The countless headaches, mood swings, lapses in memory, loss of feeling in his fingers and toes, blackouts, anxiety, depression, and suicidal thoughts. Not to mention the mickey-taking at school because he was different from the other kids.

Therapy had focussed on the benefits of forgiveness, but it was impossible to feel anything but hatred for the man who'd killed his sister and his father. Paul Whittacker was nothing but a selfish waster. Just like Jim Bentley.

He spent the next ten minutes cramming the rest of his belongings into a black leather suitcase. He added his stab vest and the certificates from the wall before leaving his bedroom for the last time. He thought he might have felt at least some degree of sadness, but he didn't. He never wanted to set foot inside there again.

Downstairs, he put the suitcase by the hat and coat stand, reminding himself not to forget to take the Burberry and the umbrella. He walked into the kitchen, stopped by the sink, and gazed out the window. The shed gave no clue to its sinister past. Just a normal wooden shed in a normal little garden.

A picture of innocence. Unless you knew the guilty truth.

He tried to force his mind to remember what had happened after he'd closed the front door on Bentley, but all he could recall was preparing Tortilla's food and being in the cave with the bats and the orb. Bentley must have put Jodie in the shed in the middle of the night while everyone was asleep. There was a small alley at the rear of the house. Just a twenty-yard walk from the road to the back gate. There was a bolt on the gate, but anyone over five foot tall could easily reach over and undo it.

The grass had sprung back to life after the recent rainfall and regained some of its colour. If only it was that simple to bring people back to life. But dead was dead, and forever was forever. Jodie, Amy, and his father were never coming back, and he would spend the rest of his life haunted by their loss.

His mother bustled into the kitchen. 'Got everything?'

Mathew nodded.

'Do you still want to have a look around the garden?'

'Why did this have to happen to us, Mum?'

'I don't know.'

'Isn't it enough that Dad and Amy were killed?'

She sat at the small table. 'More than enough.'

'Do you still miss Dad?'

'Every day. Sometimes I wake up and forget. Then it all comes flooding back.'

'I do that!'

'Then I have to get used to it all over again.'

'I wish I could remember everything that happened before they died.'

'How do you mean?'

'Remember all the things Dad and Amy said to me. Even the times we fell out. But it's as if my brain won't let me.'

'Maybe it's trying to protect you.'

'Why?'

'Because good memories can sometimes be as painful as bad ones.'

'I wish my brain would work properly.'

She touched his hand. 'I know, love. But you're still one of the loveliest people I've ever known. I wouldn't have you any other way.'

'I wish I could remember what happened when I went into the shed.'

'I don't think it would make much difference, Mathew. Not to the outcome, anyway.'

'What if Jodie wasn't dead? What if I could've saved her like Gareth saved me by calling an ambulance?'

'You can't change what's already been done. Anyway, the pathologist said she'd been dead at least twenty-four hours, so that means she was killed sometime on Sunday night.'

'How do they even know stuff like that?'

Sonia shrugged. 'They've got their ways.'

'Do you think Jodie's mum would mind if I wrote her a letter?'

'What do you want to say to her?'

'That I'm sorry. That I wish I'd been able to help Jodie.'

'I think it might be best to leave it for now.'

'Why?'

'Because her mum's upset, and I don't think it will help.'

'But—'

A loud thud in the front room interrupted the conversation. His mother stood and walked into the hall. She inched open the lounge door and stepped inside. 'Shit!'

Mathew stood beside her, surveying a huge crack in the front room window. Several smaller cracks branched out from the larger central one. Sonia turned around and stepped into the hall. She opened the front door and stepped outside.

Mathew followed her. There was a large grey rock lying beneath the window. As he bent over to have a closer look, something written on it in red marker pen stood out. Three words: *Hang the pervert!*

'Don't touch it,' Sonia warned him. 'You don't want to put your fingerprints on it.'

Mathew didn't hear her. He kicked the wall in a slow steady rhythm, chanting the three words over and over in his head like a satanic mantra.

'What does it say?'

Mathew's mind closed down in stages. He was no longer standing outside Bluebell Cottage kicking the wall. He was approaching the cave. The dark isolation of his inner sanctuary. The boulder sat in place over the entrance. The distant shrieking of bats hurt his ears.

'Mathew?'

He rolled the boulder out of the way and entered the cave. The shrieking grew louder, as if thousands of nails were being raked down a chalkboard. He wanted to pull the boulder back into place over the entrance, but he was too tired to do anything other than sit with his back against the cold stone wall.

Someone called his name from outside the cave. The voice was both familiar and alien. It belonged to another time. Another place. He needed to speak to the orb and ask it what he should do, but he couldn't just summon it like a genie from a lamp and expect it to grant him three wishes. The orb would only come when his mind was quiet and still.

'Mathew…?'

He ignored the voice. He would get up and put the rock over the entrance in a minute. He just needed to settle his nerves first.

And then, in the partial light cast from beyond the cave, three words painted on the wall opposite caught his attention. Three words which weren't there the last time he'd visited: *Hang the pervert.*

The words didn't scare him half as much as the knowledge that Jim Bentley had breached the cave's security system and got right inside his head.

CHAPTER TWENTY-NINE

After enjoying Shona's muffled screams, Jim had gone to Abbasi's to get some cans of beer and a pouch of tobacco. He'd wanted to make sure Abbasi could verify his whereabouts at the time of the murder. Not that he expected any favours from the old goat, but he was a straight-down-the-middle sort of dude, and if Jim was in the shop when he said he was, Abbasi would back him up.

By the time he returned to the flat, via stopping off at the Brooklands Estate to throw a rock through the Hillock's window, all was quiet and still. Curtis was sitting against the wall, arms draped over his knees, the blood-soaked knife discarded on the filthy carpet next to him. He was staring at the bed as if captivated by the corpse lying on top of it.

Bentley looked at the lifeless body of his ex-girlfriend. Shona was barely recognisable, thanks to the callous actions of Curtis Pollock. The bloodstained bed and her mutilated body served as a timely reminder that you couldn't trust anyone in this world. He'd taken Curtis in for the night, given him a place to stay, and this was the thanks he got. Who needed enemies when you had friends like Pollock?

Keeping his gun trained on the murderer, Bentley checked the body for any lingering signs of life. Nothing. Not even a fluttering eyelid.

'Good job, Curtis.'

Curtis didn't acknowledge him.

'I'll make sure you get what's due,' Bentley promised, walking out of the room and locking the door behind him. He wanted to punch the air. Dance on the rooftops. Go to church and praise the Lord for letting something go right for a change. Instead, he lurched forward, buried his head in his hands, and sobbed uncontrollably for almost five minutes.

This was none of that sentimental bullshit, either. These tears were siphoned straight from the heart. He had fond memories of Shona. Especially in the early days when she'd been willing to do almost anything for him. Had treated him like a god, kneeling at his altar and answering his every prayer.

As the tears subsided, his mind turned to far more important matters than mourning the loss of poor Shona. He could deal with the grief and the memories later, maybe accompanied by a bottle of whiskey, but for now he needed to make sure his story was as watertight as a submarine.

He went to the bathroom and checked his face in a small mirror fixed to the wall above the sink. His eyes looked red and puffy. Tick. No need to use the old onion and cigarette smoke trick to conjure grief. There were also bags beneath those eyes that spoke of sleepless nights and a life tormented by worry. Tick. He'd been wise enough not to touch the body, and his hands were shaking. Tick. (Although this owed more to drug withdrawal than it did to shock.) He knew his fingerprints would be all over the knife with Curtis's, but that was only to be expected, considering it was his carving knife. Tick. Curtis had gone into some sort of emotional meltdown. Tick. And Curtis's sperm would be inside the victim. Tick.

It was an open-and-shut case. The bastard had raped and murdered Shona the minute he'd turned his back. He walked back into the front room, sat on the sofa, and dialled 999. After giving his details to the operator, she passed him to a police call-handler.

'Could you please confirm your location and the nature of the emergency?'

'I just told the other woman all that shit. I'm at Flat 32, Saxon's Way in Feelham. I just got home and found my girlfriend dead. She's covered in blood and she ain't breathing or nothing.'

'Is there anyone else in the property other than yourself and the victim?'

'Yeah. The bastard who killed her.'

'Do you know the assailant?'

'Too fucking right I do. It's Curtis Pollock.'

'Where is Mr Pollock now?'

'I've locked him in the bedroom with Shona.'

'Is Shona the victim?'

No, she's my blow-up doll. 'Yeah.'

'Okay, I'll send out someone straight away. Have you any idea what Mr Pollock's state of mind is?'

'I'd say completely fucked up by the look of him. He's just sitting there staring at the bed.'

'Is he armed?'

'The knife's still in the bedroom. I didn't want to touch it.'

'Okay. The officers will be with you shortly.'

Bentley faked a sob and disconnected the call. It was time to mould himself into the grief-stricken boyfriend and prepare to launch a verbal attack if Curtis so much as dared to hint that killing Shona was his idea.

It took two uniformed constables ten minutes to reach the flat. Bentley escorted them into the living room. He recognised one of them as the wanker who'd arrested him for possession six months ago. PC Bainbridge. A complete arsehole who seemed to delight in his role as a jumped-up twat.

'What's the guy's name?' Bainbridge asked.

'Curtis Pollock.'

'How long's he been in the bedroom?'

'I dunno. I got home about half an hour ago and found him sitting on the floor. Then I locked him in there.'

'Was he conscious?'

Bentley nodded. 'But he seemed as if he was in a trance.'

'Under the influence of drugs?'

'Maybe.'

'Where were you when the alleged attack took place?'

'I went to Abbasi's to get some cans.'

'How long were you gone?'

Bentley shrugged. 'About twenty minutes.'

The other copper walked to the bedroom and tapped on the door. 'Curtis? Can you hear me?'

No answer.

The copper knocked louder. Looked at Jim. 'Are you sure he's in there?'

No. I must've dreamt the whole thing. 'He was sitting under the window, and the knife was lying on the floor next to him.'

Bainbridge asked Jim for the key, then joined the other copper at the bedroom door.

'Maybe he went out the window,' Bainbridge said. 'Done a runner.'

Bentley laughed. 'I'd like to see him try. It's about a thirty-foot drop.'

'Desperate people do desperate things, Mr Bentley. You of all people should know that.'

'What the fuck's that supposed to mean?'

'Does swallowing a bag of cocaine ring any bells?'

Jim chose not to rise to the bait. 'Whatever.'

Bainbridge thumped on the door. 'It's the police, Mr Pollock. Can you hear me?'

Again, no answer.

Bainbridge inserted the key in the lock and twisted it. He glanced at his colleague, nodded, then kicked open the door. 'Police. Don't move. Stay right where you are.'

Bentley had expected at least some resistance from Curtis. He knew he was softer than a freshly harvested cowpat, but he had to have some spunk inside him. He walked to the door and peered inside.

Shona was till in situ on the bed. Naked, battered, and bloody, one eye fixed on the doorway as if expecting help to arrive at any minute. No surprises there. No miracle recoveries. But Curtis was another matter altogether. He was lying on the floor with the knife sticking out of his bony chest. Bainbridge was kneeling beside him, checking his pulse. The other copper hovered around the bed like an expectant father awaiting the delivery of a child.

'Is he dead?' Jim asked.

Bainbridge stood. He told his colleague to radio for an ambulance and inform HQ they had a double murder on their hands. He then looked at Jim, eyes narrowed. 'I don't suppose you know anything about this, do you?'

'He was alive when I got back from Abbasi's. I just locked him in the room with her.'

'So, let's get this right – you go to the shops and come home to find your girlfriend murdered and lying in a pool of blood on the bed. Then you lock the assailant in the room with her and call us. Meanwhile, Mr Pollock stabs himself in the chest and commits suicide. Does any of that sound suspicious to you, Mr Bentley?'

'It's the truth.'

'James Bentley, I'm arresting you on suspicion of murder. You do not have to say anything, but it may harm your defence if you do not mention when questioned something which you later rely on in court. Anything you do say may be given in evidence.'

'Bollocks. I ain't done nothing. I swear on my life.'

'You could get change out of a five pence piece for your life, Jim. Now turn around.'

Bentley's thoughts hopped from hope to despair and back again in a matter of seconds. The evidence would show, beyond a reasonable doubt, that Curtis Pollock was responsible for the rape and murder of Shona, before turning the knife on himself. Why? Because, for the first time in his life, James Michael Bentley was telling the truth to an arresting officer.

As Bainbridge handcuffed him and marched him into the front room, Bentley cursed all the gods in all the heavens for his predicament. If only he could remember what had happened on the evening that Jodie Willis had walked past him on the bench. Where he'd gone for the two or three hours before he'd picked up Shona from Didcot. Now Curtis and Shona were dead, and all because he'd lost a few hours of his life to drugs and alcohol.

Sirens wailed in the distance. 'You're making a huge mistake. I'm telling the truth.'

'Then you've got nothing to worry about, have you?' Bainbridge said.

'I mean, why the fuck would I kill 'em and then call the filth? It makes no sense.'

'From my experience, Mr Bentley, very little does.'

For once, Jim was in agreement.

CHAPTER THIRTY

Mathew didn't stay in the cave for long. The screeching bats were, for want of a better word, sending him batshit. He was surprised to find himself sitting in the lounge at Bluebell Cottage. His mother was talking to a young female PC.

Sonia smiled. 'Welcome back.'

'How long was I gone for?'

'Best part of an hour. How are you feeling?

'Tired.'

The policewoman asked him if he wanted a glass of water.

'I just want to go back to Granddad's.'

'Your mother tells me you think Jim Bentley threw the rock at the window.'

'Yes.'

'Why do you think that?'

Mathew shrugged. 'Just do.'

The policewoman stood. 'Okay. I'll go and have a chat with Mr Bentley and see what he has to say for himself.'

'He killed Jodie Willis, too,' Mathew said. 'Killed her and tried to get me to take the blame for it.'

'I think it's best to leave all that up to the police,' Sonia said. 'They're well aware of what Bentley's like.'

The policewoman nodded. 'Don't worry about Mr Bentley. He's been on our radar for quite a while now. If you think of anything else, give us a call.'

Sonia showed the policewoman out, then returned to the lounge. 'Ready to go?'

'Yes.'

'Do you remember being in the fugue?'

He wanted to tell her about the cave. The bats. The orb. The words written on the wall. But it sounded bonkers. 'No.'

'Maybe we ought to take you back to the doctor and see about changing your medication.'

'I'm fine,' Mathew lied. 'I don't want any more pills.'

'Perhaps he might be able to adjust the dose.'

'I'll think about it.'

They drove back to Heritage Road in silence. There was nothing left to say.

Mathew sat in the lounge with his grandparents while his mother and Gareth attended a meeting with the loss adjustor. He didn't know what one of those was, apart from it had something to do with the insurance claim on the Book Café. He nibbled on a corned beef sandwich, trying to forget the message on the rock.

'People are nothing short of wicked,' his nan said. 'Setting fire to property and throwing rocks at windows. Bloody cowards!'

'That's a fact,' Bernard Halsey agreed. 'Wouldn't say boo to a goose if you were to come face to face with them.'

Mathew wasn't sure what geese had to do with it, but his nan was right about cowards. Or, more specifically, Jim Bentley. It was incredible how that excuse for a man could cause so much trouble.

The local news came on the TV. Mathew watched the presenter announce the arrest of a local man on suspicion of a double murder.

'The man has been taken to Oxford Central Police Station for questioning. DCI Mike Atkinson, of Thames Valley Police, today issued the following statement.'

The camera panned in on a man standing at the bottom of some steps outside the police station. His lips were compressed into a thin line as he squinted into the bright morning sunshine.

'We have today arrested a man on suspicion of a double murder in Feelham. He is currently helping us with our enquiries, and we will update you when we have any further news.'

'Can you give us any details of the victims?' a reporter asked.

'We are still liaising with the families of the deceased and awaiting formal identifications.'

'Male or female?'

'I'm not at liberty to say at this juncture.'

'Was the man arrested at the scene?'

'Again, I can't give specific details.'

'Has this got anything to do with the Jodie Willis murder?' another reporter asked, barging his way closer to the front of the ensemble.

'It's too early to say. I can't give you anything else. Thank you.' He turned and walked back up the steps without looking back.

'That was DCI Mike Atkinson,' the newsreader said. 'Moving on to other news...'

'Bloody hell!' Pam said. 'A double murder.'

'What on earth's happening?' Bernard said. 'First that poor little girl, now this.'

Pam shook her head. 'I blame it on drugs. They're like a bloody cancer eating away at society.'

'Why do people even take the damn things? It's like paying good money to become a zombie.'

'I know. Whittacker was an addict.'

'Don't remind me of that piece of scum.'

'I think they should lock druggies up and throw away the key,' Pam said. 'Give them one chance at rehab, and that's it. The trouble with this country is we're too damn soft. It's as if they know they can literally get away with murder.'

Bernard yawned and stretched. 'I wonder whereabouts in Feelham the murders were.'

'I'm sure we'll find out soon enough.'

Mathew listened to the conversation ping back and forth between his grandparents. He wanted to go back into the cave but was scared he might find more writing on the wall. And the screech of the bats was becoming intolerable in his fragile state.

Pam stood and switched off the telly as a daytime soap came on. 'I wonder if it's the same bugger who killed that little girl?'

'Seems a bit too coincidental for my liking. Three murders in a month, all in the same town.'

'Let's hope that's an end to it.'

'If the police have got the right man.'

'You have to wonder, don't you? It's not five minutes ago they had Mathew in the station for questioning.'

'Bloody ridiculous. That boy wouldn't hurt a fly.'

'Just goes to show what can happen if you're in the wrong place at the wrong time.'

'Someone must have seen who put that body in the shed.'

Mathew wanted to ask them if they actually knew he was in the room with them.

Pam hovered by the window. 'I'll tell you this much for nothing: there aren't any safe places anymore. All the worst trouble used to be in the cities, but now…'

'Can you ring the police?' Mathew said.

As if noticing him for the first time since the news bulletin, Bernard said, 'Why's that, lad?'

'To check.'

'On what?'

'Who they've arrested.'

'They won't tell us that.'

'But I need to know whether it's Jim Bentley.'

Bernard took off his glasses and rubbed his eyes. 'This isn't the same case as Jodie, Mathew. It's a different one.'

'But I know he did it.'

'Tell you what, let's wait until your mum gets home and ask her what she thinks.'

Mathew looked at the blank TV screen. The bats screeched from deep within the cave. He imagined their fangs dripping with blood as they scrawled nasty messages on the wall.

'Would you like a glass of lemonade?' Pam offered.

Mathew didn't hear her. The screeching in his head was driving him to despair. Like a symphony of sorrow. 'Jim Bentley did it,' he yelled above the sound of the bats.

Bernard stood. 'Take it easy, lad. It's all right. Don't upset yourself.'

Mathew clamped his hands over his ears. A stupid move, considering the bats were actually inside his head.

'Mathew?'

He sank to his knees as the shrieking reached a crescendo. And then he was back in the cave once more. The bats were flying around him, circling, waiting for an opportunity to strike and drink his blood. The cave was no longer a sanctuary; it was a prison, and no one could protect him now.

CHAPTER THIRTY-ONE

Dr Dark's Diary.

*C*hoices, choices, choices. The scourge of the twenty-first century. Everywhere you look, a chaotic jumble of choices designed to confuse you. From energy suppliers to TV packages. Food to phones. Cars to careers. Houses to holidays. And you know what? Most of it is pure unadulterated shite.

So, what's your poison? Are you a climate change protestor? Part of the extinction rebellion? A friend of the Earth afraid to travel anywhere through fear of the dreaded carbon footprint? Do you go to the gym and live on lettuce leaves because you think it will enrich you with immortal properties? Or do you live in McDonald's and wave a Big Mac in the face of all those do-gooders who scream abuse at you from their sanctimonious towers?

I think it's funny the way the authorities promote confusion. Do you think they care whether you snort powder up your nose or stick a needle in your arm? Whether you weigh as much as a dandelion or a baby rhino? They don't. They're happy to watch the masses living in constant fear, blaming one another for their condition, while they quietly go about their business of annihilating you by stealth.

Do you think AIDS or Ebola just happened along by chance? The virus world has its own community of scientists working on the next deadly outbreak. Perhaps you think the viruses go to the gym and workout. Pumping up their little virus bodies to make them more resistant to change. If you do, then you probably deserve to die, anyway.

Choices, choices, choices. Is the world now run by Confused.com? Or maybe it's those stupid meerkats on Compare the Market. And don't get me started on banks. Holding the world hostage and pretending to be the saviours of the planet.

Here's a question for you. Have you ever thought about killing someone? I mean, I know it's hypothetical, and I'm sure you're a fine upstanding citizen going about your daily business in this brave new Confused.com world. But have you? Maybe you've imagined plunging a knife into your partner's heart just to put an end to an argument once and for all. Or you've got a boss who is constantly sniping at you. Making you feel like an insignificant blob of snot. How good would it feel to have ten minutes in a locked room with just you, him, and a loaded shotgun? Would you pull the trigger? I think you would if you could. Give him both barrels and release all that pent-up rage.

From my perspective, there are only two choices I actually care about: to kill or not to kill. Everything else is just superficial nonsense. I eat because I have to, and I drink for the same reason. I go to work because I need money and I get dressed because, well, that's a pretty obvious one, isn't it?

So far I've killed thirteen times. Unlucky for some, you might say! A healthy number, or unhealthy if you're a victim, but I plan to kill many more. I have no limitations, other than those of opportunity. It may seem to the layperson that murder is a random act of extreme violence. This is true, but there is so much more to this dark art than meets the eye.

Choosing a victim. The meticulous planning. Watching the target's movements. Learning all there is to know about the target's friends and family. Who might pose a threat to the success of the operation? Are there any special worries concerning risk?

You must also be prepared to abort the operation if there is any doubt whatsoever of the outcome. I once spent six months planning an operation, only to find that the intended victim was in the midst of moving house. I can't tell you how disappointed I was

243

to discover this fact. There wasn't a for sale board outside the house. Nothing to suggest the coming upheaval. A massive part of me wanted to continue, but the practicalities of following the target all the way to Leicestershire made it impossible to do so.

For those of you who say there are no certainties in life, I'm inclined to agree. It's like perfection – impossible to attain. But you can get close. Maybe ninety-nine percent. The other one percent? You just have to leave that up to fate.

If you are reading this diary, you might wonder why I kill. Was I abused as a child? Locked in the closet by an alcoholic mother? Raised by religious fanatics with an insatiable appetite for biblical bullshit? Nope. None of those things. I grew up in a normal family on a normal street with normal expectations.

Foremost, I kill because I can. It's my decision. I have the power over life and death. I have to admit, I'm more thrilled by the chase than the kill itself. Identifying my target, planning everything down to the finest detail. Sometimes it can take as much as two years to plan.

I hesitate to call them victims, because we are all victims. Is there any difference between what I do and what Mother Nature does on a daily basis with her murderous streak? At least when I end a life, I make it as quick and as painless as possible. Compared to cancer, I'm a model of compassion.

I made my first kill when I was twelve. Nothing amazing. Just an old tomcat who used to come into our garden and stalk the birds. His name was Snuzzle. Probably the dumbest name I've ever heard.

Who calls a cat Snuzzle? You'd like to think it was some old granny with loose marbles, but it was actually a young family who lived a few doors along from us. The Hagans. Two kids. Mr and Mrs Perfect, with their Audi sports car and Olympic-sized swimming pool in the back garden.

Anyway, Snuzzle never caught any birds. They were always too quick for his lazy old paws. But he taught me a lot about patience. About never giving up. Biding his time. He also taught me that cats will love anyone who gives them food. Snuzzle liked to eat. Bad news for his body, good news for the birds. So I started feeding him. My mother always had a generous supply of meatballs in the freezer. I used to love them when I was a kid. Snuzzle loved meatballs, too. I'd defrost them and cut them into small pieces, then sit on the back porch and wait for him to make an appearance. He brushed himself around my legs, purring, rubbing his scent all over me as if marking his territory. It took me a few weeks to really gain his trust, then I coaxed him into the shed at the bottom of the garden.

It was a pretty safe bet Dad wouldn't be going in the shed for anything in the winter, so I executed my plan and poisoned a meatball with enough weed killer to take a stinging nettle down at fifty yards. But not enough to kill Snuzzle. Just to make him sick as a dog, pardon the pun.

I killed him slowly over the next few weeks. Every time I walked into that shed, he looked at me, hoping to be saved. I didn't have the heart to tell him he was going to die. When the time came, most of his fur was missing. I guess cats get alopecia, too.

Kudos to Snuzzle – he fought a good battle. Never complained. Unlike humans, who have a tendency to wail and screech when you do something to them they don't like. I released Snuzzle from the shed three weeks before Christmas. He was virtually dead when I put him out of his misery by tying a plastic bag over his head and letting nature do the rest.

I was sad to see him go. Not because he was dead, but because it was over. I no longer had anything to look forward to when I came home from school. Just boring homework and pretending that I enjoyed all those stupid things my parents thought I should. Going to badminton. Watching crap on telly. Talking at the dinner table about how important my schooling was. Didn't they know I needed so much more?

The only exciting thing that happened following the cat's death was disposing of his body in the Hagan's swimming pool. Imagining their shocked faces when they discovered poor Snuzzle had finally conceded his ninth life.

There were flyers stapled to just about every telegraph pole in the area asking for information concerning their precious moggy.

I went to the Hagan's house a few days later. Jessica answered the door. She was about seven at the time. She burst into tears when I asked her if they'd had any luck finding poor Snuzzle. She had to be rescued by her distraught mummy, who informed me that the cat was dead.

It wouldn't be the last time I'd have dealings with the Hagans.

Dr Dark's Advice: Look after your fucking pets!

CHAPTER THIRTY-TWO

Gareth and Sonia arrived back at the house while Mathew was still suffering his latest fugue. He was kneeling on the floor, forehead resting against the carpet as if deep in prayer.

Sonia dropped her bag on the sofa and knelt beside her son. 'How long's he been like this?'

'About three quarters of an hour,' Pam said. 'We were talking about the murders, and then he asked us to call the police to find out who they'd arrested.'

'What murders?' Gareth asked.

'It said on the news a man's been arrested for a double murder in Feelham. Mathew wanted to know if it was Jim Bentley.'

Sonia put a hand on her son's shoulder. 'Can you hear me, Mathew?'

'He sounds as if he's mumbling something about bats,' Gareth said.

Pam raised her eyebrows. 'Why would he be talking about bats?'

'It might be best to let him come back naturally,' Gareth said. 'You don't want to startle him and cause him to panic.'

'He only had one a few hours ago,' Sonia said. 'They're becoming more and more frequent.'

'Is it any wonder?' Bernard said. 'What with everything that's been going on.'

Sonia looked at her father. 'I need to take him to the doctor and let him check his medication. He's been on the same pills for quite a while now. They're probably not working as well as they used to.'

'Make them go away,' Mathew shouted. 'Make the bats go away.'

Sonia returned her attention to her son. 'It's all right. There're no bats, Mathew.'

'They want to drink my blood.'

'What in God's name is he talking about?' Pam asked. 'He sounds as if he's in a bloody horror film.'

'The poor lad is,' Bernard said. 'Maybe I should call an ambulance.'

Mathew beat his head on the carpet. 'Hang the pervert... hang the pervert... hang the pervert.'

'Mathew? Can you hear me, love?'

Mathew banged his head harder. 'Hang the pervert... hang the pervert... hang the pervert.'

Gareth approached him from behind, bent over, and shoved his hands under his brother's armpits. He pulled Mathew up and back in one swift movement so he was sitting on the floor.

'Hang the pervert... hang the pervert... hang the pervert.'

Gareth wrapped his arms around him and hugged him. 'Hey, come on now, let's get you out of the cave.'

Mathew shook his head from side to side as if trying to dislodge something wedged in his ear. 'Blood... blood... blood...'

'I've called an ambulance,' Bernard said. 'Just to be on the safe side.'

Pam stood near the door, hands clasped in front of her. 'He needs help. He needs professional help.'

'He'll be okay,' Gareth assured her. 'He just needs a bit of time to settle.'

'It's a crying shame what that thug did to him,' Pam said. 'Did to the whole family.'

Blood leaked from Mathew's nose and dribbled onto his lips.

Sonia watched her son with mounting concern. He usually went still and quiet when he had a blackout. Although worrying enough, they never seemed to have any lasting effect.

'I'll fetch some kitchen towel.' Pam bustled from the room.

Gareth bent over so his lips were close to his brother's ear. 'It's all right, Mattie. You can come out now. Everything's gonna be fine.'

'Hang... the... pervert...' This time his voice was barely above a whisper. He sounded like a dog who'd barked himself hoarse. The blood was now staining his chin and running onto his neck.

Pam returned with a roll of kitchen towel. She tore some off and told Sonia to tip Mathew's head back.

'I thought you were meant to lean forward,' Bernard said. 'Stop the blood from running down your throat.'

Sonia ignored her father and tilted Mathew's head back. Pam wedged the towel underneath her grandson's nose. 'How long's that ambulance going to take?'

'Not long,' Bernard reassured her. 'They said they'd send one straight away.'

'I know what their idea of *straight away* is like,' Pam said. 'Our Jeannie had to wait half an hour after Donald had his stroke.'

Sonia wanted to tell her mother to shut up, but she knew better than to be rude. Not even in an emergency. 'Mathew? It's Mum. Can you hear me?'

'Hang... the... pervert.' Barely audible now. Breathing slowly. Eyes rolled back.

It reminded Sonia of the night they'd found him lying on the bed after the attack twelve years earlier. Motionless. Blood all over his face. One arm hanging over the side of the bed. Gareth calling an ambulance. Getting angry with the operator because she seemed to be asking too many questions. Not yet knowing

Amy was lying dead in the adjacent bedroom. Her darling child forever frozen at eight years old.

Bernard looked out the window. 'At least Mathew seems to have calmed down a bit.'

Gareth relaxed his grip on his brother. 'I'm gonna pay Jim Bentley a visit. Tell that bastard to stop harassing us.'

'We don't know it's him,' Bernard said. 'We have to be careful about who we accuse.'

Gareth shook his head. 'I know it's him. And he's gonna regret it if he doesn't pack it in.'

Bernard moved away from the window and announced the arrival of the ambulance.

'About bloody time,' Pam said. 'Would've been quicker to take him to casualty ourselves.'

It was cold in the cave. Wind howled through the open entrance, competing with the bats to drown out Mathew's thoughts. He knew he was going to die; the bats had made that clear with their constant demands for his blood. He also knew that Jim Bentley was hiding somewhere in the shadows, waiting to give the bats exactly what they wanted.

He searched for signs of the orb, willing it to come and tell him what to do, but the orb was nowhere to be seen.

Hello Mathew, a voice whispered from deep within the cave.

The voice sounded too deep for Bentley's. Small mercies. He asked who it was.

I'm your friend, remember?

251

'No.'

We go back a long way, Mathew. Right back to the beginning of time, in fact. But that's not important right now. All you need to do is listen. Do you think you can manage that?

'Are you the orb?'

A small laugh echoed around the cave. *No, Mathew, I'm not. You know it's almost time, don't you?*

'For what?'

To die.

'I don't want to die.'

Only because you fear the unknown. But there's no need to. Death is beautiful. Peaceful. Eventual.

'But—'

You're only afraid because the body has a strong instinct to survive. Once you can override that, the rest is easy. Believe me.

Mathew shivered. 'But why should I?'

I've already told you: I am the truth. I only have your best interests at heart. Amy says she loves you and can't wait to see you again.

'Is she with you?'

No. But you can see her again as soon as you embrace the darkness.

'Are you Jesus?'

Another laugh. *No, Mathew, I'm definitely not Jesus.*

'Have you seen my dad?'

Yes. He wants you to be at peace. All you have to do is go to the bathroom when you leave the cave, lock the door, and run a bath. Let the water relax

you, then take a razor blade and cut your wrists.
Simple as ABC.

Mathew shuddered as he imagined the bathwater turning red.

No more worrying about Jim Bentley.

'Do you know him?'

I know everyone.

'Even Paul Whittacker?'

Yes. And the kids at school who used to tease you just because you were different. Sticking notes on your back saying 'kick me, I'm stupid'. Notes in your desk pretending to be girls asking you out on a date. Work ruined. Lunch stolen. Drawing pins on your chair. Hiding your shoes. Teachers sending you out of class because you couldn't stop tapping your hands on the desk or banging your feet on the floor.

'I hated school.'

Trouble is, Mathew, you've never really fitted in, have you? You've always been on the outside. A loner. A dreamer. A recluse.

'People were nice to me at the Book Café.'

Folk only pretend to be friendly. They still talk about you behind your back. It's just the way of the world. Anyway, the bookshop's gone now. Forever. So that's the end of that.

'It's not fair.'

Nothing is, Mathew. Nothing ever is. So go to the bathroom and let all your troubles bleed out of you.

A cone of light pierced the darkness. 'Mathew? Can you hear me, Mathew?'

He tried to place the female voice coming from outside the cave. It wasn't his mother's. Or his nan's.

It sounded like his cousin, Lottie, but it couldn't be because she lived up north somewhere.

'Mathew? My name's Helen. I'm a paramedic. Can you hear me?'

'I need to go to the bathroom.'

'Can you open your eyes, sweetheart?'

He gawped at the light piercing the cave. 'Where's the man gone?'

'What man?'

'The one who says I've got to kill myself.'

'No one's said anything like that, Mathew.'

'But I heard him.'

'I think you may have been dreaming.'

'But he was right here in the cave with me.'

'Cave?'

'It's just where he goes when he has a fugue.' Gareth's voice this time.

'The man's gone now, sweetheart,' Helen said. 'Can you open your eyes for me?'

Mathew wondered why she kept calling him *sweetheart*. It was as if he'd stumbled into the pages of a novel. 'I'm too tired.'

'I know. But we need to get you off the floor so I can examine you.'

'Why?'

'To check you're okay.'

'I don't *have* to go to the bathroom?'

'Not if you don't want to.'

A surge of relief went through him. He crawled towards the entrance. The cone of light was burning his eyes, but that didn't matter; he was just glad to be away from the screeching bats and the strange voice telling him to kill himself.

For the time being.

CHAPTER THIRTY-THREE

Jim didn't know whether to celebrate or phone his brief and start proceedings to charge the filth with harassment and false imprisonment. And that was just for starters. He was sure there were laws against sleep deprivation and being asked the same questions over and over. This wasn't the seventies, where the police could beat the living crap out of you to force you to confess. No, sir, this was strictly play-by-the-rules time, and the whole thing was on tape. And Jim, knowing his rights, had a copy of the tape.

Ninety-six hours was a long time under normal circumstances. But ninety-six hours without so much as a toke on a spliff was akin to mental torture. That bastard Prendergast seemed to take great delight in watching him suffer the horrors of withdrawal. Sitting opposite him with that smug smile plastered across his rubbery chops.

Well, he'd not been so smug when they'd had to release him without charge. In fact, Prendergast looked as if he'd just received news of a death in the family when the forensics came back declaring Curtis Pollock's semen had been found inside Shona. And Pollock's prints were all over the knife and Shona's body.

'That still doesn't explain the older wounds on Shona's body,' Prendergast had said as Jim had walked out of the interview room a free man. 'I'll be keeping a close eye on you, Mr Bentley.'

With a level of self-control bordering on spiritual, Jim had chosen not to respond. Given free rein to do as he'd pleased, he would have ripped Prendergast's head off and shit down his neck, but he'd simply gone on his way and caught a bus back to Feelham.

After spending a week kipping on a mate's sofa while the filth crawled all over his flat like ants on a sugar hunt, Jim had returned home to start the long arduous journey back to normality.

To say the flat needed a clean was like saying he needed a drink. There was mess everywhere. The coppers, as per usual, had shown no respect for private property. Drawers were pulled open, their contents spilled all across the floor and the sofa. The kitchen looked as if an earthquake had visited Feelham in his absence. True, the dirty dishes and discarded takeaway cartons were his own doing, as was the overflowing bin, but the rest of it was down to the coppers. No wonder they called them the *filth*.

'I'm putting in a claim for damages,' Jim told the empty kitchen. 'How would they like it if I went into their house and made such a fucking mess?'

He opened the fridge door and grabbed a can of Special Brew. At least the bastards had left something alone. Popping the tab, he walked back into the front room and swept a pile of papers and junk off the sofa. He sat and downed half the can in one go.

The sudden intake of gassy alcohol, on top of having virtually nothing to eat for days, cramped his stomach. He bent over and waited for the abdominal pain to pass. One thing was for sure: he'd have to sleep on the sofa until he could find someone willing to clean the bedroom for him. He didn't even want to think about the disgusting state of the murder scene.

He was more upset about Shona's death than he'd thought he'd be. Apart from her inexplicable aversion to razor blades, she'd been pretty good in the sack. Okay, maybe good was being a bit kind, but she'd been adequate if your expectations didn't stretch too far beyond blowjobs and sex. And she had nice tits, which was always a bonus.

He took another swig of his can and waited for the cramps to hit again. Thankfully, the lager triggered nothing more than a fart. A little too runny for his liking, but he needed a shower, anyway.

By the time he'd sunk his third can, he was feeling in a better frame of mind. If he played his cards right, he could come out of this mess a wealthy man. Not because of any potential compensation, but because the newspapers loved a good story. And what better scoop than a man who comes home to find his girlfriend stabbed to death and his best friend lying on the bedroom floor with a kitchen knife sticking out of his chest. Maybe the 'best friend' bit was elasticising the truth a bit, but the tabloids didn't care about such trivialities. Story was story, and if it sold copies, who cared what was true?

Jim raised his can at a forty-five-degree angle. 'I'm gonna get at least a hundred grand outta this. Maybe more when the compo comes in.'

An audience of junk and discarded litter remained tight-lipped about his chances. Bentley paid no heed to the surrounding mess or obstacles standing in his way. When you'd spent as much time in the shit tank as he had, good fortune was bound to come your way eventually.

A loud thump on the door interrupted his thoughts. Who the fuck was that? If it was the filth again, they could piss off. He wasn't answering any more of their poxy questions. He was innocent, and if they didn't like it, too bad. They could go pick on someone else for a change.

Maybe they've found something concerning the Jodie Willis case, paranoia whispered. *Something that's gonna lock you up for good.*

Bentley tried to tell the voice to piss off, but amnesia, and a genuine fear that he might have done something to Jodie, put a huge dent in his self-confidence.

The knocking came again. Louder. More insistent.

Jim struggled to his feet. 'All right, I'm coming.'

He looked through the spyhole. Gareth Hillock stood outside. What the hell did he want?

'I know you're in there, Bentley. Open the door or I'm gonna kick it down.'

Jim stepped back. 'What do you want?'

'To talk.'

'About what?'

'You know what. Now open the fucking door.'

Bentley finished the rest of his can and dropped it on the floor. 'I wanna know why first?'

'I already told you.'

'And I already asked you – what about?'

'Mathew.'

'The retard?'

'You call him that one more time, and I swear to God you're a dead man.'

'If you're gonna threaten me, I'm calling the police.'

'Stop behaving like a baby and open the door.'

'Curtis Pollock raped and murdered my bird, so pardon me if I'm a bit upset at the moment.'

'I don't care if he flew them to the moon. Now open the fucking door before I really lose my temper.'

Jim weighed up his options on drink-impaired scales. He knew full well Hillock would carry out his threat to kick down the door if he didn't open it. He also knew the cocky bastard wasn't the sort to just give up and go home. But he didn't want to risk

261

letting him into the flat, especially after what he'd said about Hillock's retarded brother. Jim felt as if he was trapped in a burning building, and the only thing he had to fight it with was cooking oil.

'If I open this door, do you promise to behave yourself?'

'Do you?' Gareth countered.

Jim remembered the gun he had stashed in the attic, but his head was spinning badly enough to make climbing the loft ladder a suicidal act. 'I don't wanna fall out with you.'

'Then open the door so we can have a proper man-to-man chat.'

Jim relented. He slid back the bolt at the top of the door and started to open it. He would remember very little of what happened next. The door slammed into his face and knocked him to the floor. The discarded can cut into his back, and then he was treated to sweet black oblivion.

When he came to, he was lying on the living room floor. Gareth Hillock sat in a chair next to the sideboard. At first, he thought he was dreaming. Or, at the very least, tripping on something.

'Glad you could join us,' Gareth said.

'What… the… fuck?'

'You passed out. Must have had something to do with the door smashing into your head.'

'My… head?'

Gareth nodded. 'That ugly thing sitting on top of your shoulders.'

Jim tried to get up, but the room kept swaying in and out of focus. 'What do you want?'

'Just to tell you how it's gonna be from now on. First off, you ever call my brother a retard again, I'll swat you like a fly. Understand?'

Jim thought about arguing that Mathew Hillock *was* a retard. Fact. But the look in Gareth's eyes told him it wasn't a good idea. 'But he ain't right. You know he ain't right.'

'He was attacked and nearly killed with a baseball bat when he was a kid. Left for fucking dead by some useless druggie who killed my dad and my sister. So don't you dare sit there and tell me he ain't right. It's not his fault.'

'I didn't know that.'

'Well, you do now. And, just for the record, he had nothing to do with that kid's murder.'

'So how come she was in his shed?'

'That's what the police are trying to find out.'

'But he was sitting next to the body. I mean, it's one thing saying he ain't right, and another thing altogether finding him next to a corpse.'

'Mathew hasn't been charged with anything. For a start, the glove prints around the girl's neck were too small to be Mattie's. There's not a single shred of DNA evidence linking him to the murder. Nothing. So, in my eyes, and the eyes of the law, he's innocent.'

'But I still don't get how she ended up in the shed.'

'Because someone obviously put her there.'

Jim was feeling queasy. 'But who the fuck would do that?'

'Maybe the same twat who went to the house and told Mattie to confess.'

'I only did that 'cos I thought he was guilty.'

'So you say.'

Jim sat up. 'I swear I had nothing to do with it. Anyway, the filth took my DNA, so if it was me, I'd have been locked up by now.'

'Dunno about that. The police are pretty slow off the mark when it comes to catching criminals. Especially dirty little drug addicts who go around acting the big man just because a few dopey teenagers think you're some sort of magic mushroom.'

'I—'

'Here's a question for you, Bentley: Did you throw a rock at my mother's house? One with *hang the pervert* written on it.'

'No.'

Gareth stood and walked towards Bentley. He drew back his foot and kicked him in the side of the face. 'You sure about that?'

Bentley groaned and rolled over onto all fours.

Gareth kicked him again. In the side this time. All the air whooshed from his lungs as he collapsed face down on the floor.

'You ever go anywhere near my family again, and you'll be lying in your grave before you can say *retard*, you lowlife twat.'

Bentley blacked out again. He didn't see Gareth leave the flat and gently close the door behind him. By the time he'd regained consciousness, the sky had drawn a dark shade across the window.

Jim Bentley didn't need a doctor to tell him he had several broken ribs. Or that he was hovering dangerously close to a heart attack if his thumping heart was anything to go by.

CHAPTER THIRTY-FOUR

Mathew knocked on the door to his mother's bedroom. He felt slightly better now that the doctor had prescribed him Buspirone, although the pills had made him lightheaded, and he'd suffered headaches and insomnia since taking them. But it was a small price to pay to stop unwanted thoughts of going to the bathroom and giving in to the call of a razor blade.

'Who is it?'

His mother sounded tired and throaty, as if she was suffering from a cold. Mathew knew that voice only too well. He'd heard it a lot after his father and sister were killed. He called it her *crying voice*.

'It's Mathew.'

'What do you want?'

'To talk.'

'I'm not feeling very well at the moment.'

'I've brought you a cup of tea.'

A short silence, followed by several sniffs. 'Okay. Come in.'

Mathew opened the door and stepped inside. His mother was lying on top of the bed in a pink-and-white dressing gown. Her eyes looked red and swollen.

'Put it on the bedside table,' she said. 'I'll drink it when it's cooled down a bit.'

'Are you all right, Mum?'

She shook her head. 'Everything's gone, Mattie. Everything we worked so hard for up in smoke – literally.'

'We can start again.'

'We can't, love.'

Mathew put the tea on the bedside table, then sat on the edge of the bed. He wanted to give her a big hug and tell her everything would be all right. They'd work it out. Hillocks always did. Nothing could be worse than the night Amy and his father had died. And they'd survived that, hadn't they? Kept the Book Café going.

'Did you want anything else, Mathew?'

He nodded and tugged on his earlobe.

'What?'

'You know the Book Café?'

'Yes.' Tired. Strained.

'And how you said the insurance money wouldn't be enough to get it up and running again?'

'Yes.'

'I was thinking... I was thinking we could use my insurance money to pay for it.'

Sonia stared at him open-mouthed.

'I'm twenty-one next month, so it's not as if we've got to wait very long, is it?'

'I can't take your money, Mathew.'

'But if we open the Book café again, we can live in the flat above it and sell Bluebell Cottage. Then we can start again just like we did when Dad and Amy died.'

At first, he thought she would tell him off for being silly. It was his money for when he needed it. To help support him if he ever wanted to move out of home. Then he thought she was going to cry, because her eyes misted over and looked all glassy.

But she did neither of those things. She held out her hands and invited him into an embrace. He edged up the bed and tried to manoeuvre himself into a suitable position to cuddle her, but his bulky frame and awkward demeanour resulted in him lying half across her chest and crushing her.

After a moment, she said, 'I can't take your money, Mathew. It's not right.'

'But I want you to have it. I want to work in the Book Café forever. And live in the flat. It's for me as well, Mum.'

'Are you absolutely sure?'

He nodded.

'But we'll need to replace all the books.'

'I can't think of anything better to spend the money on.'

'And it will take a long time to get the shop ready again.'

'Then we'll have loads of time to plan and get the flat ready before we sell Bluebell Cottage.'

'I don't think it's as simple as that. We can't just—'

'I want to. Please. I really want to help.'

Sonia shook her head. 'I can't.'

'You can pay me back once we sell the house.'

'It's a sweet idea, but—'

'Please, Mum. You've done so much for me.'

'I've only done what mums are supposed to do.'

A tap on the door interrupted the conversation. Bernard poked his head around the door. 'Sorry to intrude, but Gareth's here. He wants to have a word with Mathew.'

Mathew sat up. 'I'll be down in a minute.'

'I'll go put the kettle on.'

'Why don't I ask Gareth what he thinks about using my insurance money?' Mathew said as he stood. 'See what he thinks.'

'If you want to, love. But it doesn't mean I'm going to agree.'

He walked downstairs in a slightly more positive mood. Gareth would think it was a good idea. And he'd probably do a better job of persuading Mum to take the offer. Anyway, it was only a loan. She could pay him back from the sale of Bluebell Cottage if she really wanted to.

As he went into the lounge, he could tell there was something troubling his brother. Even though Gareth smiled, he looked as if he was hiding something behind his eyes

'How's it going?'

'I'm okay,' Mathew lied.

'Can we have a quick chat?'

'Okay.'

Gareth led him out into the conservatory and closed the door. 'I just wanted to warn you to be on your guard.'

A chill passed through Mathew. 'Why?'

'Because I've just been to see Jim Bentley and told him to leave you alone.'

'Oh.'

'But I'm not sure how he's gonna take it. I think he got the message, but you can never tell with the likes of him. So, just be careful, okay?'

'Okay.'

'Especially if you go out.'

'Right.'

'I don't know what's happening in this bloody town. First that poor kid, now Bentley's girlfriend gets raped and murdered by Curtis Pollock before he sticks a knife in himself.'

Mathew's mouth hung open. 'Was that the double murder?'

Gareth nodded. 'So, be vigilant, Mattie. I'm gonna suggest Granddad installs security cameras. Just to be on the safe side.'

'Who's Curtis Pollock?'

'One of Bentley's druggie mates. Anyway, he's dead now.'

Mathew thought for a few moments. 'Maybe Bentley killed them both and made it look like Pollock did it.'

'Nothing would surprise me with that tosser. Anyway, I just thought I'd let you know what's what. How's Mum?'

'Not too good. I can hear her crying at night, and she's not eating.' Mathew elected not to tell his brother he wasn't sleeping, or that the Buspirone was giving him headaches.

'Mum's a tough old bird. I'm sure she'll be okay.'

Mathew wished he shared his brother's optimism. 'Can I ask you a question?'

'Sure.'

'I've offered to use my insurance money to get the Book Café back on its feet. Just until we can sell Bluebell Cottage. But Mum doesn't want to. Says it's my money. But I want to help her after everything she's done for me.'

Gareth grinned. 'They broke the mould when they made you, Mattie.'

'Huh?'

'You're a one-off. Unique. The world would be a much better place if everyone was like you.'

Mathew wasn't sure whether a world full of forgetful insomniacs would be very productive. 'So I said I'd ask you.'

'What did she say to that?'

'That I could, but it didn't mean she would agree.'

'I think it's a great idea. Like you say, she can pay you back from the house money.'

'I also thought we could live in the flat above the shop.'

'Even better.'

Mathew's heart glowed. Gareth's approval meant the world to him.

'So can I tell her you approve?'

'Absolutely. Tell you what, why don't you come round to the flat tonight, and I'll order a pizza. We can watch a movie on Netflix and chill out.'

'Do you mean it?'

'Course. I'll pick you up around eight and drop you back here after.'

In that moment, Mathew loved his brother beyond words. He walked towards him and hugged him.

'Whoa there, big man, I want to keep my ribs intact.'

Mathew let go. 'Sorry.'

'Only kidding. See ya later.'

'Not if I see you first.'

Gareth punched him on the arm. 'You got me there, bro.'

Mathew waited for him to leave, then went back upstairs to tell his mother that Gareth thought the insurance money idea was a good one. He took several deep breaths before knocking and entering her room. This was turning out to be a good day.

Or so he thought.

CHAPTER THIRTY-FIVE

Dr Dark's Diary.

About a year after I killed the Hagan's cat, Mrs Hagan, or Valerie if you prefer, responded to my leaflet offering a grass cutting service during the summer holidays. Valerie had no idea she was the only recipient of my flyer. She was also unaware that

I had plans for her family that had nothing to do with lawnmowers.

Valerie remembered my interest in poor Snuzzle and had me marked down as a kind and compassionate boy who deserved to earn a few pounds in his spare time. She also offered me all the lemonade I could drink and insisted that I call her Valerie instead of Mrs Hagan.

By now, Snuzzle, the owner of the most absurd cat name ever, had been replaced by a Yorkshire terrier puppy called Gucci. I swear to God, that family had something wrong with them when it came to naming animals. Now, I don't want you thinking I'm cruel to animals, because I'm not. I much prefer them to humans. They're way more loyal for a start, and far less likely to tell tales. Snuzzle was just an experiment. So, before you fret about Gucci's fate, I didn't kill him. In fact, I quite liked the little fella. He was cute. A real-life cuddly toy to mess around with while taking a break beside the pool.

Valerie had all the usual crap that goes along with living in a big posh house. The husband who sometimes nodded at you if he was feeling in a generous mood. The nice car. Two kids. Boy and girl, of course. One mini-mummy and one diddy-daddy. Such a perfect family, right down to their fake pretentious smiles and perfect suburban home.

The boy was called Jonothan. He was about ten or eleven years old. Moody and good-looking. A vile combination. I can't tell you how much I wanted to drown that little bastard in the pool. Just ram his head under the water and wait for the bubbles to stop rising. But, of course, the Hagans might become

276

suspicious to find their cat and their kid dead in the same swimming pool. Plus, the police take child murder a lot more seriously than moggy murder.

The little girl was eight. Jessica. A nice My Little Pony name, don't you think? Destined to be a ballerina and play the cello in one of those fancy orchestras one day.

I sometimes watched her swimming in the pool. Imagine taking her a long way away from the Hagans. One thing I've always had is a vivid imagination. I haven't got a clue where it comes from. My father had the imaginative capacity of a wasp, and my mother was a practical woman devoted to her job and the occasional bout of baking. Both were what you might call functional and hard-working. Good honest folk who could bore the pants of anyone who wandered into their functional lair.

Here's one for you to mull over: perception. It's a funny thing, don't you think? People think they can sum you up in a few words. Friendly. Miserable. Dumb. Bright. But they're only basing their assessment on how they perceive you to be. Or, more importantly, what you want them to see. Having that vivid imagination allowed me to convince the Hagans I was trustworthy.

Before the summer was over, I had them eating out of my hand. Or, more precisely, they had me eating at their table. Even Mr Hagan was willing to offer me a few words of advice on careers when I left school. I guess he was in a good position to do so, being a lecturer at Oxford University. He told me I had a good head on my shoulders, and that if I studied hard and went to university, I would get a decent job.

With all due respect to him, I had no intention of getting on a conveyor belt of study just to sit in some rubbish job wishing my life away. Boring with a capital Bugger That. I had far greater ambitions, and, as far as I know, they don't offer degree courses in murder at university. A very interesting concept, though.

There was a wooden pool house nestled in one corner of the garden. Imagine a conservatory crossed with a shed. It had sliding glass doors at the front, and the other three walls were clad in strips of pale-green wood. There was a huge tree sitting next to it like a natural umbrella, and it was a nice place to sit and have a break.

It was also a decent spot to spy on Jessica through a knothole in the wood at the back of the building. You see, I might have a decent head on my shoulders, but it's what's going on inside that head you need to worry about. I doubt whether dear old Mr Hagan will ever get to read my journal, and that's probably a good thing, but if he does it might teach him something you can't find in any lecture hall: never make assumptions based on perception.

In fairness, if you want a better balanced appraisal of my character, I can also go the other way and give the impression that I'm as dumb as a puddle. An uneducated idiot who is only fit for cleaning toilets. But that's for another entry, when I had a brief fling with a single mother called Lexi Smith. This turned out to be another learning curve for me, but I'll tell you about that next time. For now, let's just say it was interesting, scary, and exhilarating all at once.

278

If the Hagans had paid me more money, I might have been able to buy some proper recording equipment to install in the pool house to get some moving images of Jessica. But I had to make do with taking pictures on my iPhone and using my imagination for the rest.

I also stole some of her underwear one day when I went to tea and made out I needed to use the bathroom. But that was about as far as it went concerning the Hagans. I didn't want to push my luck. I was still a novice, and I didn't want to risk going too far and ending up in some juvenile detention centre for my troubles. I was still young and had my whole life ahead of me.

Perception. Remember that next time you think old Bob up the road's a decent chap. Helpful. Always of a cheery disposition. You never know what might be lurking behind those twinkling blue eyes. They say never judge a book by its cover, but fortunately for me, most folk do. People are lazy. They don't want to interrupt their addiction to Love Island or Facebook. It's much easier to click the Like button and move on to the next meaningless discussion.

Ever wondered why everyone else's life seems so great on the internet? How they all seem to be doing so much better than you? So much happier than you? More in love than you? It's simple: Everyone's full of crap. Creating their own little illusions. Painting a distorted picture of their lives. I have to give Facebook credit here; they created a curse and disguised it as a blessing. And now all the lemmings are heading towards the cliffs chanting 'like, like, like' repeatedly, like some death-wish mantra.

279

Dr Dark's Advice: Stop gawping at the cover and read the fucking book!

CHAPTER THIRTY-SIX

Mathew forgot about his troubles as he shared a pizza with his brother. Spicy chicken. The best thing to ever come out of an oven. Hot enough to make your eyes water, and tasty enough to keep you eating right to the end.

Finished, he leaned back in his chair and stretched. 'I'm stuffed.'

'Glad to hear it. Sometimes I think you've got a bottomless pit. Or should that be a pitiless bottom?'

Mathew laughed. His brother was funny. Especially when he played around with words.

Gareth only managed a few slices before folding over the box lid and heading off to the kitchen. 'What would you like to drink?'

'Have you got any lemonade?'

'What? With you coming to tea? You shoulda told me!'

'You know I like lemonade.'

'And you know I like yanking your chain.'

Settled on the sofa, Mathew sipped his lemonade, careful not to gulp in case he got indigestion. Gareth opened a bottle of Budweiser and turned on a massive TV fixed to the wall above a black-glass-and-chrome cabinet.

Gareth plonked himself down next to his brother. 'What movie do you fancy watching?'

'I don't mind as long as it's not violent.'

'Okay. We'll have a look and see what's on Netflix in a minute.'

'Okay.'

'Did you tell Mum I thought using the insurance money was a good idea?'

Mathew nodded and wiped grease from his chin.

'What did she say?'

'That she'll think about it.'

'I reckon she'll go for it.'

'Really?'

'Yeah. It's a great idea. Especially living in the flat once the place is renovated. Tell you what, I'll have a word with her at the weekend and give her a bit of encouragement. She's probably not thinking straight with all that's been going on.'

'I wish I could remember more about what happened with Jodie.'

'It doesn't matter. The police have as good as said you're innocent. For what it's worth, I think you found the body, then just went into shock.'

'But why can't I remember?'

'Because your brain shut down.'

'Why?'

Gareth shrugged. 'Probably to protect you.'

'I hate my brain. It can be really dumb sometimes.'

'That's Paul Whittacker's fault.'

'I hate him.'

'Me, too.'

'What did Bentley say when you went to see him?'

'Nothing much.'

'I think he killed Jodie and put her in the shed in the middle of the night. Then he tried to scare me into confessing.'

'He won't be scaring you no more, Mattie. That's a promise.'

'Do you think he killed his girlfriend and that other bloke?'

'Sounds like something he'd do. But he won't get away with it if he did. They'll know from DNA evidence and the crime scene what went on in that bedroom.'

'I hope they put him in prison and throw away the key.'

Gareth raised his bottle. 'I'll drink to that, bro.'

After failing to find a movie they could both agree on, the two brothers sat at the dining table playing Scrabble instead. Mathew loved the flat. All the furniture was made from black glass and chrome, and all the walls were white. A startling combination that made the flat seem futuristic.

'What on earth does "zoc" mean?' Gareth asked as Mathew offloaded the valuable yet difficult to use zed.

'It's something you wear.'

'Never heard of it.'

'On your feet.'

'Now I'm confused.'

Mathew raised his foot and pointed at his white sports sock. 'Zoc.'

Gareth grinned. 'That's a sock!'

'Not in Germany.'

Gareth laughed. 'Aren't you the funny one.'

The theme tune to the ten o'clock news filled the room. Mathew never usually watched the news. It was too depressing. But the headlines grabbed his attention because the lead story concerned the suspected murder-suicide in Feelham.

The presenter appeared on the screen. 'Police have today announced they believe the two bodies found in the bedroom of a flat in Feelham, Oxfordshire, may have resulted from a murder-suicide. DCI Mike Atkinson said in a statement earlier today that they believe twenty-two-year-old Curtis Pollock, of Gelding Way, Feelham, raped and murdered Shona Holloway before stabbing himself in the heart. DCI Atkinson added that there was DNA evidence that confirmed Pollock had raped the victim and then stabbed her to death in a frenzied attack.'

The camera then panned to Feelham town centre and an awkward-looking tall guy with a microphone. He stood next to an elderly lady with alert eyes and a tight perm. 'I'm joined today by local resident and ex-councillor, Annie Moore. Annie, this has been a terrible few weeks for Feelham.'

She nodded. 'First, I want to send my condolences to Shona's family. My thoughts and prayers are with them. I've said for many years that the drug-related problems in this town are getting beyond control.'

'Do you think drugs played a part in this dreadful crime?'

'Without a doubt. There're dealers openly selling drugs in the town centre at night. Hanging around the war memorial with nothing better to do than cause trouble. They see reports of stabbings on the news and think it's something to emulate. It isn't, and I for one will press to see a heavier police presence on the streets at night. Successive governments have hacked away at police numbers, and I'm appalled by some of the rhetoric that comes out of Whitehall. Tough on crime, my eye. The only thing they seem to care about is austerity.'

'Do you think this latest murder is in any way connected to the Jodie Willis murder?'

'I don't want to speculate on that. All I will say is that both crimes are extremely disturbing.'

'What advice would you give to anyone watching now?'

'Be vigilant. Don't be afraid to report anything you see that appears suspicious. Monsters who commit heinous crimes rely largely on apathy.'

'Thank you, Annie.' He turned to his left and faced away from her. 'Earlier today, I spoke to James Bentley, the owner of the flat where the murder took place. Here's what he had to say.'

Bentley's face appeared on the screen. He looked as if he'd just spent the night sleeping in a thorn bush. The interviewer stood on the doorstep, microphone sitting between them like a furry arbitrator.

'Can I ask for your reaction to the news.'

'I've been through hell,' Bentley squawked. 'First, I get accused of killing Jodie Willis, then I'm carted off to Oxford nick on suspicion of raping and killing my girlfriend. I swear to God, someone's gonna pay for this.'

'How well did you know Curtis Pollock?'

'I don't wanna talk about him. I take him into my flat, feed him and give him a bed for the night, and this is how he repays me.'

'Was there ever any suggestion he might be capable of doing something like this?'

'No. But I think someone put him up to it.'

'Would you care to elaborate?'

'Gareth Hillock. He's protecting his brother. Everyone knows Mathew Hillock's sick in the head. I mean, the police find that kid's body next to him in the shed, and they still don't think he's guilty? He got away with murder, and now Curtis kills my bird for no good reason. Don't take a rocket scientist to see a link, does it?'

The reporter frowned. 'Did Mr Pollock know the Hillocks?'

'It's a small town.'

The camera panned back to the reporter standing in the town centre. A few youths were making faces behind his back.

'That was James Bentley who I spoke to earlier today. Now back to the studio.'

Gareth got up and switched off the TV. The veins in his neck were bulging. 'Don't worry about him. He'll get what's coming.'

Mathew tapped his hand against his glass of lemonade. 'Are you going to threaten him again?'

'I don't know what I'm gonna do.'

'I want the police to put him in jail.'

'Same. But sometimes they don't do their jobs properly. If they did, Bentley would've been behind bars long ago.'

'He's evil.'

'Watch your glass, Mattie, you're spilling your drink.'

'I think he'll come after us.'

'He won't.'

'He looked really mad on the telly.'

'He's a skanky little drug dealer who'd shit his pants at the first sign of trouble with anyone over the age of twelve.'

'I reckon he burned down the Book Café.'

'Or got Curtis Pollock to do it for him.'

Mathew's feet banged against the floor. 'Maybe Pollock threatened to tell the cops about him.'

Gareth pried the glass out of his brother's hand.

'What if he does something to Granddad's house?'

'He won't.'

'He burned down the shop. And threw a rock at Bluebell Cottage.'

'Don't worry about that. I've paid for a company to install security cameras at Granddad's house.'

Mathew swayed back and forth. In the distance, the bats shrieked. The man in the cave whispered in his ear that it was time to put an end to everything and be free of his mortal body.

'Mattie?'

'I need to go to the bathroom.' He walked out of the lounge and into the hallway, a faint smile on his lips.

For the first time since the girl with the startled eyes had gone missing, Mathew Hillock felt a slight sense of peace.

CHAPTER THIRTY-SEVEN

The cave was cold and dark. Gareth was somewhere outside, his voice panicked, the tone pubescent. But he didn't want to leave the cave. The world outside was too dangerous, and he didn't belong in it. Not since Paul Whittacker had smashed his skull open with a baseball bat.

'Come on, Mattie, speak to me. Wake up.'

Mathew ignored his brother. Gareth wouldn't understand how he felt. He didn't know what it was like to be bolted together with pills. Have people poking fun at you everywhere you went. Accusing you of things you'd never done. Not even knowing what you'd done yourself half the time.

'Mattie?' His name was quickly swallowed up by a crescendo of screeching bats as they seemed to grow excited by Gareth's voice.

He wanted to tell Gareth that he loved him. That he was the best brother in the world. But he was tired of fighting to get through each day. Spending sleepless nights worrying about what was going to happen to him.

I see you've come back, then.

Mathew scanned the cave for the owner of the voice. 'Yes.'

You've done the right thing.

'Who are you?'

I've already told you. I'm your friend. Are you ready to leave the pain and suffering behind and go to a better place?

Mathew nodded. 'Does Heaven really exist?'

Depends whether you want it to. Everyone gets to go where they deserve.

'What do I deserve?'

Only you can answer that, Mathew. You're the only one who has the key to your heart.

'I want to go to Heaven if Amy and Dad are there.'

They are. Now lock the bathroom door.

He did as he was told.

Sit on the toilet for a minute. Take some deep breaths and prepare yourself for the journey.

Mathew sat and rested his elbows on his knees. He breathed slowly in and out through his nose.

Better?

'A bit.'

Stand up and take the Stanley knife out of your pocket.

'What Stanley knife?'

The one you took from the kitchen drawer at your granddad's house.

Mathew was shocked to find another chunk of his life missing. He stood and took the knife out of his pocket. Slid out the blade. A small triangle of steel, like a shark's dorsal fin, and every bit as threatening. 'Will it hurt?'

No. It's just like letting all the bad stuff out. You know, like when you're bursting for the loo and you finally get to go. Just a slight sting, then sweet release.

'Will Gareth be mad at me for doing it in his bathroom?'

He'll understand. He knows how much you've suffered.

Tears stung the backs of Mathew's eyes. He would miss Gareth. And his mum. 'What about the Book Café?'

You don't have to worry about that. It's just a building.

'I told Mum she could have my insurance money to buy new books for it.'

Then that's what she'll do.

'How do you know?'

I know everything.

A knock on the door. 'Mattie? You all right in there?'

Don't answer him. Just do it, Mathew. Do it now!

He rested the blade on a bunch of veins half an inch from the heel of his hand. The ceiling light shone down on the blade, glinting off the steel.

You need to cut deep, Mathew. Don't just scratch the surface.

He dragged the blade across his skin and watched blood leak from the wound.

You need to go deeper.

He jabbed the tip of the blade hard into his wrist, and this time used a sawing motion to chop through the veins as deep as he could go. Blood splashed onto the floor, adding its own deathly shade to the black-and-white tiles. The voice was right: there was something liberating about letting the blood flow. It was as if all the bad things anyone had ever done to him were leaving his body with the blood.

Feels good, doesn't it?

Mathew tried to speak, but his thoughts wouldn't form into words. The bathroom spun round.

You need to do the other one before you pass out.

He tried to switch hands, but the blood had greased the knife and made it almost impossible to grip the handle.

Quick! Cut the other one, Mathew.

Gareth's bath appeared to set sail on an invisible ocean. It bucked and rolled and swayed.

The other wrist, Mathew. Cut the other wrist!

He dropped the knife. It landed in a small puddle of blood with the blade pointing at his feet. The bath turned into a dark shapeless blob as he fell to his knees, blood gushing from his wounded wrist. Then he crashed to the floor, head resting against the side of the bath.

No more pain. No more voice.

CHAPTER THIRTY-EIGHT

Mathew spent the night in the John Radcliffe Hospital. He had no recollection of locking himself in the bathroom, or of Gareth breaking down the door and administering first aid. He also remembered nothing of the ambulance taking him to hospital, or his brother sitting in the back with him and holding his hand. After being given a local anaesthetic and having his wound stitched, he'd been put in a small private ward where he'd spent the rest of the night hovering in and out of consciousness.

'Mathew?'

The voice sliced through a dream he was having about Jim Bentley setting fire to all the books in the Book Café. Murdering them one by one and grinning like a Halloween pumpkin in the orange glow of the flames.

'Mathew? Can you hear me?'

The voice was soft. Perhaps that of an angel come to take him to Heaven. He tried to speak, to tell her he was ready to go, but his mouth refused to operate.

'Your mum's here to see you, Mathew.'

Why was she here? Was she dead, too?

'Is he going to be all right?' His mother's voice, thin and broken.

'He'll be fine. Just a few stitches. He'll be okay to go home later this morning.'

'I can't believe this is happening. It's just been one thing after another.'

'Try to focus on the positives, Mrs Hillock. Mathew's going to be okay. Just make sure you give him all the love and support he needs.'

'We'll take good care of him.' Gareth's voice this time. Strong. Positive. Safe.

'Come on, sleepyhead,' the angel said. 'It's almost nine o'clock. Time to wake up.'

He tried to open his eyes, but the lids felt weighted down.

'Come on, bro, shake a leg.'

What was that supposed to mean? Just another one of those silly sayings that made no sense.

'Would you like some toast and marmalade for breakfast?' the angel asked.

This time Mathew managed to half-open his eyes. He squinted at a blurry figure standing beside the bed. As his eyes grew accustomed to the light, he saw a nurse dressed in a light-blue uniform. His mother was sitting on a chair next to her.

The nurse smiled. 'Good morning, Mathew. How are you feeling?'

'Where am I?'

'You're in the John Radcliffe Hospital. Would you like some toast?'

He shook his head. 'Just water.'

She smiled again. 'Coming right up.'

Gareth walked around the bed and sat in a chair next to his mother. 'Morning, Big Guy. You gave me one hell of a shock last night.'

'I'm sorry.'

Gareth shook his head. 'No need to apologise. It's my fault. I should've been taking better care of you.'

Sonia sniffed and dabbed her eyes with a tissue. 'Do you want to talk about what happened?'

'I don't remember.'

'You must remember something.'

'I don't.' The truth. All he could recall was Jim Bentley making threats on the news, and then the rest of it was a blank canvas.

'Why didn't you talk to your brother if you were feeling so upset?'

Mathew shrugged.

'I think he had another fugue,' Gareth said. 'It was straight after Jim Bentley was on the news.'

Sonia balled her tissue up and produced another one from her sleeve. 'What was *he* doing on the news?'

'Doing what Bentley does best – talking crap and making threats.'

'I can't understand why that man's still walking the streets.'

'He wouldn't be breathing if I had my way,' Gareth said. 'Just the sight of his ugly mug makes my blood boil. With a bit of luck, he'll get hit by a bus.'

'What did Bentley say?' Sonia asked.

'That I was the reason Curtis Pollock murdered his girlfriend.'

'How on earth does he work that one out?'

'God knows. His head's so puddled with drugs that his brain's facing east and his mouth's facing west.'

Sonia turned back to her son. 'How are you feeling?'

Why does everyone keep asking me that? 'Tired.'

'Does the wound hurt?'

'Not really.'

'I wish I could get my hands on that swine.'

'You and me both, Mum,' Gareth said. 'You and me both.'

'Where's it all going to end?'

'With Bentley in jail hopefully.'

'When can I go home?' Mathew asked. 'I don't like it here. It smells of disinfectant and sick.'

Gareth grinned. 'Might have something to do with it being a hospital.'

'I thought the nurse was an angel when I woke up. I thought she was an angel, and I was up in Heaven.'

298

'Nurses *are* angels,' Sonia said. 'Doing God's work.'

'I wish I was in Heaven. Then there'd be no more pain. Just nice things and nice people.'

Gareth ran a hand through his hair. 'You're far too young to go to Heaven.'

'Amy went.'

'She didn't have a choice. But you do. And you've got a lot of living to do before you're allowed to go anywhere near Heaven.'

'Do you think God's real?'

'He is if you want Him to be.'

'That's what the voice said.'

'What voice?'

'The one in the...' He hesitated and glanced at his mother. 'The one in my head.'

Gareth looked at Sonia. 'You need to get his pills checked out again. Maybe the Buspirone doesn't suit him.'

Mathew shook his head. 'I don't want to take no more pills. They just give me bad heads and keep me up at night. Then I get exhausted, and my brain gets all confused.'

Sonia stroked his arm. 'I know it's hard, but it's important to let the doctors keep trying different things until they get the balance right.'

'I just want to go back to Granddad's and stay in my room.'

Gareth leaned forward. 'That's not such a good idea, mate. I don't think you should isolate yourself when you're feeling like this.'

'Why does everyone keep telling me what's best for me? Doesn't anyone care about what I think?'

'Of course we do,' Sonia said. 'We're only trying to help.'

'Then leave me alone.'

Sonia flinched.

'I'm sorry. I didn't mean to be rude. I just need some time on my own to think about things.'

'A problem shared is a problem halved, bro. Tell you what, why don't I come and stay with you at Granddad's for a day or two, and then we can have a bit of time to ourselves. I won't let anyone hurt you, I promise.'

Mathew couldn't think of anything he'd like better, but Gareth couldn't protect him from the man in the cave. Or from Jim Bentley setting fire to Granddad's house – CCTV cameras or not.

'We could do a spot of fishing up by the weir.'

'Maybe.'

'It's gonna be okay, Mattie. You just have to forget about Bentley and focus on positive things like getting the Book Café up and running again.'

'And I'd like to take up your offer of using the insurance money to help stock the shop,' Sonia said. 'If it still stands?'

Mathew nodded. 'I want you to have the money whatever happens.'

Gareth clapped. 'That's great news. I think we should celebrate tonight with a fish and chip supper. My treat.'

Mathew forced a weak smile as his mother leaned forward and squeezed his hand. 'Love you.'

'Love you, too.'

Unfortunately, as Mathew had come to realise, love was not the all-conquering hero it was sometimes made out to be.

CHAPTER THIRTY-NINE

Dr Dark's Diary.

I met Lexi Henderson down by the river two years *after working for the Hagans. I was seventeen, and the need to satisfy my sexual urges was growing stronger by the day. I'd done a lot of thinking, and an even greater amount of imagining, since my time with the Hagans. Going over what I could have done better. Watching Jessica through the pool house wall was not enough to quench my insatiable thirst. I needed more. Always needed more.*

I'd stalked one or two potential targets before I met Lexi, but nothing had materialised. I had to be sure I wouldn't get caught. The target had to meet certain criterion before I'd make any serious move on her. She had to be single. The last thing you need is someone that's got a bloody gorilla waiting in the wings to punch out your lights. She also had to have at least one child, preferably pre-teen, docile and easy to manipulate. And last, but definitely not least, the mum had to be desperate for a man in her life.

Lexi had long dark hair and grey eyes. She also had a hooked nose and a set of front teeth that would have made a beaver proud. She was thinner than a bamboo cane and tall enough to bump her head on the clouds. But she had a nice enough personality, and she could be funny when she had half a bottle of wine sloshing around inside her. Lexi also had a daughter called Paige, so as far as lights go, this one was racing-green.

Lexi was sitting with Paige on a wooden bench near the splash pool. I kept my distance for a while, just observing the two of them to make sure they were on their own. This was a huge step up from the Hagans, and the last thing I wanted was some bloke turning up and asking what I was doing hanging around his wife and daughter.

One of my greatest strengths is being a good judge of character. I won't lie and say I've always got it right, but I'm accurate enough most of the time. I studied mother and daughter for at least half an hour before making my move. I took off my watch and wandered over, looking as nonchalant as I could. It's a good job they couldn't see my heart clambering all over my ribs. As I said, it's the thrill of the chase that really turns me on and gets the blood pumping.

'Sorry to bother you,' I said, careful not to let my eyes roam somewhere they shouldn't. 'Have you got the time?'

Lexi glanced at her watch. 'Just gone two.'

'Thanks. Do you know when the next bus to Oxford is?'

Despite her friendly demeanour, she put a protective hand on her daughter's arm. 'I don't. Sorry.'

'Do you know if there's a public phone box anywhere around here? I've lost my mobile.'

'There's one just over the bridge near the pub.'

'Thanks.' I gave a nervous laugh. 'I don't suppose you've got 50p I can borrow? I wouldn't normally ask, but I'm in a bit of bother.'

Her eyes asked what sort of bother? Her mouth said, 'Oh.' She took off her shoulder bag and rummaged inside. Pulled out her purse and opened it. 'Sorry. I've got no change.'

I shrugged. 'That's me dead, then.'

'Sorry?'

'Someone's after me?'

'Who?'

'It's a long story. I'm sure you've got better things to do than listen to my problems.'

'When are we going to the pool?' Paige asked.

'Soon.'

'I'm hot.'

305

'I'm Mummy. Pleased to meet you.'

I smiled at Lexi's response.

Paige asked me how I would catch a bus to Oxford when I didn't have any money for the phone.

Good question. I'd have to watch this one. She was sharper than a compass point. 'I've got a bus pass.'

'You're not old.'

'I'm a student.' A spur-of-the-moment lie, but it seemed to satisfy her curiosity. Be careful, I thought. It wasn't so long ago that curiosity killed the cat. Literally!

Lexi shot her daughter a look as if to say mind your own business. 'You can borrow my phone.'

'I don't want to take advantage.'

'It's no bother, I've got enough credit.' She handed it to me. A plain black Nokia.

'Are you sure?'

She nodded and treated me to a toothy grin.

I walked a few yards away and stood under the shade of an oak tree. I dialled my own mobile number and had a two-minute argument with my voicemail facility, then disconnected the call and did my best to forge a distraught look on my face.

'Everything okay?' she asked as I handed back the phone.

'Not really. I tried ringing my dad to see if he'd let me stay for a while, but he doesn't want to know. Reckons he had enough of wiping my backside when I was a kid.'

'I wanna go to the pool now,' Paige said.

She really would have to learn some manners. And she would if things went to plan.

'Be quiet,' Lexi snapped. 'If you keep going on, you won't go at all.'

Paige opened her mouth to say something else, then seemed to think better of it.

'Tell me to mind my own business if you like, but who's after you?' Lexi asked.

I glanced behind me to give the weight of my next words a confidential air. 'You promise you won't say anything?'

She nodded.

I leaned closer and whispered, 'I owe money to someone. A lot of money.'

'How come?'

'It's a drug debt.'

'Are you an addict?' Worry in those grey eyes now.

'Never touched the stuff. It's my brother. He got in way over his head, and they beat him black and blue. I promised to pay them off if they left him alone.'

'But how can you do that if you're a student?'

'I don't know. I had a few hundred quid saved from a part-time job in a bar, but the trouble with dealers is they keep adding interest. So, you start off owing them a grand, and before long it's trebled.'

'I'm glad I never got involved in drugs. Paige's dad was a bit of a... well, never mind what he was.'

'I heard you call him the C-word on the phone to Granny Dottie,' Paige said. 'And—'

'And I told you not to listen to my conversations!'

'I'd better get off,' I said. 'See if I can find somewhere to doss down for the night.'

'Where will you go?'

'Wherever the wind takes me, I suppose.'

After a short silence, she offered me the use of her sofa. *'Just until you get yourself sorted out.'*

'I can't do that. It wouldn't be fair on you.'

'It's up to you. The offer's there if you want it.'

'Are you sure?'

She nodded. *'It'd be nice to have a man about the house for a change.'*

I stuck out my hand. *'I'm Tommy.'*

She grinned. *'Lexi.'*

'And this young lady is?'

The child gawked at me for several seconds before saying, *'Paige.'*

So, the deal was sealed. I went to live in their small terraced house on St John's Road for the next few weeks. I made Lexi swear on her daughter's life that she wouldn't tell anyone I was there because of the drug dealers, and in return, I promised to help out around the house as much as I could.

I enjoyed my time with the Hendersons. I have to say, the most surprising aspect of all was my feelings towards Lexi. I actually liked her. Not sexually. God, no! I'd have rather gone to bed with a lizard. But she was a decent woman as far as women go, and I had a certain amount of sympathy for her for trying to make the best of a bad lot.

Paige, though, was not a likeable child. She was the epitome of a spoiled brat. Not in a materialistic way; Lexi didn't have enough money for that, but in an I've-always-had-Mummy-to-myself way.

I knew I had to be careful. Be patient and wait for the right opportunity to take my career to the next level. The opportunity came one evening after Lexi had consumed a bottle of cheap plonk from Abbasi's.

Her little treat when her Universal Credit got paid into her bank. Lexi was no drunk. It was just something to reward herself with once a month, so think again before you get on your high horse about benefit scroungers – they don't all live in that pathetic television programme.

By about half eleven, Lexi was too sloshed to make sense. Once asleep on the sofa, I covered her with a duvet. I waited a while to make sure she was in the Land of No Return, then made my way upstairs.

There are some things in life that take you by surprise. Paige's resistance to my attention was one of them. So was her failure to keep our secret a secret, despite being warned I would kill her mother if she dared to breathe a word about it.

Paige left me with very little choice. It was either strangle her with a dressing gown cord or risk her bringing an abrupt end to my career before it had barely got going. Now, I don't want to make excuses, because it's fair to say I had a choice, but I had to kill Lexi because she was the only other person who knew I was there.

At least she didn't suffer. I smothered her with the pillow from Paige's bed. I found that one simple act comforting. To know that the two of them would be reunited in death.

I stayed at the Hendersons' place for another day, taking photos of the bodies on my phone and sitting with the corpses. Savouring the stillness of death.

I occasionally visit the graves of Lexi and Paige. Just to pay my respects, you understand. There will always be a spiritual link between the three of us.

One that can't be broken. And that, my friend, is a beautiful thing.

Dr Dark's Advice: Be careful who you invite into your home!

CHAPTER FORTY

Alison couldn't feel her legs as she walked out of the church with Terry and Christine supporting her. Her mother kept sniffing and clearing her throat. Dabbing her eyes with a cotton handkerchief. Nodding at some of the mourners as they stood aside like some macabre guard of honour.

There were at least a couple of hundred people gathered in the market place to pay their respects to a child most of them probably didn't know. The same folk who were most likely responsible for the dozens of cards, flowers, and stuffed animals filling the front garden and spilling onto the pavement outside Alison's home.

Terry's sister had travelled from Portsmouth for the funeral. Under different circumstances, Alison would have been pleased to see her. She liked Janice. A plain-spoken woman who was easy to get along with, Janice was the only one, other than Terry and her mother, she wanted anywhere near her. Terry had arranged for drinks and sandwiches at the Cross Keys pub after the funeral to take care of hospitality, but Alison and Janice were going to go straight home to share a bottle of wine.

As they were about to get into the car, Colin stepped forward and said,' Well, isn't this cosy. The mother who couldn't be arsed to go to the shop for a pint of milk, and the dodgy stepfather acting as if butter wouldn't melt. Say what you want about Mathew Hillock, but I reckon Stevens is the one who killed Jodie.'

Alison stared into his red, bloated face. He was barely three feet away, and he stank of booze.

'Go home, Colin,' Christine said. 'Go home and sleep it off. No one wants you here.'

'Is that right. And who the fuck do you think you are, you sanctimonious old bag? The world's oldest guardian angel?'

'Shut up,' someone said from the crowd of mourners. 'Don't do this today of all days.'

Colin didn't seem to hear him. 'Hey, Stevens, why don't you tell the truth about what you've done?'

Terry turned to face him. 'What did you say?'

'Leave it,' Alison said. 'Just leave it.'

'Nine times outta ten it's the stepfather,' Colin persisted. 'Preying on kids. Is that why you moved in with her? To get at Jodie?'

'I'm warning you,' Terry said. 'One more word and I'm gonna flatten you.'

'Is that right, big man. Come on then. Let's see what you've got.'

Alison shook with rage. Even her heart felt as if it was vibrating. 'Terry's more than of a man than you'll ever be. You're not fit to breathe the same air as him.'

Colin laughed. A nasty, bitter sound rounded off with a sneer. 'That ain't no man. It's a dirty lying weasel who's gonna get what's coming to him.'

Christine pulled on her daughter's arm. 'Come on, Ali. Get in the car. Ignore him.'

'That's right,' Colin said. 'Run away like you always do.'

Terry squared up to Colin. 'Go home. Final warning.'

'That's enough,' a deep, authoritative voice boomed. Reverend Chase moved through the mourners. He stopped next to Colin and Terry. 'Have you no respect?'

'I'm just telling it like it is,' Colin said.

'You're making a show of yourself, Mr Pitman. Goodness gracious, man, we're about to bury your child.'

Colin jabbed a finger in the direction of Terry's chest. 'Because this bastard killed her.'

'That's a matter for the police,' Chase said. 'Today is about paying our respects to that poor child and laying her to rest. I know you're hurting, Mr Pitman, and I sympathise for your loss, but you really need to get a grip of yourself.'

'Amen to that,' Terry whispered.

Chase turned his attention to Terry. 'I think it best that you get in the car now and do nothing further to exacerbate the situation.'

Terry stared at Colin with eyes that looked capable of firing lethal weapons. He nodded and helped Alison into the car.

'You should be ashamed of yourself, Colin Pitman,' Christine said. 'You're an utter disgrace.'

Colin looked about to respond, then seemed to think better of it. He barged his way through the crowd and headed off down the alleyway opposite the church towards Saxons Green.

Alison would later remember nothing of the short journey along Castle Street to the cemetery. It was as if her physical body was in the car, but her mind was elsewhere searching for Jodie. She would have given anything to have just a few minutes with her daughter to tell her how sorry she was that she'd let her down. That she would gladly take her place if God was open to such requests. But, of course, this was the cold mortal world where no such deals could ever be done. Done was done forever, and history would show that a million mothers' tears could never bring back a child.

Terry kept rubbing her arm as if trying to wear a hole in her black jumper. Although the weather was warm, rain splashed onto the car roof.

'I can't believe how many people turned up,' Christine said as they pulled into the gravel turnaround behind the hearse. 'It's comforting to know that so many people care.'

Terry nodded. 'It's a shame Pitman didn't have the good sense to stay away.'

Christine. 'He makes me sick to my stomach.'

'If he says anything at the funeral, I swear to God I'll put the bastard in the ground.'

'Is that right?' Alison said. 'You think that's going to help matters, do you?'

'No, but—'

'You want me to lose you as well?'

Terry shook his head. 'I'm sorry, love. He just gets right under my skin.'

One of the funeral guys, attired in a black suit and sporting an appropriate sombre expression, opened the door and helped Alison out of the car. The cemetery was veiled in a misty gauze of drizzle. Alison shivered and wrapped her arms around her chest. The gravestones stood like monuments to mortality.

Terry climbed out of the car and put an arm around her shoulder. 'You okay?'

Alison didn't answer. She'd had enough of dumb questions to last her a lifetime. *Do you need anything? Would you like a cup of tea? How are you bearing up? Is there anything I can do?* Why couldn't anyone see that the only thing she wanted was the one thing no one could give her?

315

As if to amplify her thoughts, the coffin was brought out from the back of the hearse and hoisted onto the shoulders of six men from the undertakers. They made their way along the gravel track leading to the bottom of the cemetery.

Alison, flanked by Terry and Christine, followed the coffin with fifty or so mourners falling into line behind them. Christine continually sniffed and dabbed at her eyes as they approached the freshly dug grave. Gravity and grief tried to force Alison to her knees.

The rain fell harder as they gathered around the grave. Someone Alison didn't recognise offered her an umbrella. Christine thanked the woman and held it over her daughter's head.

After several minutes, Reverend Chase took his position at the head of the grave. Decked in a black gown and clutching an open Bible, he looked briefly at the mourners before saying, 'In the Name of God, the merciful Father, we commit the body of Jodie to the peace of the grave.'

Alison watched the coffin being slowly lowered into the ground. A few minutes later, at the invitation of the reverend, Terry and Alison stepped forward and threw a handful of earth onto the coffin.

Chase nodded at Alison, but her feet felt as if they'd taken root in the wet earth.

'Take your time,' Chase prompted.

Alison shook her head. She didn't want to throw a stupid handful of earth into her daughter's grave. She wanted to jump on top of the coffin, rip off the lid, and take Jodie back home where she belonged. Not leave her here in the cold damp earth for the maggots and worms to devour.

Chase nodded politely, made the sign of the cross, and said, 'From dust you came, to dust you shall return. Jesus Christ is the resurrection and the life. Lord God, our Father in Heaven, Lord God, the Son, and Saviour of the world, Lord God, the Holy Spirit, have mercy on us. At the moment of death, and on the last day, save us, merciful and gracious Lord God.'

Alison lurched forward and fell to her knees. 'Why has this happened?' she screamed, beating her fists against the ground. 'Why has this happened to my baby?'

Terry and one of Alison's uncles rushed to her side. Helped her to her feet.

She glared at the reverend. 'Why Jodie? Why her?'

Chase seemed to have no answer to that. He merely shook his head and shifted weight from one foot to the other.

'Ask God now. I want Him to tell me why He's taken my baby.'

'Come on, Ali,' Terry said. 'Don't—'

'Don't what? Don't get upset? Don't blame God? Don't put the vicar on the spot?'

'Please, love. Let's just get this over with and get you home.'

Alison tried to tell Terry to leave her alone. There was nothing left in this world for her anymore. Just a long empty road of pain and misery. She felt as cold and dead as her beautiful child, and no one was ever going to change that. Not even Reverend Chase with his direct line to the Lord. When it came down to it, people were just powerless pawns in some stupid game of life and death. Insignificant specks of dust in the universe. And God, if He really did exist, didn't give a damn about how much they suffered.

People gathered around her at the end of the service. Offering condolences. Telling her not to hesitate asking if there was anything she needed. Well-meaning decent folk who cared about her. Aunty Joyce. Her friend Caroline. Terry's sister. A middle-aged guy with long hair who she vaguely recognised but couldn't quite place. But they might as well have all been aliens from a distant planet as far as she was concerned.

There would be no way back from this. Her life had been turned into a living hell, and only death held the key to release her.

CHAPTER FORTY-ONE

Alison couldn't process the fact that her precious daughter was lying in the cold earth at Feelham cemetery. It didn't seem real. Almost as if it had happened to another Alison in another lifetime. Jodie's brief, but eventful, eleven years on this planet gone in the blink of an eye. She would never forgive God for letting an evil monster take her child's life. Why couldn't He have taken Colin instead?

Her mother handed her a glass of wine.

Alison drank half of it in one go. 'What the hell am I gonna do now?'

Christine lit a cigarette. 'Just try to take it one day at a time, love.'

'It feels as if there's nothing left inside me. Just this gaping black hole where Jodie used to be.'

'Jodie's still here, darling. It's just you can't see her right now.'

'How do you work that one out?'

'My little brother died when he was twelve. Got hit by a car and knocked off his bike up near the school when I was fifteen.'

'You never said.'

'It's not something I usually talk about. Anyway, I didn't know how to feel about it. I mean, I loved him because he was my brother, but I wasn't his biggest fan because he could be an annoying bugger at times. It was almost as if I wanted to laugh and cry all at the same time. Anyway, to cut a long story short, I pleaded with Mum to let me have his room because it was much bigger than mine. But she wouldn't let me. She wanted to keep it the way it was when Graham was alive.'

'That's what I'm gonna do with Jodie's room. I'm gonna make it up nice and put all her favourite things on the shelves.'

Christine nodded. 'I think she'd like that.'

'So, what happened with your brother?'

'I know this is gonna make me sound like a right little bitch, but I used to sneak into his room when my parents were out and lie on his bed. Pretend it was my room. Imagine it was filled with my stuff, and I was like some stupid queen and this was my castle.'

'Sounds… weird.'

'I know. Anyway, one night, I couldn't sleep, so I snuck in there and got into his bed. I didn't intend to go to sleep. Just lay awake awhile and play daft games of imagination. But as the time wore on, my eyelids started getting heavier and heavier. Closing and then springing back open. And that's when I saw Graham. He was sitting on the end of the bed dressed in his school uniform. I pinched myself really hard to make sure I wasn't dreaming. But he was there, Ali. I swear on my life. He really was there.'

'Did he say anything?'

'Not out loud. But he seemed to speak in my head. You know, like telepathy.'

'What did he say?'

'He said, "Don't worry, Goldilocks. I won't tell Mummy Bear you've been sleeping in my bed." Then he grinned and vanished into thin air.'

'Bloody hell.'

'I ran back to my room and pulled the duvet over my head. Then I spent the rest of the night sobbing my heart out.'

Alison finished her wine, then said, 'You might've dreamt it.'

Christine fetched her handbag from the sofa and opened it. She took out her purse and pulled out a small card. She handed it to her daughter.

'What's this?'

'One of Graham's football cards. When I got up in the morning after he'd visited, I found it lying on my bedside table. It was his favourite. One that he wouldn't loan out, even to his mates.'

Alison studied the picture of a bearded footballer in a white shirt. 'Are you serious?'

321

'I'm a lot of things, Ali, but I'm not a liar. That card was by my bed, and there's no way on earth anyone else could've put it there.'

'I don't know what to say.'

'You don't have to say anything. Just remember it when you can't bear the burden of Jodie's loss. Know that she's still with you, and maybe one day she'll come to see you like Graham did me.'

Alison handed back the card. 'I hope so.'

'There's so much more to life than meets the eye, Ali. It took me ages to come to terms with what happened that night, but now I know Graham was just trying to tell me he's okay. There's no such thing as death. At least, not in the way most people think of it.'

'It still doesn't alter the fact that Jodie never got to live her life because some sick bastard couldn't control himself.'

'I know. But she's safe now. Somewhere no one can hurt her.'

'You know what gets to me the most?'

'What?'

'The way the police keep arresting people and then letting them go.'

'I still think that Hillock boy had something to do with it.'

The letterbox rattled and interrupted the conversation. Christine stood. 'I'll get it.'

'If that's another request for an interview, put the bloody thing straight in the bin.'

Christine returned with a brown envelope. Alison's name and address were printed on the front, and it was postmarked Oxford. She took it from her mother and opened it. Pulled out a sympathy card. The front had a brightly coloured butterfly sitting on a daffodil. The message read: *Someone so special can never be forgotten.*

'Who's it from?' Christine asked.

Alison opened the card. Two pages of printed A4 paper fell into her lap. 'What the hell…?'

There was no name attributed to the card. No message.

'Ali?'

She picked up the note paper and read:

Hi, Alison,

Sorry to trouble you at what must be a very difficult time for you. First of all, please accept my condolences for your loss. I just wanted to write and tell you that Jodie was a credit to you. A real fighter, right to the end. How old was she? They said "eleven" in the papers. Let me tell you, that girl acted like someone twice that age. She nearly convinced me to let her go at one time. Smart girl. I almost believed her when she said she loved me and wanted to spend the rest of her life with me.

A word of advice if you ever have any more children, Alison: Take better care of them. Run your own errands. Don't be lazy. Just an observation. Please don't be offended.

I suppose you're dying to know what happened, right? No pun intended. I find the English language is a minefield of ambiguity. Have to be so careful with the words you say, lest they get you into trouble.

Anyway, back to the night in question. Thursday, August 6th, I believe. Yes. That's the one. I've just

323

checked it in my diary. Hot as hell's kitchen, as I recall. If it's any consolation, I didn't plan this one like I have the others. It was spontaneous. A golden opportunity way too good to pass up.

Jodie was ambling along the alleyway at the back of the garages adjacent to St John's Road. As with all kids these days, she was fully engaged with her phone and not looking where she was going. A dangerous combination for a young lady out on her own. Like I said, nothing was pre-planned – I just happened to be taking a shortcut along the same alleyway.

I asked her if she'd seen a dog. Told her it had escaped out the back gate. Obviously, she said she hadn't, because the escaped dog story was a lie. Then I asked her if she'd help me to look for it. Said his name was Pongo. She thought that was a funny name. Sounded like it was stinky.

She said she would, but she needed to get home soon because her mum would wonder where she was. I told her that was okay, because I would give her a lift home once we'd found the dog.

See how easy it is, Alison? All that advice about speaking to strangers, and what does she do? Walks off searching for a make-believe dog with me. You know the biggest problem with kids, Alison? They're too trusting. Especially when you throw a cute little doggie into the mix. Not that you can blame them. They don't know any better. Parents need to step up. How far's Abbasi's from your house? Two hundred yards? And you send your own daughter to get the milk? Shame on you!

We ended up along the Bunky Line. Then she started getting all jittery, thinking you'd be mad at

324

her for not coming straight home. I persuaded her to go as far as the derelict farmhouse. I don't think she wanted to, but by then she seemed genuinely worried about the poor doggy.

I always carry a bottle of Coke laced with sleeping pills for these types of encounters. You never know when a golden opportunity will present itself, do you? So we stopped by one of the old air-raid shelters and had a short break before heading home. She drank most of that Coke in one go. Went out like a light, as they say.

I carried her into the shelter and laid her on the ground. It was pretty whiffy in there, and there were quite a few bugs crawling around, but it was cosy enough once you got over the initial shock. Now all I had to do was wait for it to get dark and take her home.

Risky? Perhaps. But then that's half the fun of what I do. The excitement. The thrill of the hunt. I spent four wonderful days with Jodie. Got to know her better in that time than you did in her entire life. Just for the record, Alison, she loved you. Said you were a good mum, even if your choice of boyfriends left a lot to be desired. Not her exact words, but close enough!

Before I sign off, I just want you to know that Jodie gave me more pleasure than you could ever imagine. She was a joy to be with, and I regret I had to kill her.

I suggest you make better choices in the future, Alison. For your sake, and for the sake of any further children you may have.

Dr Dark's advice: Know what is precious and guard it with your life.

CHAPTER FORTY-TWO

Jim was not in a good mood. No, scrub that, he was raging. Not only had he been accused of crimes he'd not committed and dragged through an ordeal that made Jesus's time on the cross look like a walk in the park, the newspapers had refused to offer him any money for his story. Why? Because he was still a suspect in an ongoing investigation.

What a load of bollocks. You read about stuff in the papers all the time. False arrests. Scumbag journalists hacking into victims' phones. The filth up to all sorts of bad shit to get a conviction. So why the sudden need to uphold moral values? He couldn't even get a booking on *Jeremy Kyle* because the do-gooders had shut that fucker down with all their sentimental claptrap.

Two lines of coke and half a bottle of vodka had failed to ease the pressure building up inside his head. True, he was buzzing like a fly in a jam jar, but he was also filled with a desperate need to exact revenge on the Hillock family. Particularly Gareth, who'd not only assaulted him but had defended his retard brother as if he was some sort of national treasure.

He'd bought a gallon of petrol earlier in the day, and now it was time to construct a makeshift bomb. Or a gasoline incendiary device as the voiceover man had called it on the TV programme.

The arsonist had filled plastic containers with petrol and then used a sock as a fuse. Hardly something that needed specialist training. Then he'd gone to the target's house, lit the sock, and left the device on the front doorstep to do its thing. A successful operation the guy had repeated over two hundred times across central America.

If it was good enough for Uncle Sam's children, it was good enough for Gareth Hillock. The only downside to the plan was he wouldn't be around to watch the fucker burn. But how was he going to get inside the block of flats late on a Saturday night when there was only controlled entry? The answer came to him as he smoked a second spliff. Buzz one of the other flats and make out he had a pizza for Hillock but couldn't get an answer. Ask if they could let him in so he could knock directly on the door.

Fool proof? No. But if he was carrying the petrol bomb in a canvas bag, no one would get suspicious if they clocked him. His black hoodie and jeans would also make it impossible to identify him if there were any cameras in the corridors and stairwells. Anyway, Hillock lived in the basement flat, so he didn't need to go trudging up and down the stairs. Just get in, light the fuse and get out.

Arson. Boom. Cremation.

For once, he laughed at the voice in his head. He finished the spliff and studied the tools of his trade lying on the table. One two-litre milk carton, one can of petrol, one unwashed sock, one funnel, and one black canvas bag.

He checked the time on his phone. 10:17 p.m. Time to get cracking. First things first – transfer the petrol into the milk carton.

Sometimes things were easier said than done. And sometimes they were damn near impossible. Especially when the milk carton kept introducing a twin and making it impossible to know which one to aim for. Unfortunately for Jim, he kept picking the wrong milk twin and missing the target.

'Fuck it! I need a drink to steady myself.'

Bad move. A massive swig of vodka only added another milk carton. Not only that, but all three cartons seemed to defy the laws of physics by swaying on the table to an imaginary tune.

Jim abandoned proceedings and went to the bathroom to splash some water on his face. Sharpen up a bit before embarking on Operation Hillock.

The water went some way to reviving him, but when he looked at his reflection in the mirror above the basin, Jodie Willis's face was staring back at him.

He splashed his face with more water. 'Not there. Not there.'

Maybe you were the one who killed her, Jimbo. Strangled her and put her in Mathew Hillock's shed.

'I wouldn't kill a kid,' he squawked. 'I don't even like kids.'

We all have our guilty secrets.

He took a cautious peek at the mirror. This time his own haunted face gawped back at him. He didn't know whose features scared him the most – his or Jodie's.

It had taken him the best part of three days to go back to sleeping in the bedroom again. To get over the horror of discovering Shona brutally murdered by Curtis Pollock. Now the bathroom would be out of bounds for the immediate future.

He lurched back into the living room. At least the shock of seeing Jodie in the mirror had reduced the milk triplets to a single entity once again. He wiped an arm across his forehead, took a few deep breaths to calm his nerves, and set about transferring the petrol again.

This time he managed to half-fill the carton. A major success considering his hands were shaking. But success was success, even if there was a puddle of petrol on the table. He'd have to clean up tomorrow. And air out the flat. Smash that fucking mirror in the bathroom.

He sat and attempted to insert the sock into the end of the carton. It was like trying to stuff a marshmallow into a slot machine. His unsteady hands didn't help matters. Nor did his continuous need to keep checking on the bathroom door to make sure Jodie's ghost didn't wander into the hallway.

Maybe you ought to leave it until tomorrow when you're not so freaked out.

Good advice. But he wanted Gareth Hillock barbecued tonight. Then he could start planning a new life away from Feelham. Maybe go down to the coast. There was no way he could stay in the flat after what had happened to Shona. It was too upsetting. Too raw. Her murder would forever mess with his head and make it impossible to relax. Seeing Jodie in the mirror had only confirmed his belief that his future lay a long way from his past.

'I'm outta here as soon as I've sold my story,' he announced. 'Sort myself out a nice little flat in Brighton and use some of the money to buy some decent gear and begin dealing again.'

Good plan.

His phone told him it was now ten twenty-nine. Time to go. Just one problem – he was too knackered to walk all the way into town.

Take a cab.

Great idea. But what if the cabbie remembered a stoned guy getting a ride into town with a bag stinking of petrol? Saw news of the fire on TV and put two and two together?

Drive your own car, then.

331

Better. But there was no way he was gonna take the car anywhere when he was off his face. He'd end up wrapping it round a tree and spending the night in the cop shop trying to explain why he was carrying a Molotov cocktail in the back of his car while under the influence.

He felt trapped in a no-man's land of indecision. 'I'm gonna fucking burn you to a crisp, Hillock. You and that retard brother of yours. You just see if I don't.'

He stood and went into the bedroom. Checked the room for signs of Shona and Jodie. Nothing. Just a pile of dirty clothes littering the floor along with several foil dishes and empty cans of Special Brew.

He fished in the bedside table for his weed. Thought he saw something moving in the corner of his eye and span round. Nothing. Just his reflection in the dressing table mirror.

Nice one, Jimbo. Jumping at your own shadow now!

'Fuck you!' He went back into the living room and sat in a chair next to the TV. It was no good. He'd have to abandon the mission tonight. One more spliff and he'd hit the hay. Live to fight another day.

As sometimes happened, one spliff led to another, and by the time he was halfway down the second joint, he was feeling ready to go into battle again and torch Hillock's flat. He felt as if he could fly all the way into town on Black Leb wings.

'I'm fucking invincible,' he slurred, staggering towards the bomb-making table with a spliff dangling from the corner of his mouth. 'Hillock the pillock's gonna regret the day he ever threatened Jim Bentley.'

That's better, Jimbo. Strike while the iron's hot!

The voice in his head seemed to be that of his old man. The bastard who'd taught him the only way to raise a kid was with violence and constant criticism. It was a shame he'd died when Jim was twelve, because it had deprived Jim of the pleasure of killing him.

You need to soak the sock in petrol first, Bentley Senior advised. *Otherwise it might not burn.*

Jim glanced behind him, expecting to see his dad with Jodie Willis on one arm and Shona on the other. He tried to remember the TV programme and whether the arsonist had primed the sock with petrol first.

'Well, it ain't gonna hurt to soak it, is it?' he said, turning back to the table. He put the sock next to the petrol can and then emptied some fuel onto it. The stench of the petrol was overbearing, filling his nose and making his eyes water.

'That should do.'

As he spoke, the spliff fell out of his mouth and ignited the sock. He watched for a few seconds, stunned, as it engulfed his wannabe fuse in a ball of orange and yellow flame. It looked so pretty. The colours so vibrant. Then the puddle of petrol on the table ignited and engulfed the rest of the paraphernalia scattered across the surface.

Jim was transfixed as the flames reached up towards the ceiling, consuming the plastic milk container. In his stupor, he could see the outline of an exotic dancer in the fire, wiggling her hips and thrusting her crotch at him. She appeared to invite him into the flames.

The milk carton exploded and showered him with burning liquid. He only had a few seconds to realise he'd been turned into a human torch. He staggered across the living room, trying to make his way to the bathroom. He just needed to get in the shower and douse the flames. Then he could call an ambulance.

His body felt as if it had been submerged in acid. He tripped over a pair of boots and fell against the sofa. Within seconds, the sofa was ablaze, and Bentley was beating his fists against the cushions.

He didn't hear the petrol can explode or see the flames devour the curtains and the other soft furnishings. The rubbish strewn across the floor acted as stepping stones for the fire as it headed off towards the kitchen to see what it could cook up.

For Jim, it was over. No more pain. No more disappointment. No more Hillocks.

CHAPTER FORTY-THREE

Mathew sat in his room, which wasn't really his room at all; it was the one which had belonged to his mother when she was a child and still had dreams of a happy life. There was even an old rag doll of hers called Fifi sitting on top of the pine wardrobe. She was unloved and alone, her sad eyes fixed on the door as if waiting for another kid to walk into the room and play with her again.

He knew he'd upset his mum by cutting his wrist in Gareth's bathroom. It was bad enough that she'd already lost Amy, without him doing something stupid like that. But the worst thing of all was not being able to remember very much about it. One minute he'd been watching Jim Bentley on the news, and the next he'd been in hospital having his wrist stitched up.

He knew he'd suffered another fugue. But that was just a name; it did little to explain what was really going on inside his head. The most frightening aspect of these 'blackouts' was the lost time. How he could sit in the shed with the dead body of a child all day and not even be aware of doing so.

Worse than that, though: what if he really was the one who'd taken Jodie and hid her somewhere along the Bunky Line? He knew he would never do such a thing in his current state of mind, but what about the Mathew in the fugue state of mind? The one who cut his own wrist? That Mathew was someone he didn't know at all. It was like having an evil twin living right inside his body.

He was still trying to digest the news that Jim Bentley had died three days earlier in a fire. Although he hated Bentley with every bone in his body, it was still a terrible way to die. His bandaged wrist reminded him just how close he'd come to dying himself. If Gareth hadn't smashed the bathroom door open, it might have been a very different story.

A knock on the door interrupted his thoughts. His granddad poked his head inside. 'Can you come downstairs a minute, lad? The police are here.'

Mathew's heart picked up speed. 'What do they want?'

'Just to talk to you about something.'

'I don't want to see them. I'm too tired.'

'I'm afraid you have to, lad.'

'Why?'

'Because they're the police.'

He followed his granddad downstairs, shoulders slumped, legs heavy. DS Palmer was sitting at the dining table. A shiver rolled along Mathew's spine.

Palmer smiled. 'Hello, Mathew. How are you?'

'Tired.'

The detective nodded as if tiredness was his specialist subject. 'Take a seat. I won't keep you long.'

Bernard offered Palmer a drink which he declined. 'I've already got half a gallon of tea sloshing around inside me.' He turned to Mathew. 'I'll get straight to the point. After receiving information from a member of the public, we have reason to believe that Jodie Willis was kept in an air-raid shelter along the Bunky Line on the evening of Thursday, August 6th. Upon investigation of the shelter, we found a four-pint milk carton with Jodie's fingerprints on it, and other DNA evidence proving her presence there.'

Bernard cleared his throat. 'That's good news, Detective. But I can't see what this has to do with Mathew.'

'Mathew told us he went to the river on the evening of the abduction. He later admitted that this was a lie and said he went along the Bunky Line instead.'

Bernard asked Mathew if that was correct.

Mathew nodded.

'Why did you lie?'

'Because I thought Mum would be mad at me.'

'Thing is, Mathew,' Palmer said, 'we need to know exactly where you went that evening.'

'I don't remember. I walked along the Bunky Line to see if Jim Bentley had taken Jodie to the farmhouse.'

'Did you go into the farmhouse?'

'No.'

'Did you see Jim Bentley anywhere along the Bunky Line?'

'No.'

'How long did you spend there?'

'I can't remember.'

'You must have some idea.'

'I got back home around half eight.'

'That's about two hours after your sighting of Jodie. What did you do after you went to the farmhouse searching for Mr Bentley?'

'I don't remember.'

'Did you go to the air-raid shelter?'

'No.'

'How do you know if you can't remember?'

Mathew tapped his right hand on the table. 'Because I'd have no reason to go there.'

'Not even to look for Mr Bentley?'

Mathew didn't answer. He watched his hand like a cat watching a bird.

'He's already told you he has blackouts,' Bernard said. 'He's had three in the past week alone.'

Palmer stared at the bandage. 'What happened to your hand?'

'I cut my wrist.'

'Deliberately?'

'Yes.'

'Why did you do that?'

'I don't know.'

'Another blackout?'

'Yes.' Mathew thumped the table harder.

'Do these blackouts often lead to acts of violence?'

'No.'

'So, why this time?'

'Does it matter?' Bernard asked. 'I can't see how this is relevant.'

'Just trying to establish Mathew's state of mind.'

'If you're alluding to what I think you are, it's already been proven that the marks around that child's neck were caused by someone with much smaller hands than my grandson.'

This seemed to stop Palmer in his tracks. 'Things don't always turn out the way they seem.'

'And there's not one shred of evidence linking Mathew to the murder.'

'I'm not suggesting Mathew is guilty of anything.'

'Then what are you suggesting?'

Palmer seemed thoughtful for a moment, then said, 'That he may have witnessed the murder.'

'Don't you think he'd have said?'

'Not if he can't remember… or if he was involved in some other way.'

Mathew clamped his bandaged hand on top of the other one to stop it tapping. This was the cue for his feet to take over instead. 'I think the detective's right. Maybe I killed Jodie. Maybe I killed her in the air-raid shelter and I just don't remember.'

Bernard grabbed his arm hard enough to pinch the skin. 'No. You. Didn't. You hear me? Don't let anyone put daft ideas into your head.' He turned to Palmer. 'You've got Mathew's DNA, right? Was there anything found at that shelter to link him to it?'

'We're still carrying out tests.'

'You ought to be ashamed of yourself, coming here making unfounded allegations. The boy suffers blackouts because of being attacked. He cut his wrist because of all the pressure he's been under lately. As for taking part in that girl's murder... bloody hell, it's like accusing Mother Teresa.'

Palmer seemed undeterred. 'Are you aware that Mr Bentley is dead, Mathew?'

'Yes.'

'How do you feel about that?'

'That it was a horrible way to die.'

'You didn't like him, though, did you?'

Mathew shrugged and chewed his lip. 'Not really.'

'Would it be reasonable to say you hated him?'

'Yes.'

'That you're glad he's dead?'

'Of course he's pleased,' Bernard interrupted. 'That man made my grandson's life hell. If you ask me, Bentley's the one who killed that poor child. End of story.'

Palmer seemed to weigh this up for a moment, before saying to Mathew, 'It seems odd that Mr

Bentley thought you were the one who killed Jodie, and you think Mr Bentley killed her. Extremely odd considering you two were the last people to see her alive.'

Mathew tried to speak, but his tongue seemed glued to the roof of his mouth.

'It also seems odd that Mr Bentley died in a fire and you tried to kill yourself.'

'Is that all, Detective,' Bernard said. 'Because my grandson is in a delicate enough mental state as it is without your half-baked accusations upsetting him any further.'

'With all due respect, I'm investigating the murder of a child. Sometimes people get upset when being questioned. But let me tell you this: no one's anywhere near as upset as Jodie's mother. Alison Willis is in pieces, so just remember that the next time you want to accuse me of upsetting anyone.'

'I'm well aware of what it's like to lose a child. My granddaughter and son-in-law were killed. My heart goes out to Mrs Willis. But we're all victims here, Detective. All of us.'

The bats shrieked in the cave. Calling him home.

Palmer stood. 'If there's anything else you remember, Mathew, anything at all, no matter how insignificant you might think it is, please let us know straight away.'

Mathew didn't hear him. He walked into the cave, rolled the boulder over the entrance, and sat on the cold stone floor. He drew his knees up to his chest as icy shivers rolled along his spine. The screeching bats sounded like the Devil's private orchestra. Written on the wall to the right of *Hang The Pervert,* an additional four words which said: *I Am The Pervert.*

And that was the truth, wasn't it? Just because he couldn't remember, didn't mean he was innocent. He closed his eyes and prayed for the orb to help him.

CHAPTER FORTY-FOUR

Mathew stayed in the fugue state for about an hour before being coaxed out of it by his mother. After she'd persuaded him to come downstairs and have something to eat and drink, he found himself at the centre of a mini-inquest.

'Are you absolutely sure you didn't see Jim Bentley when you went along the Bunky Line?' Sonia asked.

'I don't think so.'

'Did you see anyone else?'

'I can't remember.'

Pam took a sip of tea. 'What does it actually feel like when you have one of those fugue things?'

Mathew decided not to tell her about the cave. 'It's a bit like sleepwalking, I suppose.'

'How do you know where you're going?'

'I don't.'

'How come you don't trip over things?'

Mathew shrugged.

Pam turned to her daughter. 'Maybe we could get him hypnotised.'

'Whatever for?'

'To see if it can help jog his memory.'

Bernard shook his head. 'I don't think that's a good idea, love.'

'Why?'

'For a start, evidence obtained under hypnosis isn't recognised in court.'

'Why not?'

'It's got something to do with suggestion. Anyway, it's not very clever messing with the lad's head with... well... you know.'

'I don't want to be hypnotised,' Mathew said, fearing it might reveal a truth nobody wanted to hear. 'I just want to be left alone.'

'It's all right,' Bernard assured him. 'No one's going to force you to do anything you don't want to.'

'Are you sure you went nowhere near that air-raid shelter?' Sonia asked.

Mathew shrugged. 'All I know is I went to see if Jim Bentley took Jodie to the farmhouse. Then I came home. That's it.'

'What I want to know,' Pam said, 'is how come the police knew to look in the air-raid shelter in the first place?'

'They said they were given information,' Bernard said.

'By who?'

'I know you think I'm clever, dear, but I'm not a mind reader. Someone probably found the milk carton in the shelter and remembered Jodie went missing after she bought milk.'

'For what it's worth, I think the police are just fishing,' Pam said. 'Trying to make things fit. It's clear to anyone with half a brain that Bentley killed that little girl and tried to drag Mathew into it by hiding the body in the shed.'

'Maybe I helped him,' Mathew said. 'Maybe I did it and I just can't remember.'

Bernard touched his arm. 'Don't talk like that, lad. The police are just trying to confuse you. Make you think you're guilty. They do it all the time. You just have to ignore them.'

'What if they're right? What if I kept Jodie hidden in the shelter? Then went out in the middle of the night and put her in the shed?'

'I'd have heard you leaving the house,' Sonia said. 'I barely sleep these days.'

Pam asked Mathew if he could remember anything about finding the body in the shed.

'No.'

'But you remember Bentley coming to the door?'

'Yes.'

'And he told you to confess?'

'Yes.'

Pam shook her head. 'But why would he do that? It makes no sense.'

'None of it does,' Bernard said. 'And now Bentley's dead, I doubt whether we'll ever get to the truth of what really happened. That evil swine took his dirty little secret to the grave with him.'

'Crematorium, more like,' Pam said. 'Talk about divine retribution.'

Mathew stared at his bandaged wrist. He wanted to get up and leave the table, but it was rude to do so before everyone else had finished.

Pam buttered a scone. 'Everyone gets what they deserve, eventually.'

'Does that mean I deserve to go to jail?' Mathew asked.

Pam shook her head. 'Don't be silly. You've done nothing wrong.'

'The police think I have.'

'The police can whistle up a wind tunnel. Everyone knows you're not capable of hurting anyone, let alone a child.'

'I cut my wrist.'

'That's an entirely different matter.'

Mathew's eyes widened. 'Is it?'

'Yes.'

'I don't remember doing it.'

'That's because you had a blackout,' Sonia said.

This only deepened Mathew's doubt about his own involvement. 'What else have I done in a fugue, Mum?'

'Nothing.'

'How do you know?'

'You're my son. My wonderful brave son who's battled against incredible odds to become the man he is today. I know, Mathew. I just do.'

'Your mum's right,' Bernard said. 'So, let's have no more of this self-doubt nonsense. We're all here for you. And we all believe in you.'

Mathew wished that positive words alone could mend his fractured mind. Allow him to fill in all the blank spaces in his life and show him the truth. But nothing could help him. He was who he was, and nothing other than death could change that. 'Can I leave the table, please?'

Sonia asked him if he wanted any scones.

'I'm not hungry.'

'Not even for strawberry jam?'

'No.'

'Please don't hide yourself away in your room, Mathew. It's better to have people around you at a time like this.'

'Why?'

'Because it's not healthy isolating yourself.'

'It's not healthy being accused of murder, either,' Mathew said.'

'No one's accused you of anything.'

'The detective did.'

'Just ignore him. There's not one shred of evidence to suggest you did anything to that child.'

'Apart from I went along the Bunky Line, and they found the milk carton there.'

Bernard laid a hand on his grandson's arm. 'It's just a coincidence, lad. Like your nan says, they're just fishing to see what they can catch.'

'Can I leave the table, please? I'm tired. I need to lie down.'

His mother nodded. 'Go on, then. But if you feel as if you can't cope, or you need to talk, come and get me straight away.'

Mathew promised he would, then went to his room. How could anyone understand how he felt when he didn't even know himself? He knew they were only trying to help, trying to encourage him, but it only seemed to be making things worse.

He sat on his bed, a headache pulsing behind his eyes. It felt as if all his thoughts were banging against the inside of his skull, demanding to be let out.

Looking at his hands, he tried to imagine them strangling Jodie.

But the marks around her neck were made by much smaller hands.

Tortilla's words startled him. He gawped at the vivarium sitting on his dressing table. 'Maybe Bentley was the one who strangled her, and I just helped him.'

Why would you wanna help a piece of scum like him?

'I wish I knew.'

It's been a while since we had a proper chat.

'I'm sorry.'

I get lonely in here.

'I know.'

I miss the garden.

'Me, too.'

Are we ever going back to Bluebell Cottage?

'I don't think so. Do you wanna come out of the vivarium for a while?'

Thought you'd never ask.

Mathew walked to the dresser, took Tortilla out, and went back to the bed. 'I'll get Granddad to get you some more food tomorrow. Any requests?'

Dandelions.

'Is that all?'

I'm not fussy. You know I love dandelions and cauliflower.

'Dandelions it is, then.' As he went to put Tortilla on the bed, he dropped him. The tortoise flipped over onto his back.

Hey, put me the right way up, I get dizzy upside down.

'Sorry. It's awkward with this bandage on.' He was about to turn him over when he noticed a patch of white fur stuck to the bottom of the shell.

What are you looking at?

'You've got fur stuck to you.'

Must have come from the shed.

Mathew put Tortilla back in the vivarium. 'Wait there. I'm just gonna get Granddad.'

As if I've got a choice!

Two minutes later, Mathew and Bernard were both staring at the fur as if Tortilla had started to morph into an unknown species.

'It looks like cat's hair,' Bernard said. 'But how would he get that on him? He's been in the vivarium ever since he's been here.'

Mathew's heart picked up speed. 'Maybe it was on Jodie when she was put in the shed, and Tortilla crawled over it and it got stuck to his shell.'

'Maybe,' Bernard agreed. 'Leave Tortilla in the vivarium and don't touch the hair. I'll call the police.'

Mathew tried not to get too excited. The hair could have come from anywhere. Blown into the garden. Got carried in on someone's shoe. Been deposited by a bird.

Snowy's got white fur, hasn't he?

Mathew gawked at the tortoise as if it had just revealed the meaning of life to him. But the fur couldn't belong to Snowy; the cat only had three legs, and he never left the flat.

Another thought: Maybe he'd got Snowy's fur on his own clothes and transferred it to the shed. Gareth was always moaning about the cat moulting.

By the time his granddad came back to the bedroom, doubt had virtually extinguished Mathew's excitement. Nothing new there!

CHAPTER FORTY-FIVE

A young PC called Denver came to the house to take the fur away for analysis. He asked Mathew to hold the tortoise upside down while he shone his torch on it. 'Looks like cat's hair to me.'

'That's what we thought,' Bernard said. 'But Tortilla's been in his vivarium ever since the body was found.'

Denver used a long pair of tweezers to extract the fur. He put it in an evidence bag and sealed it up. 'And you haven't got a cat?'

Mathew shook his head. 'But Gareth has.'

'Gareth?'

'My brother. But Snowy doesn't go out because he's only got three legs.'

'Has Snowy got white fur?'

'Yes.'

He put the bag down and took out his notebook. 'Could you give me Gareth's address, please? Just so we can check Snowy's fur to see if it matches.'

'It's flat 5C, St Peter's Place,' Bernard said. 'But I can't see how Snowy's fur could turn up in the garden at Bluebell Cottage.'

Denver shrugged. 'Let's see if it belongs to Snowy first before we speculate. I doubt Snowy's the only white cat in Feelham. Anyway, we'll get this looked at and see what's what. If you think of anything else, please let us know.'

'Is there any news on what happened to Jim Bentley?'

'It seems he was messing around with petrol in his flat and somehow caught himself on fire. Other than that, we're still investigating it.'

'He got what he deserved. Good riddance to bad rubbish.'

Denver didn't respond. 'Right, I'll get this back to the station. Thanks for bringing it to our attention.'

After Bernard had showed him out, Mathew and his granddad sat at the kitchen table sharing a pot of tea.

'What will happen if the fur belongs to Snowy?' Mathew asked.

'I don't know, lad. I suppose they'll try to figure out how it ended up in the shed.'

'Maybe I brought it back with me last time I visited Gareth.'

'Who knows? Like the policeman said, it's best not to speculate until we know for sure.'

'What do you think happened with Jodie, Granddad?'

'I think Jim Bentley killed that little girl. I also believe he killed his girlfriend and made it seem like that other lad did it.'

'Do you think I helped him?'

'Of course not. You've got to get that silly idea right out of your head.'

'But I can't. What if I went along the Bunky Line that night and saw him with Jodie? What if I saw him kill her, and he made me help him? Then I had a fugue, and now I can't remember anything?'

'I'm sure you'd remember something like that.'

'Not in a fugue.'

'What actually happens when you have one of these blank episodes?'

Mathew took a deep breath and told him about the cave, the bats, and the orb. The bad voice that had told him to go to the bathroom and cut his wrists, and how everything after that was wiped from his memory.

After a few seconds, Bernard said, 'I think the orb might be your dad. The one true light in the darkness.'

'Really?'

Bernard nodded and lit his pipe. 'Makes sense to me, lad.'

'But what about the bats and the voice that told me to kill myself?'

'Maybe the bats represent the chaos going on inside your head, and the voice is telling you to take the easy way out.'

'I've never thought of it like that. Do you believe in God, Granddad?'

'I do.'

'Do you think Dad and Amy are in Heaven?'

'Absolutely.'

'Does that mean Jim Bentley's in Hell?'

'I hope so.'

'I think I might go to my room and read for a while. It makes me feel better sometimes.'

'I used to like a good book when I was younger. I loved Catherine Cookson novels. She had a knack of making you feel as if you were right there in the story.'

'I like romance stories best.'

Bernard smiled. 'Each to their own, lad, each to their own.'

Mathew walked upstairs. He would have a chat with Tortilla first and apologise for all the disruption, then settle down with a good book and try to take his mind off murder.

After chatting to Tortilla, he fell asleep in a chair by the window. He was awoken nearly two hours later by his mother knocking on the door.

'I'm going into town with Nan and Granddad for a while.'

Mathew rubbed his eyes. 'Why?'

'I need to see my solicitor about the Book Café, then we're going shopping.'

He yawned and stretched. 'Okay.'

'Do you want anything?'

'Just some lemonade.'

'Will you be all right on your own?'

'Yes.'

'Make sure you call me if you have any problems.'

'Okay.'

'See you later.'

'Not if I see you first.'

'Ha, ha, Mathew, I'm splitting my sides.'

'Ha, ha back. Watch your kidneys don't fall out.'

A little joke they'd shared for years. Same words, but now they seemed to be devoid of genuine humour. He watched the car pulling out of the driveway, then selected a novel from a tall mango bookcase. *Deadly Desires.* A tale of a blossoming romance against all the odds. He sat in a chair and read the blurb on the back cover before diving into the story.

But the text kept blurring on the page, and the storyline was impossible to follow. Autumn rain lashed against the window. He welcomed the drop in temperature, but nothing could alter the endless cycle of misery each day brought with it. As far as his heart was concerned, it would always be winter.

The doorbell rang as he was about to put the book down. He got up and peered out the window. Gareth's car was parked in the driveway.

The bell rang again, this time accompanied by a fist banging on the door. He didn't really want to talk to anyone, but he couldn't just ignore him. Gareth was his brother. The man who'd saved his life. Taught him to ignore people who made stupid remarks about his appearance. Put an arm around his shoulder when the bullying got too much for him at school. Told him to keep believing in himself.

'Granddad? Mum? Anyone home?' Gareth called through the letterbox.

Mathew trudged downstairs.

Another knock on the door. 'Mattie? You in there?' Gareth's voice didn't sound very friendly. 'Mathew? Granddad?'

He opened the front door. Apologised. Said he was on the toilet.

'Where're the others?'

'Gone into town.'

Gareth stepped inside. 'What for?'

'To see a solicitor about the Book Café, and then they're going shopping.'

Gareth shut the door. 'So, what have you been up to, bro?'

'Reading.'

'Anything good?'

'Not really. Do you want a drink?'

Gareth went into the lounge and sat on the sofa. 'I'm good, thanks. Have you heard any news about the investigation?'

'Only that Jim Bentley had petrol in the flat and set himself on fire.'

'Sounds about right for that idiot. Anything else?'

'Not really.'

'That's strange, because I had a visit from DS Palmer and some forensic guy this morning. They wanted to take a sample of Snowy's fur and swab his cheek. You know anything about that?'

Mathew hesitated. He could tell by the look in Gareth's eyes that he was mad at him.

'Well?'

'I found some fur snagged on the bottom of Tortilla's shell. I thought he must have picked it up in the shed. Then Granddad called the police because he thought it might have something to do with Jodie's murder. They took it away to examine it.'

'Nice one, Mattie. Now they're treating me like I'm a criminal.'

'Why?'

'Because the police are suspicious by nature. That's why they join the police force in the first place.'

'But even if the hair does belong to Snowy, it doesn't mean anything. I could have taken it back to Bluebell Cottage after I visited you.'

Gareth's stance softened slightly. 'True.'

'Or you could have brought it into the house, and I transferred it to the shed.'

'You're right. Sorry, bro. I've been under a lot of pressure at work trying to meet targets and stuff. I think I'll ask Mum for a job in the Book Café when it opens again.'

'But I thought you enjoyed selling houses.'

'I do. But not enough to put me in an early grave.'

'Your job sounds exciting.'

'That's because a lot of things *look* glamorous until you do them.'

'Did you always want to sell houses?'

'I wanted to be a butcher when I was at school.'

'Yuck!'

Gareth grinned. 'Someone's gotta get the meat prepared for all the hungry carnivores. I'm just gonna nip to the loo, then I'd better get going. I told the guys in the office I had a dental appointment.'

Mathew watched him stride into the hall. So confident. So in control. He sometimes wondered what it would have been like if it had been the other way round. If Mathew had been the elder brother and saved his mother. If everyone looked up to him the way they did with Gareth.

He wanted to ask his brother what it was like to be normal. Go to work and makes lots of money. Have his own flat and a nice car. Get to choose who he dated rather than plead with the heavens above to send him anyone to make his life worthwhile. But that could never be. His imagination was his only hope of finding romance. Walking the pages of a novel and pretending that he was the hero who swept the pretty woman off her feet and whisked her off to a country retreat to live happily ever after.

'I'll see you later,' Gareth called as he opened the front door.

Thankfully, Mathew had no idea of the circumstances this would be under.

CHAPTER FORTY-SIX

Two days later, Mathew and his granddad were sitting at the table discussing a visit to the museum when DS Palmer turned up with a search warrant. His usual cordial manner was absent as he swept into the living room with a uniformed officer in tow.

'I don't know what you think you'll find,' Bernard said.

'We're just following a line of enquiry,' Palmer said. 'We'd like to have a look in Mathew's room.'

'Don't tell me you still think the lad has something to do with Jodie's murder?'

'We don't think anything, Mr Halsey. We follow leads and look for facts.'

'What facts?'

'I'm sorry. I'm not at liberty to discuss the investigation.'

'Really? But it's all right for you to come into my house and demand to search it?'

'I'm afraid the warrant says *yes*.'

'Then the warrant's a bloody joke.'

'Did you find out something with the cat's hair?' Mathew asked. 'Does it belong to Snowy?'

Palmer softened. 'I'm sorry, but—'

'You're not at liberty to discuss it,' Bernard finished. 'We know.'

Mathew's stomach turned into a coffee percolator. You didn't need to have a sharp mind to know the police were searching for something specific. He sat in a chair by the window and gazed outside. Imagined Palmer reading him his rights and leading him out of the house to a waiting police car.

'Don't worry about it, lad, they won't find anything here.'

Mathew wished he could believe him, but his blank memory was telling him otherwise. He was gripped by a sudden urge to run. Anywhere would do, just as long as he didn't have to wait here for the police to arrest him.

'Mathew?'

'What if I did it, Granddad? What if I did it and I just can't remember?'

'You didn't.'

'But you don't know that for certain, do you?'

'I know *you*, lad.'

'How can you, when I don't even know myself?'

He didn't have an answer to that. They sat in silence, Mathew's heart stomping all over his ribs.

Twenty minutes later, Palmer and the uniformed officer returned to the lounge. Palmer was holding a clear plastic evidence bag. He held it out in front of Mathew. 'Do you recognise this?'

Mathew stared at the purple ponytail band sitting inside the bag. 'No.'

'Can you explain why we found this hidden at the bottom of your sock drawer?'

Mathew's insides crumbled to dust. 'No.'

'Who else has access to your bedroom?'

'What the hell is this?' Bernard asked. 'There's just me, my wife, and Mathew's mother living here. Are you suggesting one of us put it in there?'

'I'm not suggesting anything, Mr Halsey. I just want to know how a ponytail band matching the one Jodie Willis was wearing on the night she vanished turns up in your house.'

'Maybe it's one of Sonia's. Mathew's room used to be hers when she was a child.'

Palmer didn't seem convinced. He turned to Mathew. 'Are you certain you have never seen this hair band before?'

'I don't know.'

'Has your brother ever had access to your room?'

'Gareth? Only when I've been here.'

'Are you sure?'

Mathew nodded.

'How well do you get on with Gareth?'

Great. A question he could answer. 'Brilliant. He saved my life once.'

'Wow. That's impressive. So, would it be fair to say you'd do anything to help him if he asked?'

'Yes.'

Pam walked into the room and placed a pile of ironing on a chair. 'What's all this?'

Bernard looked as if his wife was the last person he wanted to see. 'The police have found a hair bobble in Mathew's room.'

'And?'

'It matches the one Jodie was wearing the night she went missing.'

Pam inspected the bobble. 'Might've belonged to Sonia.'

Bernard nodded. 'That's what I said.'

Pam turned back to Palmer. 'Why are you even searching Mathew's room? That boy wouldn't hurt a fly.'

Palmer didn't seem to be interested in character references. 'I'm going to get the hair bobble examined.' He then told Mathew not to go anywhere without telling the police.

'Why?'

'Because you're still a part of an ongoing investigation.'

'Is he a suspect?' Pam asked.

Palmer repeated his initial assessment and walked to the front door. 'In the meantime, if you remember anything at all, I'd be grateful if you'd get in touch with the incident room or call me directly. I'll see myself out.'

After they'd gone, Pam pulled out an ironing board from the side of a large mahogany display cabinet and set it up. 'Part of an ongoing investigation, my eye. It's beyond me how anyone could think that lad's involved in any of this.'

'They've got no evidence,' Bernard said. 'Otherwise they'd have arrested him.'

Pam set the iron to steam. 'Who's to say someone never planted that hair bobble in the drawer. You hear about that sort of thing all the time. I don't trust the police one jot.'

Bernard nodded. 'I've always respected the law, but now I'm wondering whether my trust has been misplaced.'

Pam started ironing one of Mathew's tee-shirts. 'Where's Sonia?'

'Gone to the Book Café to make some plans about the refurbishment.'

'I'm going to ask her about that hair bobble when she gets home.'

'It seems to me as if someone told the police to search his room.'

'But who? Bentley's dead, and he killed that druggie mate of his.'

'I'm sure he's got other druggie mates.'

Pam disappeared behind a cloud of steam. 'Drugs seem to be at the root of all evil these days. None of that rubbish ever appealed to me. I can't understand why anyone would want to poison their own body.'

Mathew watched the conversation ping back and forth. He felt as if he was floating outside his body and observing the scene from a neutral perspective. He wanted to tell his grandparents he was probably the one who'd put the hair bobble in the drawer. The one who'd helped Jim Bentley hide the body.

He walked upstairs unnoticed while his grandparents offered their perspective on the failings of society. He closed his bedroom door and sat on the bed. Every drawer in his dresser was pulled out, and his wardrobe door was open. Clothes were piled onto the chair next to the dresser. A lot of them had spilled onto the floor. His books were all messed up on the shelves, and Tortilla's vivarium had been moved.

This was the end. There was no going back now. Darkness fell around him, luring him into the cave. 'I must have done it,' he said as he sat and rested his back against the cold stone wall. 'Why else would Jodie's hair bobble be in my sock drawer?'

The screeching bats instantly gobbled up his words.

He tried to think back to the night the girl with the startled eyes had walked past him on the bench. Fill in the blank space between going to the Bunky Line and returning home. What did he see? What did he do?

Fresh words written in blood on the cave wall. *Everything comes to those who die.*

Suddenly, it all made sense to him. Everything was nothing. And nothing was everything. The culmination of every second spent on this earth was just an endless black sanctuary. No more pain, no more heartache, no more murder. Death was the final reward. The true meaning of closure. Of peace.

The orb appeared in front of him, its light illuminating the cave.

'I see you're back again. It's over. The police found Jodie's hair bobble in my room. I killed her.'

How can you be so sure?

'How else could it have got there?'

Perhaps Gareth put it there. Maybe he's the one who killed Jodie.

'Gareth wouldn't do that.'

And you would?

'I might if I was in a fugue.'

But it's not in your nature.

'So everyone keeps saying.'

Because it's true. Face up to the truth, Mathew: Gareth isn't who everyone thinks he is.

'Don't talk about my brother like that. Gareth's a hero.'

You think he is, but nothing could be further from the truth.

'Stop saying things like that. Me and Bentley killed Jodie. No one else. We kept her in that air-raid shelter, and then we moved her to the shed. I wish it wasn't true, but it is.'

Why was Gareth so upset about the fur on Tortilla's shell, then?

'Because he thought the police would get suspicious of him.'

Or because he's guilty.

'No way.'

Maybe it was Gareth who put the hair bobble in your sock drawer.

Mathew clamped his hands over his ears. 'I'm not listening to this.'

Blocking your ears won't help. I'm inside your head, Mathew. Have been ever since the day you were born. Remember I told you that courage is having the strength to do something that you don't want to do?

'Leave me alone. Gareth saved my life.'

Be strong. See Gareth for what he really is. A liar and a murderer.

Mathew bowed his head and prayed for the first time since he was a young child with a fully functioning mind.

CHAPTER FORTY-SEVEN

DS Palmer returned to the house that evening. Mathew watched him pull into the drive in a dark-blue unmarked car. This was it. He'd come to arrest him for Jodie's murder. It didn't matter what the orb said, nothing could protect him from the law. They'd probably found his fingerprints all over the hair bobble and gathered enough evidence to lock him up for the rest of his life.

But Palmer hadn't come to arrest him. He just wanted to know where Gareth was. If they'd seen him in the last couple of days.

Sonia frowned. 'What do you want him for?'

'We need to clarify one or two things with him, but he's not at home and he hasn't been to work.'

Sonia's frown deepened. 'Not at work? But he never misses work.'

Palmer nodded. 'That's what they said at the office.'

'But Snowy will be on his own,' Mathew said. 'Someone needs to feed him.'

'Don't worry about the cat,' Palmer said. 'We'll make sure it's all right.'

Mathew thought about the orb. 'Is Gareth in trouble?'

Palmer's eyes remained neutral. 'We just need to ask him a few questions.'

Mathew almost blurted out what the orb had said about Gareth putting the hair bobble in his sock drawer. But who would listen to him rambling on about an orb in a cave? Instead, he asked if the fur on Tortilla matched the cat.

'Yes. But the fur isn't the issue.'

'What is, then?' Sonia asked.

'It's something else concerning the cat, but I can't discuss it with you at the moment. We need to speak to Gareth first.'

'First Mathew, now Gareth. It seems to me you've got it in for my sons.'

'Trust me, Mrs Hillock, we haven't *got it in* for anyone. We're trying to solve the murder of a child, and we think Gareth may be able to help us with our enquiries.'

Sonia sat and rubbed her forehead. 'When is this nightmare going to end?'

'I understand how you feel,' Palmer said, 'but—'

'You don't have a clue how I feel, Detective. First Mathew's more or less accused of killing that girl. Then the Book Café's burnt to the ground and a brick's thrown at my window. Now you want to question Gareth.'

'I know it's—'

'Have you got any closer to finding out who set fire to the Book Café?'

'We're following several lines of enquiry regarding the arson attack.'

Sonia snorted. 'Is that the best you can do?'

'It's all I can tell you at the moment.'

Bernard stepped between them. 'We'll let you know if Gareth turns up, Detective. I promise.'

Sonia looked at him as if he'd just trodden on her foot.

Palmer nodded. 'Thank you.'

'And in the meantime,' Sonia said, 'we just have to sit in a goldfish bowl of misery, wondering what the hell's going to happen, do we?'

'I know it's tough,' Palmer said. 'But please try to remember how Jodie's mother must be feeling.'

'I've got all the sympathy in the world for that poor woman,' Sonia said. 'But that doesn't mean we all deserve to suffer, does it?'

After a short awkward silence, Palmer excused himself. 'I'll be in touch if there're any further developments.'

'I'm bloody sick to death of this,' Sonia said as the front door closed. 'What in God's name does he want to talk to Gareth about?'

'I'm going to my room,' Mathew said, before the orb's words accidentally popped out of his mouth.

Sonia shook her head. 'You stay downstairs with us.'

'Why?'

'Because it's better for you to have people around you.'

'Why?'

'You know why, Mathew; you keep going into those bloody fugues, and I need to keep an eye on you.'

Mathew almost laughed. Did she really believe that having company would stop the blackouts? That he could stay out of the cave if she was with him? Didn't she remember the one he'd had outside Bluebell Cottage when she was standing right next to him?

'Anyway,' Bernard said, 'we like having you around, lad.'

He looked at his granddad. He loved him as much as he loved his mum and Gareth. Possibly more. Granddad never judged anyone. Was always calm and polite, even when provoked.

Bernard smiled. 'We could have a game of Scrabble.'

'I'm not in the mood, Granddad.'

'How about that visit to the museum we were talking about?'

Mathew shook his head. 'I just want to see Gareth.'

'Why?'

'I have to talk to him.'

'What about?'

Mathew hovered on the brink of telling him everything the orb had said to him about Gareth planting the hair bobble. That his brother was a liar and a murderer.

'Mathew?'

'It's nothing important. We just talk sometimes, and he helps me to straighten out my thoughts.'

'I don't understand where he could have gone,' Sonia said. 'He never misses work.'

'Maybe he's got a girlfriend,' Bernard suggested.'

Pam laughed. 'That'll be the day. I've never seen him with a woman.'

'Maybe that's because he likes to keep his private life private.'

'Or maybe he just doesn't like women,' Pam said. 'He wouldn't be the first one in this family to be gay.'

'Don't be ridiculous,' Sonia snapped. 'He's not gay.'

'Children don't always tell their mothers everything,' Pam said. 'Your cousin Lottie was a lesbian, and she didn't tell her mum until she was dying from breast cancer.'

Bernard shook his head. 'What a lovely story. That's cheered me up no end.'

'Just saying.'

'Do you believe in spirits?' Mathew asked.

His mother frowned. 'Why do you ask that?'

'Just wondered.'

'You must have a reason for asking.'

'I think I see one sometimes.'

'Where?' Sonia asked.

'In my head.'

'How do you mean?'

'Sometimes when I have a fugue, I see this blob of light in my head, and it occasionally speaks to me.'

Sonia's mouth hung open. 'What the hell...?'

'I'm sorry. I shouldn't have said anything.'

'It's all right, lad,' Bernard said. 'We're all on your side here. Tell your mum what you told me.'

After a few seconds deliberation, Mathew told his mother about the cave and the orb. How the voice in the dark had told him to go to the bathroom and cut his wrists. Insisted he cut both of them. And that the orb had told him to face the truth.

'What truth?' Sonia asked.

'About...'

Bernard touched his arm. 'Come on, lad. It's fine. You can tell us anything. We love you.'

'The orb said... Gareth put the hair bobble in my sock drawer.'

Sonia's eyes widened. Her hands flew to her mouth as if trying to stop any words escaping.

'But it doesn't mean it's true. It's just what the orb told me. I don't believe it.'

Sonia looked as if she'd just had all the life sucked out of her. 'It's absurd. I've never heard such a load of rubbish in my life.'

'Is it, though?' Pam said. 'First the cat's hair, now Gareth's gone missing and the police want to talk to him.'

Sonia turned on her. 'If you can't think of anything sensible to say, keep your mouth shut.'

'Don't talk to me like that! Show some respect.'

'You earn respect, Mum, you don't demand it.'

'I'm not demanding anything. I'm just asking you to keep a civil tongue in your head and remember that you're in my house.'

'Oh, here we go. How many times did I hear that when I was growing up?'

'If you don't like it, then you can always go back to Bluebell Cottage. It's no skin off my nose.'

'I can't believe I'm hearing this. First you as good as accuse Gareth of killing that child, then you—'

'I said nothing of the sort. All I did was repeat what the detective said. If that doesn't look suspicious to you, then perhaps you need to open your eyes a bit wider.' Pam turned away and strode out of the room.

Sonia gawped at her father. 'What do you think?'

'That it's strange Gareth has gone missing. But that's all. I'm not prepared to make any wild guesses about anything until I know the full story.'

Mathew's phone beeped. He checked the screen. Gareth.

We need to meet. It's vital you tell no one. I've got a key to Bluebell Cottage. Come round at 7 p.m. Alone!

'Who was that?' Sonia asked as Mathew stuffed the phone back in his pocket.

'No one.'

Bernard grinned. 'The invisible man, eh, lad?'

Mathew shook his head, trying to construct a lie from his jumbled thoughts. 'Just one of those cold-call things.'

Bernard stood. 'I'd better go and see how Pam is.'

'Tell her I didn't mean to snap,' Sonia said. 'I can't seem to get my bloody head straight.'

'Little wonder with all this wretched business going on. It's affecting us all.'

'Maybe it would be better if me and Mathew went home. It's not fair on you and Mum having us here.'

'I don't want to go home,' Mathew said. 'I like it here.'

'Then I'll go home. Get the place ready to sell.'

Mathew's mind conjured up an image of Gareth walking through the door to meet him and finding his mother there instead. 'No! I want you to stay here with me.'

'No one's going anywhere,' Bernard said. 'I'll have a chat with Pam and iron things out with her.'

Mathew almost fell to his knees and kissed his granddad's feet.

'Okay. But I'm not having Mum treat me as if I'm still at school,' Sonia said. 'I respect her, and I'm sorry I snapped at her, but I won't hold my tongue when she makes stupid allegations. It's ridiculous to even think Gareth has done anything wrong. He's one of the nicest people I know. He saved my life. Mathew's, too. I'm his mother, for God's sake, and I'll defend him until my dying breath.'

Mathew didn't hear his mother's impromptu speech. His mind was on other things – like how he would go out later to meet Gareth at Bluebell Cottage.

CHAPTER FORTY-EIGHT

DS Palmer rang the buzzer to flat 5C. Accompanying him, DC Halliwell, a uniformed officer by the name of Maxwell, and the estate manager from Lassiter's, Derek Broadbottom, who had a master key to the front door and a spare key to Gareth's flat. He waited a few seconds, then buzzed again. Still no answer.

Broadbottom asked if Palmer wanted to be let in.

Palmer nodded.

'Is he in trouble?'

Palmer sidestepped the question. 'He's just part of our enquiries.'

'What are you investigating?'

'Could you just open the door, please?'

Derek looked as if he'd just slipped down several rungs on the importance ladder. 'There's talk going around the office that he's got something to do with that kid's murder.'

Palmer sighed. 'Talk is cheap, Mr Broadband.'

'Bottom.'

More like arsehole. He followed Derek into the communal hallway and down some steps to the basement flat. Even though it was still only early September, the air was chilly. Flies buzzed around the landing and the stairwell, as if seeking suitable winter accommodation.

Palmer swatted several away from his face as Broadbottom opened the door to the flat.

'Do you want me to stay?' Derek asked, as the three cops filed into the flat. 'Just in case you need access to anywhere else.'

'I think we'll be all right,' Halliwell said. 'You can get off now.'

Derek seemed disappointed that he was no longer a part of the investigation. 'Are you sure?'

'Yes,' Palmer said. 'Unless you've got any idea of Mr Hillock's whereabouts.'

'I know he goes down to Brighton sometimes.'

Palmer smiled. All patience and no humour. 'Brighton's a big place. I think you need to be a little more specific than that.'

Derek shrugged. 'Dunno. I've heard he might be gay or something.'

This time Palmer's smile was genuine. 'That narrows it down. A gay man in Brighton. I think we'd better get down to the seaside pronto.'

'No need to be like that. I'm only trying to help.'

'And we appreciate it,' Halliwell said. 'But I think we can take it from here. Thanks for your help, Mr Broadbottom.'

Derek trudged back up the stairs, keys jangling on his belt loop.

Palmer closed the front door. 'Can you believe him? Tosser.'

Halliwell pushed a strand of hair out of her eyes. 'The world's full of them.'

Palmer held up a hand. 'Right, we know that the cat's DNA matches the DNA from the scratch on Jodie's leg. So, unless a three-legged moggy abducted Jodie and took her along the Bunky Line, I think it's safe to say Gareth Hillock's our man.'

'Where's the cat now?' Maxwell asked.

'Still in here as far as I know,' Palmer said. 'So be careful when entering the rooms. Make sure you all put on gloves before touching anything. Me and DC Halliwell will take the bedrooms, you search the front room and keep an eye on the door in case our man comes home.'

Maxwell nodded.

'And get that computer over there unplugged and ready to go.'

'Okay.'

'Any questions?'

'What are we gonna do if we find the moggy?' Maxwell asked. 'I'm allergic to cats.'

Palmer sighed. 'We'll keep it shut in a room, then see if anyone in the family wants to take it in. Right, let's get this done.'

Palmer and Halliwell walked along a narrow hallway with three doors leading off to the left. Palmer opened the first door and peered into a small room that had all the hallmarks of a man cave. A large plasma TV fixed to the wall, an Xbox, a laptop on a black-glass-and-chrome desk, a gaming chair, and two speakers in an alcove three quarters of the way up the wall. There was also a pink mini-fridge in one corner, and a large wooden chair with leather restraints fitted to the sides.

'What the fuck is this?' Halliwell said.

Palmer looked at a video recorder mounted on a tripod in one corner of the room. 'A bloody pervert's paradise.'

'Do you wanna do this room if I go next door and make a start in there?'

Palmer nodded. He took a deep breath. There was a pungent smell mixed in with the two air fresheners plugged into a double socket near the fridge.

He went to the desk, opened the laptop and flashed it up. He knew there was very little point in checking files and search history; bastards like Hillock always covered their tracks. That was a job for the forensic guys. He just wanted to get a feel for the man they were looking for.

While he was waiting for it to boot up, he turned his attention to the chair. It didn't take a degree in perversity to realise it was a bondage chair. And it didn't take a vivid imagination to realise it would probably have Jodie's DNA all over it.

Palmer had been in the force long enough to know there was no limit to human depravity. He'd investigated some sickening cases in his time. A homeless man set on fire by teenagers. An elderly woman robbed and beaten for a few pounds in her purse. Stabbings. Rapes. But nothing disgusted him more than the abuse and murder of a child.

'Is this where he kept you, Jodie?' he whispered.

The cold, heavy atmosphere in the room told him it probably was. He tried not to think about how terrified that poor child must have been. How helpless she'd felt, alone with no one to help her, wondering what that sadistic bastard would do next and crying out for her mother.

'We're gonna get him,' he promised. 'Get him and lock him up for life.'

Empty words. There was no real justice in this world. Even if you tied Gareth Hillock to a tree, doused him in petrol and set fire to him, it would never come close to punishing him for his disgusting behaviour. It wouldn't bring Jodie back or give her mother closure. Nothing ever could.

He walked back to the laptop and sat down. A picture of Pocahontas filled the screen. Clicking on *documents*, he scanned the files. One, titled *Alison Willis Letter* caught his attention. Chills ran down his spine as he read a draft copy of the letter which had been sent to Jodie's mother. Not that he needed any confirmation that Gareth Hillock was their man, but the letter would add significant weight to the forensic evidence provided by the cat.

Another file. *At Home with the Hagans,* confirmed Hillock's propensity towards cruelty and perversion.

His time with Lexi and Paige Henderson was followed by another entry entitled *Dream Trip.*

I met Paul Whittacker when he was sleeping rough in a run-down flat we'd been instructed to sell. A Grade-A waster who was of no use to society. But I had a use for him. One I was prepared to offer a lot of money for. Five grand to kill everyone in the house except my mother. I needed her to be alive to witness me saving the day and stabbing Whittacker to death before he had a chance to open his mouth and blab to anyone.

I know you're probably dying to know why I wanted them dead, but I need to make a separate entry regarding that one. It's far too intimate to write about without first giving it careful consideration. I want to do it justice.

The plan to kill the family went as well as can be expected with a junkie for an assassin. He killed Amy and my father but left my younger brother still alive. Brain-damaged. I'd like to make it clear that it was never my intention to burden my mother with the responsibility of looking after Mathew. It remains one of the few things I am truly sorry for.

I can't describe what it was like waiting for the police to turn up with Whittacker lying dead on the floor in the master bedroom. Wondering whether I'd covered all the bases. Trying to comfort my mother and mould myself into a paragon of grief when I felt no remorse whatsoever.

Reports later showed that some of the blows missed Mathew's head and hit the wooden headboard. I suppose I must accept some of the responsibility for hiring a bloody junkie in the first place.

I can't tell you how much I hate Mathew. What makes it even worse is he thinks I'm some sort of hero for saving him. If only he knew how many times I wished I'd checked him over before calling the police. Finished the little bastard off.

Maybe I'll do it one day, but for now I think it's best to leave well alone. I don't want to tempt fate by shitting on my own doorstep again. Still, as they say, every experience is a lesson learned, and the murder of my family taught me a lot about the importance of due diligence.

Dr Dark's Advice: Never assume anything; it may come back to haunt you!

DC Halliwell knocked on the door and entered the room. 'Any luck?'

'We've got him. We've got the bastard bang to rights. There's a shedload of stuff on his computer. Dr Dark's fucking diary, if you can believe that.'

'No way!'

'And he paid that junkie Whittacker to kill his family.'

'You're kidding me.'

'Wish I was. And here's the good bit – he killed Whittacker to make it look as if he'd saved the day.'

Halliwell shook her head.

'What about you? Find anything interesting?'

She nodded. 'A bag of children's clothes in his wardrobe. Some of them match the ones Jodie was wearing the night she disappeared. There're also various items of kid's jewellery and a load of hair accessories.'

Palmer nodded. 'Right, we'll get the forensic guys round to go over the flat, then we'll pick up Hillock. I reckon Jodie Willis is just the tip of the iceberg. I dread to think how many other kids he might have killed or abused.'

'The sooner that sick bastard's locked up the better.'

Palmer agreed, but he couldn't help thinking it was like closing the stable door after the horse had bolted.

CHAPTER FORTY-NINE

Mathew's stomach tightened as he walked downstairs and prepared to lie to his mother about where he was going. Upon reaching the front room, he was convinced she'd be able to see the deceit in his eyes. At least his grandparents were visiting relatives, so he wouldn't have to endure a three-pronged inquisition.

Sonia was sitting at the dining table with several documents spread out before her. She looked up as he entered the room.

'I'm going out for a while,' he blurted, before guilt got the better of him.

'Where to?'

'Just for a walk.'

'Anywhere in particular?'

'No.'

'You're not going along that Bunky Line again, are you?'

His cheeks flushed. 'No.'

'Would you like me to come with you?'

'Don't you trust me?'

'Of course.' Her eyes seemed to contradict her words. 'I'm just concerned about what might happen if you have another blackout.'

'I'll be fine.'

'Have you got your phone?'

He nodded, terrified she might ask to see it and read Gareth's message.

'Is it charged?'

'Yes.'

'How long do you think you'll be?'

'I don't know, Mum. I just want to get some fresh air and be on my own for a while.'

'Make sure you call me if you need anything.'

He assured her that he would and left before he lost his nerve.

The walk to Bluebell Cottage took Mathew just over twenty-five minutes. He spent ten of those minutes sitting on a bench near Druid's Lane contemplating all the reasons he should turn around and go home. Tell his mother that Gareth had sent the text message and was waiting for him at Bluebell Cottage. But he loved and respected Gareth too much to betray him. He owed his life to Gareth, and no amount of doubt or suspicion would ever change that.

He stood on the front doorstep preparing to ring the bell. Sweat dampened his forehead, and his right eye twitched.

Maybe it was Gareth who put the hair bobble in your sock drawer.

The orb's words, loud and insistent in his head, demanding attention.

Be strong. See Gareth for what he really is. A liar and a murderer.

The front door opened. Gareth beckoned him inside. 'I was wondering if you were gonna show, Mattie.'

He checked his watch. Seven-twenty. 'Sorry. I've had a bad tummy all day.'

'Never mind. You're here now.'

Mathew stepped inside the house and shuddered. It felt cold and hostile, as if the negative energy from all the bad things that had happened was still stored within its walls.

'Would you like a drink?' Gareth asked.

'I'll have some lemonade if there's any.'

'Coming right up.'

Mathew sat on the sofa. He put his hands on his knees and pressed down as hard as he could to stop his feet tapping against the floor.

Gareth handed him a glass of lemonade, then sat in a chair opposite him. 'So, how's life with the folks on the hill?'

'Huh?'

'Heritage Road.'

'It's okay.'

'How's Mum?'

'Tired.'

Gareth shook his head. 'Poor woman. I feel sorry for her.'

'Me, too.'

'Do you, Mattie? Do you really?'

'Yes.'

'Even though it's all your fault?'

Mathew's mind suddenly tipped upside down. 'Pardon?'

'I mean, it can't be easy for her. Especially having to look after you on top of everything else.'

'I don't understand.'

'No, I don't suppose you do. But that's always been your trouble, Mattie. Too blind to see and too dumb to notice.'

Be strong. See Gareth for what he really is. A liar and a murderer.

'Do you know she was still wiping your arse when you were twelve years old? Potty-trained at two, crapping yourself again at twelve.'

'I can't help the way I am.'

Gareth reached behind him. He pulled out an air gun and a large carving knife with a chrome handle. 'You were meant to die that night, you fucking freak.'

Mathew's heart stalled. He gawked at the gun. The muzzle seemed to wink at him, as if mimicking his twitch. 'I—'

'You've made everyone's life a misery. Do you realise what you've done by telling the cops about Snowy?' He didn't wait for an answer. 'Given them a chance to match the cat's DNA to a scratch on Jodie's leg.'

Mathew's heart stopped. 'Huh?'

'If you say that dumbshit word one more time, I'm gonna put a pellet right between your eyes. If you hadn't turned up unannounced at the flat that day, I wouldn't have had to shut the bloody cat in the Play Chamber with Jodie.'

Mathew closed his eyes and tried to force his mind to open up the cave and let him come inside. But, as usual, his mind failed to respond to a direct order. He pounded his feet against the floor and his hands on his knees.

'Stand up and empty your pockets. And take that bloody coat off while you're about it.'

As he stood, Mathew's legs shook badly enough to wobble his body.

'Turn around.'

'Why are you doing this to me? I thought you loved me.'

'Love you? I love Snowy fifty times more than you, you fucking half-wit. Now turn around, get on your knees, and put your hands on your head.'

Mathew did as he was told.

'I shoulda finished you off the night Whittacker messed everything up. But enough about regrets. Onwards and upwards, as they say. Let's start by rewinding twenty years. Back to the day Dad took me to the hospital after you and Amy were born.

'Mum looked so happy. As if her life was finally complete. I wanted to be pleased for her, but I couldn't help thinking that everything was gonna change. I was no longer her priority. The twins would always come first from that day on.

'Don't get me wrong. I'd always wanted a baby sister. Someone who I could protect. Pass on advice to. But I hated you from the first time I set eyes on you. You wanna know a secret, Mattie?'

Mathew didn't.

'I never liked Dad. He was a self-righteous arsehole. Strutting around as if he had all the secrets to the universe stored in that stupid head of his. But he didn't have a clue. Couldn't see what was happening right under his nose.

'You reminded me of him as you got older. Same crazy hair. The way you'd stick your tongue between your teeth and tilt your head to one side when trying to concentrate on something. I used to watch you at the dinner table shovelling food into your mouth and dream about poisoning you.'

Mathew sobbed. 'But why?'

'Because you disgust me.'

Mathew searched his mind for the entrance to the cave, but everywhere was shrouded in a thick blanket of fog. 'Please don't do this, Gareth.'

'Sorry, bro, I think we've gone past the point of no return. Maybe it would have been different if you hadn't started blabbing to the police about Snowy, but done is done, and the consequences are forever.'

'What about Mum? She's done nothing to deserve any of this. It's not fair on her.'

Gareth laughed. 'Who said life was fair? Anyway, this isn't up for debate. As soon as I've finished with you, I'm outta here.'

'You won't get away with it. The police will be looking for you.'

Gareth fired the air gun. The pellet slammed into the wall next to Mathew's head. 'Do you really think I care about the police? They couldn't catch a plane at an airport.'

'I feel sorry for you,' Mathew said. 'I thought it was bad enough living inside my head, but it must be ten times worse being inside yours.'

'I'm touched that you care, Mattie. Truly I am. But it's time to shut the fuck up and listen.'

Tears streamed down Mathew's face. 'You were my hero.'

'Ironic, eh? First, I want to say that I never planned to fall in love with Amy. It just grew from an original thought. I mean, incest is a big deal, right? Not something you should enter into lightly. I know some cultures encourage it, but this is England, and even relationships with cousins are taboo. Not that you'd think so when you see some of the stories reported in the press. Whole sections of the land seem to have been built upon the practice of inbreeding.

'Anyway, it just happened one night after I couldn't sleep. I went into Amy's room and sat on the edge of her bed. I watched her sleeping for about half an hour. She looked so peaceful. So sweet. So innocent. In some ways she reminded me of Jessica Hagan.

'I started stroking her hair. Touching her skin. Listening to the rhythm of her breathing. The cute

389

little sigh she gave when I tickled her neck. I held her hand for a while, imagining things a big brother isn't supposed to imagine. Then I climbed into bed with her. Just to feel her warmth and taste her innocence.

'I was drifting off when she woke up and started screaming. I want to make it clear I never intended to harm her. Or frighten her. Just to love her and let my imagination do the rest. With Mum and Dad sleeping in the next room, my first instinct was to clamp a hand over her mouth. This only made her kick and struggle. I tried to calm her by telling her it was only me, but this just seemed to fire her up further. I slapped her across the face. Not hard, but enough to shock her into silence. Then I told her over and over that I wouldn't hurt her. I was just protecting her. Doing what big brothers do.

'I don't know how long we stayed that way, with me trying to reassure her I wasn't the bogeyman, but I eventually took my hand away from her mouth and sat up. Told her I was going back to my room and that she needed to get some sleep because she had school in the morning.

'As far as I was concerned, that was the end of the matter. Never shit on your own doorstep as they say, especially when that doorstep is right next to your parents' bedroom. But the following day, I could tell she wasn't ready to forgive and forget. She kept staring at me at breakfast as if I was some kind of monster. I tried to disarm her by smiling my best *Love you, sis* smile, but she looked at Mum as if she was about to tell tales.

'I offered to drive her to school, just to try to explain that she'd got the wrong end of the stick.

Mum was grateful because you were sick in bed with a stomach bug and it would save her doing the school run. Amy insisted she wanted to walk to school. A lot of kids in her class did, but Mum wasn't having any of it.

'So Amy had no choice. I gave her a lift to school and asked her why she was being so grouchy. She didn't answer at first. Just sat in the passenger seat like a spoiled brat ignoring me and staring out the window. I asked her if it was because I'd got into bed with her. Told her I was only trying to be nice. And then she accused me of touching her private parts. I told her I'd only stroked her hair and cuddled her, but it made no difference. She said she was gonna tell Mum because it was wrong.

'I told her Mum would never believe something like that. We spent the next few days in a kind of standoff. I could tell she wanted to say something but was scared to in case Mum didn't believe her. But as time rolled along, I started to wonder if she would tell. A teacher at school. One of her friends. The fucking lollipop lady on the crossing outside the school.

'I don't mind telling you, my head was getting in a right pickle. Kids are unpredictable at the best of times, and the more I thought about it, the more convinced I was that I'd have to make sure she couldn't tell. I thought about threatening her. Telling her I would kill you if she ever said anything. But how could I be sure it would work? Threats can be effective, but they can also come back to slap you round the face.

'So I arranged for Paul Whittacker to kill everyone. Well, everyone except Mum. I needed someone left alive to prove that I had no choice but to kill Whittacker.'

Mathew slipped through the entrance to the cave as the screeching bats finally drowned out his brother's words.

CHAPTER FIFTY

Sitting with his back against the cold stone wall, Mathew could hear his name being called from outside the cave. No prizes for guessing who that voice belonged to: the fallen hero. The child murderer. The man who thought it was okay to get into bed with his own eight-year-old sister and get someone to murder his whole family.

It's nearly over, Mattie, a voice whispered in the darkness. It was the same voice that had told him to go to the bathroom and cut his wrists. The one that belonged to death. *You had a chance to end it yourself, but you chose not to take it. Now you must face the consequences.*

'I never had a choice,' Mathew argued. 'Everything that's happened to me is because of Gareth. He's the reason I'm like this. The reason Amy, Jodie, and my dad are dead.'

I admire your capacity to blame others, Mattie. You should've been a politician.

'It's the truth!'

Do you really think the truth matters?

'Yes.'

Don't be so naïve. It's what people believe that matters. The truth isn't worth a damn if everyone thinks it's a lie.

'God knows the truth.'

Is that so? So where is He now? Hiding behind the curtains waiting for the right time to come out and blind us all with the truth?

'I don't care what you say. I'd rather die honest than live as a liar.'

How noble of you. I'll try to remember that when I come to pay my respects at your graveside.

The orb suddenly appeared in the cave, its light extinguishing the darkness. The bats ceased shrieking. Everything around Mathew became calm and still. His heartrate slowed and, for the first time since he was a young child, his mind cleared.

You must stand up now and face the truth. Be strong. Stand tall. And don't allow the lies to penetrate your heart.

Mathew stood and walked towards the entrance. The boulder rolled out of the way on its own, and he stepped straight back into the living room at Bluebell Cottage.

Gareth was waiting for him, knife in one hand, gun in the other. 'Get back on the floor, you fucking freak. Get back on the floor or I'll shoot you!'

Mathew ignored him and took a few steps towards him. He gazed into Gareth's dark eyes. It was like looking into an empty chasm.

'I'm warning you, bro – get back on the floor or I'll shoot you.'

Mathew continued to move towards him, each step slow and measured, robotic, as if in a trance.

Gareth fired. The pellet hit Mathew in the chest. The stab vest prevented it from piercing his skin. He stopped about six or seven feet in front of his brother.

'I'm warning you, freak! Get back over there, or I'll empty the whole fucking gun into you.'

'I am the truth,' Mathew said, his voice calm and even. 'Your lies can no longer penetrate my heart.'

'What the fuck...?' He fired again. The second pellet thudded into his stomach.

Mathew lurched towards him. A third pellet struck him in the front of his shoulder. A fourth in the midriff.

Gareth dropped the gun and held the knife out in front of him. He flipped it from one hand to the other. 'One more step and I'm gonna cut your fucking heart out.'

Mathew lunged at him. His momentum forced Gareth backwards, and they tumbled onto the floor in a tangled heap of twisted limbs and breathless curses. After several seconds thrashing around on the floor, Gareth rolled on top of Mathew. He straddled his chest and raised the knife.

Mathew held out his hands as if trying to ward off an evil spirit.

'Why didn't you just keep your fucking nose out?' Gareth brought the knife down.

The blade sliced through the edge of Mathew's hand on its way to his chest. He cried out as the blade hit the stab vest. Gareth tried to stab him again. Same result. He was about to take aim at Mathew's throat, when the younger brother bucked and threw him sideways onto the floor. Gareth dropped the knife due to the sudden movement.

With an agility previously unknown to his bulky frame, Mathew rolled over, grabbed the knife, and stood. Held it out in front of him.

Gareth pushed himself onto his knees. His eyes looked as if they were about to burst into flames. 'What're you gonna do, goody two-shoes? Stab me?'

Mathew glanced from the knife to his brother and back again. 'I'm not gonna do anything if you don't move.'

'Is that right?'

'Yes.' The knife juddered in his hand. He grabbed his wrist to steady it. 'The police know what you've done, Gareth. Everyone does.'

Gareth manoeuvred himself into a crouching position. 'Then I ain't got nothing to lose, have I?'

Mathew backed away a step. 'Stay where you are. I mean it, Gareth. If you try anything, I'm gonna kill you.'

'You ain't got the guts to kill a fly, Mattie.' He stood. 'Just give me the knife, and I'll go. You won't ever see me again.'

'No.'

'Give me the knife.'

Don't allow the lies to penetrate your heart.

'No.'

Outside, the faint sound of a police siren. Gareth glanced at the window behind him. 'Did you call the police?'

Mathew didn't answer.

Gareth took several steps towards his brother. 'Just give me the knife.'

The siren grew louder.

'It's over. You have to face up to the truth now.'

After checking behind him one last time, Gareth rushed towards his brother, hands raised, lips twisted. He made a noise that sounded somewhere between a scream and a howl.

Mathew didn't mean to stab him. He just shifted the blade out the way of Gareth's flailing arms. It pierced Gareth's stomach, the force of his momentum and weight thrusting it deep into his abdomen.

Gareth froze for a moment, eyes wide, mouth hanging open. And then he staggered backwards, the blade pulling free. He gawped at Mathew as if he'd just appeared out of nowhere in his worst nightmare.

Mathew held the blade out in front of him, the silver steel now coated with Gareth's blood.

Gareth clutched the wound with both hands. 'You've done it now, bro.' He lurched forward, knees buckling, blood bubbling on his lips.

Everything seemed to be moving in slow-motion as Gareth fell forwards onto the knife. Mathew let go of the handle as the blade cut deep into his brother's chest. Gareth made a high-pitched whistling sound and fell to his knees, gargling blood.

Gareth's eyes glazed over. He pitched forward, landing face down on the floor. Blood spread out from his body, staining the carpet crimson.

After Mathew stared at his brother's motionless body for several minutes, there was a loud knock on the door. He would later have no recollection of answering it or letting the police inside. Or the commotion that followed and the journey to Oxford Police Central Station.

For Mathew Hillock, it was over. He was the truth. And that was all that mattered in a world full of liars.

EPILOGUE

One year later.

Mathew and his mother sat at a small table out the back of the refurbished Book Café. He was getting used to his newfound status as a cult hero, although he didn't view himself as anything other than someone who'd done what he'd had to – stand up and face the truth that his brother was a paedophile and a murderer.

He'd not visited the cave since his brother's death. No more orbs. No more voices. No more screeching bats. His therapist had taught him that these things were all just an integral part of the subconscious mind. A deep-seated protective sanctuary in the brain to help humans cope with traumatic situations. Mathew wasn't sure whether that made the orb and the dark voice real, but it went some way to explaining their existence in his head.

The police had found thousands of disgusting images of children on Gareth's PC, along with Dr Dark's Diary and a list of future victims with coloured stars next to their names. It could only be assumed that the colours denoted some kind of rating system. According to the diary, Gareth Hillock had been responsible for thirteen deaths in total.

An inquest into Gareth's death had concluded that Mathew had acted in self-defence and was not to be held accountable for his brother's passing. The ruling was of little consequence to Mathew. He felt no joy or satisfaction knowing that Gareth was dead. In fact, he'd have rather seen him spend the rest of his life behind bars where he'd have plenty of time to reflect on his evil deeds.

Mathew's mother was still trying to come to terms with giving birth to such a monster. Wondering if there was anything in his childhood that could have triggered such dreadful behaviour? Any warning signs? Anything she could've done differently? But Mathew knew Gareth was just a monster of his own making. No Dr Frankenstein involved.

In a strange twist of fate, one of Gareth's lesser-known victims had seen Gareth entering Bluebell Cottage on the day he'd died. Jessica Hagan had called the police after seeing on the local news that the police were searching for him. She'd paid close attention to the story because she remembered him from her childhood.

Mathew asked his mother if she would like another cup of tea.

Sonia shook her head. 'I drink any more of that stuff, I'm gonna end up looking like a bloody teacup.'

Mathew smiled. 'We've sold four novels and two autobiographies this morning.'

'I know.'

'When's the flat going to be ready?'

'Soon.'

'I think it'll be cool living above the shop. I can get an extra half an hour in bed.'

'Lazybones.'

The shop bell rang. 'Would you mind getting that, Mathew? I've got a headache.'

Mathew walked into the main body of the shop. The smell of the books seemed to travel right to the centre of his heart. This was a brand-new start. Time to make fresh memories. Happy memories. Maybe even meet the girl of his dreams and live happily ever after.

The woman standing by the cash register appeared vaguely familiar, but he couldn't quite place her. Maybe she was an old customer from way back. 'Good morning. Can I help you?'

Dark smudges beneath her eyes and her badly stained teeth spoiled what was probably once a pretty face. Her grey hair was tied back in a ponytail. 'I just wanted to thank you.'

He smoothed down a clump of hair hovering just above his ear. 'What for?'

'For putting that monster in his grave.'

'Gareth?'

She nodded.

'Do I know you?'

'I'm Alison – Jodie's mum.'

Mathew opened his mouth to say how sorry he was. That he wished he could have stopped his brother from killing her. But no words seemed adequate.

She handed him a folded piece of notepaper. 'I want you to have this.'

'What is it?'

'Something for you to keep.' With that, she turned and walked out of the shop.

He opened the piece of paper. On it, a neatly written poem. Some of the words were smudged, and there was a drawing of a smiling sun in the top right-hand corner.

I wish I was a flower,
Sitting in the sun,
Watching all the children play,
Having lots of fun,
Hoping I'll be picked,
To be a special friend,
Someone to depend upon,
Until the very end.

Beneath the poem:

I hope you have a wonderful life, Mathew. I'm sure if Jodie could have chosen anyone to be her special friend, it would have been you. Alison x.

ACKNOWLEDGEMENTS

Thanks to:

Sarah Hardy, Jill Burkinshaw and Jen Lucas for kindly beta reading the story.

Emmy Ellis for the great editing and eye-catching cover.

Jacqueline Beard for proofreading the book.

All the book bloggers for their invaluable help in spreading the word.

Alison Willis for allowing me to use her name.

The UK Crime Book Club on Facebook for all their support and encouragement.

This book is dedicated to my lovely niece, Louise. Always in my thoughts.